Praise for *P*

'Funny, moving, philosophical a
life, loss, and the murky depths
charming and utterly hilarious.' – Emma Jane Unsworth

'Lisa Blower takes us on a mysterious quest along the dual carriageways and B roads of the West Midlands. Her great talent is to make compelling characters of normal people, and show us all the strangeness they contain.' – Chris Power

'A novel that dares to find the lyrical, the luminous and the hilarious in the kind of people and places that literature often overlooks. Down arterial roads and a variety of stops and diversions, *Pondweed* finds humour and enlightenment in a Britain of caravans and out-of-town aquatics dealers.'
– Stuart Maconie

'Lisa Blower is a highly regarded short-story writer whose new novel tells the tale of an unlikely road trip undertaken by Selwyn and Ginny, two endearing and idiosyncratic sixty-somethings. Blower has drawn an unlikely romance between two people who are meant for each other, but don't know how to be together.' – Dan Brotzel, *iNews*

'Her characters are wry and complex, despite the apparent mundanity of their surroundings.' – *Big Issue North*

'A tale of the extraordinary within the ordinary... Blower's sketches of minor characters are delicious [and] her taste for drama, when present in her scene descriptions and characters, works brilliantly.' – Mandy Sutter, *New Welsh Review*

'*Pondweed* is superb and I was entirely drawn in. Lisa Blower has the knack of making the most mundane and unlikely worlds become full of depth and colour. The concept is high comedy but these folk become so quickly, quietly tragic and more tragic because they had so little to lose in the first place, and yet somehow managed to lose it. This is a delicate, careful novel about people we are forced to care about.'

– Jonathan Davidson, Writing West Midlands

'Lisa Blower is an excellent storyteller. It's a phenomenal talent, to be able to make people care about the history of people that they don't necessarily even like that much, and Lisa manages it brilliantly.' – Ninja Book Box

'Edgy, raw and just a little bit dark, Lisa Blower's prose is biting and fresh. This is a book to lose yourself in, filled with simple yet devastating truths and razor-sharp observations. And it is funny, laugh out loud funny. In the way that snatches of life and overheard conversations take on meaning and mirth. For every pool of darkness, there is a glorious patch of light. Without a doubt, one of my reads of the year.'

– *Book Bound*

LISA BLOWER

PONDWEED

Myriad Editions
An imprint of New Internationalist Publications
The Old Music Hall, 106–108 Cowley Rd,
Oxford OX41JE
www.myriadeditions.com

First published in 2020 by Myriad Editions
This Myriad paperback published in 2021
First printing
1 3 5 7 9 10 8 6 4 2

A CIP catalogue record for this book
is available from the British Library

ISBN (paperback): 978-1-912408-72-6
ISBN (ebook): 978-1-912408-73-3

This is a work of fiction.
Names, characters, places, businesses, locales, events and incidents are the products of the author's imagination or have been used in a fictitious manner. Any resemblance to actual persons, living or dead, or actual events is purely coincidental.

Designed and typeset in Sabon
by www.twenty-sixletters.com

Illustrations by Ramiia Tiugunova

Printed and bound in Great Britain
by Clays Ltd, Elcograf S.p.A

For Dave
My big adventure

PARKED OUTSIDE THE HOUSE is the Toogood Aquatics Swift Conqueror caravan with its saucy mermaid curtains, fully stocked bar, and the words *For your pondlife and beyond* stuck on the side, in the sort of red slanted font favoured by pound shops.

A man stands aside of this caravan as if he's just birthed it. This man is tall, but not imposing. His hair is a nest of fag-ash grey. His face like an ornate clock. He is wearing a suit jacket with patched black slacks and an XL red-and-white-check shirt with a button missing across the chest. This is a man I do not know, yet he is instructing me to pack what I need and to get in our car, which he's attached to the caravan. Behind me, a couple put in an offer on *A Place in the Sun* on the telly.

He says, 'The sooner you get in the car, the sooner we can get going.' He scans our road as if expecting something to happen.

Nothing is happening. Nothing ever is happening. He raises his voice as if this is something happening.

I ask him, 'What's happening?'

He says, 'I'll tell you everything in the car, but please. Pack what you need. We have to go. We're running out of time.'

By now, I've forgotten everything about us and all reasons for us being together. I try to remember when he was so irritatingly handsome he would admire his own reflection in a cheese grater.

'Are you leaving me, or am I leaving you?' I ask.

He grunts as if he's just passed a kidney stone. 'Ginny,' he says, giving me the same look as he does when he's seen our winter heating bill. 'We're finished. The bastard's gone and blown the lot.'

We all whimper at the faint whiff of romance, yet it is such a grub. I met Selwyn Robby in the garden centre. Almost fifty years had lumbered by since we'd parted ways and then he was right there, in the aquatics franchise selling garden ponds. I heard him before I saw him. He was talking intently to a couple about pond liners as if they might repair a doomed marriage. 'The most durable in the world with a lifetime guarantee,' he was saying. And there it still was: that Welsh borders accent with its fat and thick vowels that used to soothe my mother like a dose of laudanum, and no doubt doing that thing he used to do where he pinches his nostrils together and sniffs. 'This is top-quality Swedish Butyl rubber. One hundred per cent watertight, even in swell.'

For the size they wanted – 'Because you must consider the edging excess for the expansion during the water fill' – this particular liner was going to set them back £85.99 a square metre, and this was apparently without underlay, which was going to cost them another fifty quid per square metre if they went with the tight-mesh he was recommending with hand sewn trims. The couple looked as if they were having to share their lottery win with a family they despised. This was a little out of budget for them, they said. They were only in a retirement new-build with a lawn the size of a postage stamp. Not that this mattered to Selwyn. He pattered on: told them that the Swedish Butyl rubber comes with its own ecosystem, assuring an ecological balance that would filter rainwater and siphon off the right nutrients, as it would with any uneaten fish food. 'It's the effect of a million tiny teeth chewing on algae,' he said solemnly. 'On my mother's grave, you will never find a suffocated fish if you line with this beautiful tarp.'

Impatience had got the better of me – I'm the same with sweets: I'm a cruncher not a sucker – and I'd inched myself forward enough to see who he'd become.

Yes, I'd thought. It could only be you. You: from next door who'd count my hiccups through the wall. And me. Just sixteen then, and ripe as a bowl of apples. Now – happening upon one another again, and it was just as we were, as if time hadn't passed and he still took three sugars in his tea. Though I could tell straightaway that the world had pushed him to one side, as it had with me, as it does with those of us born on our bones. And his left hand then, smoothing down his hair at the back before placing it on the man's shoulder. 'I'm wondering,' he'd said, 'if you've been considering a submersible or external surface model?'

The man looked at Selwyn as if his affair with a submersible model had just been exposed, and his wife clamped her hand over her mouth and gasped that she'd not given it a thought either. 'There is so much to think about,' she'd exclaimed. 'It's like a whole new world.'

Selwyn led the distressed couple to the pond pumps where he got them to cradle each one as if choosing a new born. This one was more economical and practical and likely to sleep through the night. This came with an external pressurised filter – a squawker, if you like – and this one came with a removable leaf trap, which clogs less often: they generally last longer and they're easier to repair and replace parts.

And he doesn't know about her, I kept thinking to myself. I'm going to have to explain, show him a photograph and hope he won't mind. *Understand*, I shall have to ask. *Please. You must understand.* I watch the couple spend over five hundred quid at the till without buying a single fish: Selwyn's knack for selling you his promised version of how your world could be still terrifying.

He *won't* understand.

He will *never* understand.

Except that's when he caught sight of me, and not a bit of me but all five foot nine of me: just another one of those women who's standing behind you in the supermarket queue and dressed as if applying for a job in a department store that will let me down gently. I felt magnified.

You couldn't have counted a blink between us as he swam up to me. A musty aftershave, boots laced with military precision, and *that* smile. God. I remember that smile: I'd thought only freshwater habitats could bring that sort of smile to the hoover parts of Selwyn Robby's leathered face; flagellating moss on the manhole; a soft-boiled egg.

'You remember me,' I'd said, which wasn't the thing I'd wanted to say having had so much to say over the years and thinking about this moment, should it ever happen, and practising what I would say, which would not have been, 'It's been so long I thought you'd have forgotten me.'

He dropped down on one knee and said, 'Marry me.'

Ten months later and here we are. Not married. Not sweethearts. Not quite a couple, or partners in crime, but next-door neighbours, once, who became something else because of the something we did, which I did without thinking when all I felt was rage. A monstrous rage that changed everything. I think about it a lot now – our small story that was over before it was started. I ask Selwyn a lot about it. He says he understands it, so I ask him to explain what he understands. He says, *There's nothing to understand. Just swimmer's itch, that's all.* But it is not all and it is not enough and whenever I tell him that it's not enough, he gives me his choking fish look and says, *How is that perspective working for you?* because salesmen don't just turn the tables, they set them up with such clean cutlery, you can't help but keep looking at yourself.

So, I say to him again, 'I don't understand what's happening, Selwyn. What have you done?'

He says, 'It's not what I've done but what I haven't done. Now, pack what you need. We need to go. Do *you* understand?'

And he's galloping up the stairs, despite the grinding cartilage in his knees, and two at a time, me chasing after him with every fuse blowing in my head.

'No, I don't understand,' I shout at his back and pelt him with questions as hard as I can. 'What's happened? Why are you behaving like this? Are you drunk?'

He flings open the wardrobe door. I watch him shrink back from my hanging clothes as if they're about to sting him. Then he thinks of something else, more important, and reaches up for the suitcase on top of the wardrobe.

It's heavy – he hadn't expected it to be heavy – and he buckles and it lands on the bed with a *thunk*. He stares down on it, frowning. Selwyn's frowns are a foot long and bleed into his neck.

I hold my breath and something sticky lodges in my throat as I watch him look for the zip.

That's when I launch myself on top of the suitcase shouting, 'No. Nothing is going to happen until you tell me what's happening. You need to tell me what is going on.'

I am lying on the suitcase.

He says, 'What's in the suitcase, Ginny?'

I say, 'No. You tell me what is going on.'

He says, 'Why's it so heavy?'

I have both of my hands atop of the suitcase and my breasts pressed into the canvas with my full bodyweight behind them. I say, 'It doesn't matter what's in the suitcase. What matters is you telling me what is happening right now. Why that caravan is outside our house.'

He blows out his cheeks and puts his hands on his hips. He does this when I've burnt the toast.

'You've been leaving me, haven't you?' He points at the suitcase. 'It's why it's so heavy. You've already packed to leave.'

I lift myself off the suitcase and stand up. This is the same suitcase I arrived with when I first moved in with him – ten months ago now – and what's still packed in there I have never worn. I have moved in and not moved in. Lived here and not been living – like a bee that butts our bedroom window, until I've dug the sting into myself and given up. I have wished floods on this house, mini earthquakes and other natural disasters that might bring it down brick by brick. Left the front door wide open, and not a single burglar or even them dregs from the cuckoo's nest chancing their luck.

My eyes settle on my suitcase on the bed. In another life, I could've been a mountaineer with that case. Instead, I have only unpacked it and repacked it and then ironed what had creased.

I say, 'What's in the suitcase is only what I've not taken out.'

Selwyn starts to cough. I ask him if his throat's still sore. Did he gargle with TCP like I told him to? He takes out a handkerchief – man-size, white – the sort my mother always said you should bury with the dead. 'You're not well, Selwyn,' I say. 'What have you taken?'

I mean pills, tablets, he's allergic to everything and probably me, but he tells me, 'The caravan. And we need to leave.'

He looks down at the suitcase again, which is bottle green with a black leather trim, and frayed, ever-so frayed around the edges. He asks me if I have already packed a toothbrush. I tell him, 'I don't know,' so he heads for the bathroom. I follow him in and say it again – 'Selwyn, you really need to tell me what the bloody hell is going on' – and by now I am nuclear with rage. *That* rage. 'You can't just turn up towing that fucking caravan in the middle of the day and start ordering me about without telling where, or why, or– For God's sake, Selwyn!'

He pushes past me, a warrior with our toothbrushes in one hand and his razor in the other, and heads back out on to the landing.

'We really have to go,' he says again. 'Please, Ginny. I will tell you everything, but we need to go. Please.'

What a word it is – *please* – it comes at the beginning and end of everything, and he says it so morbidly that I wonder if he's going to leave flowers like they do on roadsides when someone's life's been snatched by a hairpin bend. I grab his shirtsleeve and tell him that I am going nowhere until he tells me what is going on because this is bloody ridiculous and he's behaving like a madman and making no sense. He hangs his head and scrunches his face and shouts, 'Goddamn you, Ginny! We're going to Wales!'

'Wales? What do you mean, Wales? Why?'

He's made it sound like a punishment when this is positively exotic for the likes of us.

'Snowdonia,' he sighs. He's good at sighing. He sighs so much they form their own opinion. 'It's our nearest New Zealand. I want to see how she handles the roads.'

'New Zealand?'

He suddenly looks very pleased with himself.

'In that caravan?'

He's practically at bursting point.

'Are you fucking serious?'

He tells me again to get in the car. He will tell me everything, but I need to get in the car.

'Is this to do with Mia?' I start to panic. 'Has something happened? Is it Anthony? What's he done?'

My daughter will be fifty next month. Half a century and half a world away. Her being over there, in New Zealand, with one of my old flames, is the stuff of theatre.

'It's nothing to do with Mia.' Selwyn pushes past me to go back into the bedroom. 'I'll explain everything in the car, but we really have to go. You need to get in the car.'

If Mia was here now, she'd just tell me to go with him. *You don't deserve him anyway*, she'd say, and don't I remember how I gave her a map of the world and a box of drawing pins at eighteen and told her to go and adventure? This should suit me down to the very ground I refused to be rooted in. *Like mother like daughter like daughter again*, she would say. To know that you do not know everything about each other should be enough. And that none of us make our mistakes with such purpose.

'Please, Ginny,' he says it so sadly I wonder if he's been given a diagnosis and three months. He coughs again.

'It's lung cancer, isn't it?'

I imagine the next few weeks spent carting about breathing apparatus and being hoodwinked by reincarnation.

He covers his mouth with his handkerchief. 'I'm not ill, Ginny,' and he even laughs it off. 'But for me, for us, *please*. Just get into the car.'

'Because we're going on holiday,' I say. 'To Wales.'

He nods his head, and lifts my suitcase off the bed with a stiff grunt.

'You're just taking me on a holiday. To Wales.'

He says, 'Is this everything? What's in here, it's all you need?'

'Just a holiday to Wales,' I say again.

'Yes,' he says wearily. 'Just a holiday to Wales. Now, please. For the love of God, and whatever it is you think of me. Please. Get into the car.'

I move towards him and take what he'll let me of his hand. 'Is it really such a terrible thing that's happened that we have to leave right now?' I try and make it sound like I'm asking if my lipstick goes with my blouse.

His fingers curl around mine and for a moment I think I have him, and all to myself. No Louis. No bladderwort. No Val from next door. But he pulls his hand away and tells me to stop asking questions. 'You can ask as many of them as you want as soon as we get into the car.'

'Then what about your water butts,' I snap. 'You never leave your water butts.'

He lifts up the suitcase, and at the same time lifts his head slightly so that our eyes should meet – there's little more than an inch in height between us – but we both do what we always do which is remember who we were and not who we are now.

'Okay,' I tell his shoelaces. 'I will get in the car.'

He gives me the same sigh of relief as I make when I've finished the ironing. 'Good. Thank you.'

He leaves the bedroom with my suitcase and I suddenly want to ask him if he's packed enough plasters. Selwyn's blisters can be biblical.

Then I remember my box, at the bottom of the wardrobe. A cardboard box and not at all heavy, but I will go nowhere without it when it is everything and nothing. I tuck the box under my arm and look out of the bedroom window and down on to our street. I watch Selwyn go into the caravan with my suitcase. I wait for him to come back out like he is always waiting for me. He waits and he waits and I still don't truly arrive.

A learner driver pulls up to practice a three-point turn. I watch Selwyn watch the car stall, the car start, the car be thrust into reverse. The car stalls again. The car will not start. The learner driver gets out flinging her arms – *She can't do it! She won't do it!* – and the instructor takes over. Like Selwyn does with me. Holds umbrellas. Opens doors. Licks my stamps. Tells me to put my purse away, he has enough. And, when I'd first arrived, he'd bought me a dress I wouldn't wear, rusty chiffon with bouffant sleeves, to attend some wedding of a friend of a friend where he introduced me to everyone as his like-wife – like it was a thing we'd agreed to do, along with shopping on a Thursday and a run out on a Sunday that always ends with me following him around a pond. Where are you really going, old man? I think, as I straighten the net. This is not like you. This is not what you do. Perhaps I really don't know you at all.

I know you like an under-sheet with hospital corners on your bed; an eiderdown, four pillows, a valance that I refuse to iron. That you talc between your toes and sleep with your eyes open, like a fish; that you and Louis have been the sort of chums that might share kidneys. So what has he done to you, Selwyn? What has happened between you for you to behave like you've disturbed a snake pit?

I close the bedroom door and head back downstairs with my box. I see that Selwyn has left the front door on the latch for me. A slight wind catches it. It opens. *Out.* It closes. *In.* It opens again. *Out.* Enough of a gap to squeeze through. Another breath and *out* again, wider. I have left other places with that suitcase and less thought. I have left and left again, from one rut to the next, and not looked back. When Selwyn sleeps with his eyes open, he is beautiful.

I close the front door behind me and look down at my feet. I do not know the name of this particular species that wraps itself around my ankles, ties itself into a tight bow and pulls, but it's pondweed all the same. I close my eyes and let it take me towards the car.

And so, on the First Day

'There is a great necessity to create ponds in our lifetime for the generations we will never meet. Our country needs them. A pond is the most diverse source of life. It begins with no history and focuses only on its future self.'

~ *The Great Necessity of Ponds*
by Selwyn Robby

SELWYN STARTS THE CAR and straps the seatbelt across his chest like he means it. He has both hands on the steering wheel, his heart in the right place, and driving gloves. He is an unknown species. One that bites his nails to the point they're no bigger than a battery hen's claws. When he talks about his work in pond supplies, he can be as interesting as a dead phone. I have long accepted that if I was a puddle, I'd be of more use to him. And though he insists that this is the beginning of something, when it's way past that and nearing the end, we are going somewhere, and there is something to be said about that. Then he remembers to release the handbrake.

He says, 'It can only ever happen to us, Ginny. Luck favours the wicked.'

I tell myself not to look at who I am but to remember who I've been, and I concentrate on my hands. I settle on the bit between the life line and the love line and the creases that tell you how many children you'll have, which doesn't so much as make me feel disappointed, but reminds me that I know all my lies like the back of my hand. We set off in a shell-shocked silence that neither of us will interrupt.

Selwyn slams on the brakes.

Val.

'WHAT'S TO-DO HERE THEN?' Val coos, gesturing towards the caravan. 'Going anywhere nice?'

Val is our next-door neighbour, not attached. A master of bereavement who makes a fortune out of dead pets, yet she lives like she's only doing a paper round. She's one of those who's always got something wrong with her and, if she didn't have something to complain about that day, she'd be expecting it by the end of the week and probably up at A&E. But her ailments she saves for Selwyn, and for me just sneers and grunts. Most times, she looks straight through me and will even cross the road before she will look me in the eye and say hello.

She chuffs gamely on a Consulate, filling the car with smoke. I cough for effect. She has her arms folded, a polo neck of maroon velour, and looks at me as if measuring me up for a coffin. There are moccasins on her feet. Bunions, I expect. Splayed toes.

'Just a little holiday,' Selwyn offers, as he gets out of the car to speak with her. 'Hardly running off to the other side of the world.'

Yet now we seem to have all the time in the world.

There are many things I want to say to Val but none of them come to me. Instead, I pass the time trying to guess her weight in telephone directories.

Val is a different species entirely. I know only three things about our next-door neighbour, not attached:

1. She's been with her husband Alan since she was twelve, celebrating more anniversaries than the Queen. Rumour has it that they even cut each other's hair at the kitchen sink.
2. She's one of those who's stockpiled for the apocalypse and learnt how to use a gun, while you're still battening down the hatches. The contents of her chest freezer will take your breath away.
3. She spends hours on her hands and knees in the backyard peeling the labels off the tins for the recycling, as if hiding what they eat.

It's not healthy for two people to be together as much as they've been, but Selwyn disagrees. 'We could've made it, too,' he told me. 'If you'd tried.'

Val stands with one hand on her hip looking like she can smell a gas leak. I wonder where Alan is when he normally exists behind her knees. Selwyn is telling her something that I can't lip-read. She is listening. She has been listening through the drainpipes for the thirty years Selwyn has lived aside of her, and it's a slippery relationship. I can't fathom it at all.

She'd mistaken me for his cleaner when I'd first moved in. She'd straddled the paving stones with her hands on her hips, hankering after a truth I couldn't give her. She'd said, 'Selwyn usually tells me everything.' And I'd blathered away – we were next-door neighbours, fifty years back. We've met again. So, I'm here. It'd sounded like an ultimatum. She'd said, 'He keeps that house spotless. Even that gas oven.' And I'd agreed, 'It looks brand new. I'm scared to use it.' In the fog of her fag, her eyes had narrowed. She didn't believe me and she certainly didn't like me. 'Just you make sure you look after it,' she'd said, flicking her cigarette over the hedge. I found myself assuring her that I would.

I watch the two of them together. She nods at Selwyn. Selwyn nods at her. Val nods again and stubs out her cigarette. Then she steps towards him and hugs him. It is the most sincerely given hug I have ever seen a woman give to a man, or a man give to a woman. I expect to feel jealous, but I don't. Selwyn gets back in the car.

'She'll keep an eye on things,' he says.

'You didn't need to *ask* her to do that.'

He pretends he doesn't hear me. He does that a lot.

'Did you tell her where we're going?'

He adjusts the wing mirror and mutters something about not recognising the place, it's been that long, and that if he doesn't go now, he never will.

He turns the ignition. Val turns her back on us.

I suppose this is where we finally begin.

WE'RE SAT ON THE very dual carriageway I can see from our bedroom window. I can still see our bedroom window peeping out from under the flyover and realise that I've forgotten to draw the curtains and put the plants in the bath. The traffic is bottleneck because they're doing something to the flyover that's taking years to finish. Selwyn chose to live under the flyover so he can be *on his way*, as he calls it, when needing to get on the M6. Salesmen, I've come to find, do not like to waste time queuing on flyovers to get on to slip roads. They also keep properly clean cars. Which is why, as I shift my foot and hear the crunch of an empty crisp packet, I smell a rat.

I look around his car and start to see other things I wouldn't normally see. Like a smeared plastic lunchbox and empty sandwich cartons stashed behind the driver's seat. There are blankets on the back seat, covering something large, aside of a body of files he usually keeps in a plastic tub in alphabetical order in the boot. There's also a funny smell. Like hairspray. I turn back around and look out of the window again. In the car aside of us, I see a woman is on her mobile phone.

'I've left my phone,' I say to no one in particular. 'At home. On the bed.'

Selwyn's reply is that Malcolm Gallagher bought a caravan with his redundancy pay out. They're still in Spain. I don't know Malcolm Gallagher. I've never been to Spain. 'It's what folk do with their nest eggs,' he says.

'Folk like us only rent the nest,' I reply. 'And this isn't our caravan.'

He tells me he's just giving me perspective. I tell him I don't want perspective. I want him to tell me what's going on, and ask him to pull over. He tells me he will, as soon as we get going.

'Going where in Wales exactly?' I shout. 'I still don't know what's actually happening.'

'I've told you,' he says. 'It failed to yield.'

I feel like I'm holding on to my temper with a paperclip. 'You *haven't* told me,' I say. 'I don't know what that even means. *What* failed to yield?'

'So, I took the caravan. Reckon it's worth between forty and fifty grand with all the renovation of it. I did the sums.' He pauses to look at me as if calculating what I'm worth.

I tell him we're having two separate conversations, make two fists and wonder what to do with them. I am so wound up I've given myself a stitch.

I wonder which house in Majorca the couple put in an offer for on *A Place in the Sun*.

'I don't understand what you're telling me,' I say again.

He asks me which part I don't understand. I tell him all of it. He uses the words compensation, recompense.

'For what?' I ask.

He tells me I'm not listening. 'The problem with you, Ginny, is that you never listen.'

'I am,' I say. 'You're just not telling me anything that makes any sense.'

'Dennis Glass,' he says. Dennis Glass is someone else I don't know and will not ever know because he died, exactly a week after retiring, from a clot in the leg. 'Joe Salt,' Selwyn presses on. I don't know Joe Salt either. 'He got the cancer as soon as he stopped work.' I try and persuade Selwyn that Joe Salt probably had the cancer before he stopped work, just as comparison can root like cancer if you let it. 'Peter Hale.' Again, I've never heard of Peter Hale. 'Saves up for a holiday of a lifetime, never comes home.'

I'm starting to feel disaster weary.

'Selwyn,' I say solemnly, 'death at our age comes with a free bus pass, but that doesn't mean it's going to happen to you. And this isn't you. You don't do things like this. You don't let things like this happen. You would not have let whatever has happened happen.'

'And you of all people can't really be thinking that I should go back as if nothing has happened, that none of it matters,' he says. 'I'm taking a stand, Ginny. Isn't that what you've always wanted?'

'No,' I reply quickly. 'It's not what I wanted at all.'

'Then what was I supposed to do?' he snaps back. 'What would you have liked me to do?'

'I don't even know what he did, Selwyn. What did *he* do?'

He looks out of the window on his side of the car.

'I'm asking you a question!'

He punches the steering wheel. 'Goddamnit, Ginny! He invested everything and lost it all. All of it. It's gone. There's nothing left.'

'What do you mean he invested everything? What is everything?'

He takes a deep breath and pulls his chin into his neck. 'What bit I had in my pension. And that thirty-grand lump sum.'

'Oh, God.' I clutch my chest.

'Which is why I walked out and took what I could.'

Selwyn has never walked out on anything. Not even me, despite me.

'Well, walk back in,' I say. 'With a lawyer. Haven't you got grounds for embezzlement?'

'Not when I'm in possession of stolen property. No.'

'What are you talking about? It's not stolen. You were his partner. Did he lose all his money too?'

'Of course he lost his money.'

'What the hell did he do?'

'What you have to understand, Ginny, is that sometimes, when an offer is a put on the table that glows gold, you have to take it.'

'You knew about it?'

'I didn't know all of it.'

I find myself looking for sharp objects. A biro. Even a hairgrip. I once read that you can kill a man with a single blow to the temple with a frozen sausage. 'This is not happening,' I mutter into my lap. 'This cannot be happening.' I duck my face into my hands. 'For fuck's sake Selwyn. How the hell did you let this happen?'

'Will you please stop swearing at me,' he asks. 'I hate it when you swear. It makes you sound like a trucker.' He unbuckles his seatbelt then and slumps over the steering wheel. Remorse is a great tactic of the salesman. When the patter has failed, that *look* of astronomical exhaustion – *well, that's that then*. It all comes to nothing in the end.

'Why didn't you just retire when you were supposed to retire last summer?' I try to sound like I've just asked if he still wants three sugars in his tea. 'You had a pension, Selwyn. A thirty-grand lump sum. I told you to take it.'

'And the only way this is going to work, is if you put our future in this caravan and not any of our past.'

I know this is pillow talk but– 'Bollocks. You should've taken the money when he had the money, instead of pretending you still had it in you. The money was there. It was right there, offered to you on a plate, and I said to you, 'Take it. Please. Take it.' You are seventy-one, Selwyn. Retirement is there for a bloody good reason.' And I am so angry I am punching my own knees. 'But you didn't take it, did you? Too bloody-minded to take it. Thought you still had something to prove. Well, here's your proof, because now we have no money. Sod bugger all. And you have us running off to Wales with a mobile fucking pub.'

'No, Ginny. We have a renovated Conqueror with fully stocked bar and leather seats,' he corrects. 'Collectors will salivate over it.'

'Stop the car.'

He takes his hands off the steering wheel because the car *is* still stopped in this traffic jam.

'You wanted me to tell you everything, and I am telling you everything,' he says. Then he drops his eyebrows and asks me why I'm so angry when it's not my money. 'This is all coming from the woman who hates being still.' He starts to mock. '"When are you going show me the world, Selwyn? Why don't you and me just take off? What are you waiting for, Selwyn? What do you think is going to happen if you stick around?"'

'But not like this!' I fold one lip over the other to stop anything I might regret coming out of my mouth and see that he is the doing the same. I start to wonder if this is what rubber bullets feel like.

'Well, this is it,' he suddenly says. 'This is me showing you my world.' And just like that, the traffic starts moving and so do we.

Strictly speaking, we met because of kippers.

A man with a cart with his sprats and dabs and winkles from the west would wheel down the road every Friday – Meg would send me out for a cod head, and to make sure it still had its eyes.

Picture the scene: Joiners Square, Stoke-on-Trent, circa 1966, the year of the Barclaycard and hovercrafts. We spluttered and strutted under smog on the slag, workers but not earners, walkers but not explorers, side by side and hand-to-mouth in a wedding ring of terraces werriting about the weather – *to peg out, or not to peg out?* – and what we had left over in the larder for our teas. There were gamblers and grafters in numbers one to ten; hoodlums and hairdressers from eleven to twenty; then Nora the war nurse and Teapot Marge who'd read your tealeaves for a tanner but chuck her another and she'd have you think you were going to change the world. Across the way, Tracy Spooner pushing her phantom baby, and always with her mother, wicked Ethel, who'd grow parsley the size of a hedge. We lived in twenty-three with new neighbours in twenty-four, and no one knows any different and less is definitely not more, but it's Friday which means the Social Club, Babycham, fags, and necking and a cod head for our tea. And *we* were the lucky ones.

We is me, Meg, and the Bluebird. One mother is a butcher, the other never leaves the house – we don't talk of a father but believe in miracles and storks – and I'm a sneeze off sixteen, caring for nothing but boys and petticoats. My hair has never met with scissors, so it's as bushy as a squirrel tail and a weird mushroom-grey. I wear it like a cape that hides the unfastened zips or missing buttons on the backs of dresses my mother makes me wear – woe betide I ever forget that I'm a girl – which have been someone else's and fitted them better. She's a brontosaurus of a woman who casts shadows in the street, and I'm not allowed to call her Mother, Mum, or even Ma. She is only Meg. As if we are roommates. And she calls me Imogen Dare because, goddamnit, I *will*. Yes, I have to pay her board and lodgings, which I do by working in the butchers with her on weekends, and she even puts the coins in an envelope and gets me to hand it her back like we're traders. My other mother says nothing, yet sees everything, drifts from room to room as if on casters, and blends into the walls.

And it really was a wooden-slatted cart filled with wooden ice boxes. The fishman would be looking at me as I'd be looking at the fish who'd sometimes be looking at me and sometimes not, and when they weren't looking at me – which meant their eyes had been plucked out – then I'd look up at the fishman and say, no thank you. Except, this one Friday, the fishman has nothing but kippers and he's trying to get rid of them by offering them at half their price. So, this man appears – and Selwyn is a man, even at twenty he had a face like a barbed-wire fence, all twisted and crinkled like he was permanently puzzled – and he looked too old to be living at home, which he was, our new next-door neighbour at number twenty-four. He'd moved here with his mother and been very vague in where they were from. There was something about them both that made you wonder if snow had fallen and frozen solid – their lives seemed so still.

So, I was looking at the fish which were looking at me and also at the fishman who was looking at me along with this other man, being Selwyn, being our new next-door neighbour in number twenty-four, and Selwyn asks the fishman for how far the fish have travelled because he's not yet found a pond. And he doesn't talk like us, not at all, but with a Welsh lilt that makes the fishman ask him what he's doing round here. Selwyn says something about settling his old dear and he'd be much obliged if the fishman knew of any ponds, lakes, or streams nearby.

'Angler, are you?' the fishman goes. 'Eater or sport?'

And Selwyn says, 'I'm not fishing. I'm interested in the weeds and what's submerged.'

Except I start to realise that Selwyn's not telling any of this to the fishman but to me. He can't stop looking at me, as if he's shocked by the look of me. So, I look back at him, and almost straight in the eye because I've got that tall, and he says, 'Do you mind all those bones, in kippers? Because if it's not what you want, you mustn't let him persuade you. You keep to what *you* want.'

And I just keep looking at him because there's something familiar about him, something I can't put my finger on. Because we've met, haven't we? is what I wanted to say. You and me. Somewhere, somehow, we've been together. And that's when it suddenly occurs to me that there are all kinds of truths, and I could have this all wrong, when Selwyn is more than capable of diddling Louis.

LOUIS TOOGOOD IS A corny, smarmy sort who'd sell you the sunshine if he could. He spends the bulk of his life under the harsh fluorescent lights in his Portakabin, parked at the back of the Toogood Aquatics yard on a blot of land he'd inherited from his father, who for years kept it as a car park for an office block across the way. Louis and Selwyn had met as boys fishing at Rudyard Lake, thrown together in a thunderstorm so fierce they were forced to camp out in a disused fisherman's hut and eat what they'd caught with a fire they'd started by rubbing sodden twigs against a breezeblock. When they ever talk about this night, they make it sound like they'd endured trench warfare and eaten each other's legs to survive. Because that's how Selwyn behaves around him – like he and Louis have drank each other's blood. And like he has no mind of his own.

Selwyn would call Louis Toogood a hybrid species: one of us who wants to be one of them who wouldn't be seen dead with him because they see nothing but themselves. Still, God loves a trier and Louis does nothing but. He tries and he *tries* and then he tries some more.

I first met him four months back. I'd not long had a bath and was coming down the stairs in my dressing gown all pink and woozy, and there he was, stood in the hallway in a cheap navy suit, starched white shirt and holding a bag from the Chinese takeaway.

'Oh,' I'd said. 'I didn't know,' and asked for five minutes to go and get dressed. But Louis was already bulldozing his way up the stairs to meet me and, before I knew it, he was on the step below me, leaning in to kiss my cheek – God, it was good to meet me, finally, and did I like Chinese?

His aftershave took my breath away. He'd already been drinking, and the coarseness of his stubble could've struck a match. I concentrated on the dandruff in his hair.

By the time I came back downstairs, he'd hammered his way through a bottle of red and was enquiring of a second. I wondered for his leash. I'd known wives like that. And also drunks. They'd laid out the Chinese on the dining-room table and both of them were eating out of the silver trays and sharing curry sauce by the spoonful. Louis talked so fast he spat rice. Selwyn agreed with everything he said and didn't look at me once.

'Share, or nothing,' Louis kept saying. 'It's what it's come down to, old boy. Share, or nothing.'

That was the moment when Louis Toogood offered Selwyn a partnership. Until then, Selwyn had been his sole employee and was thinking about retiring. He'd not long celebrated his seventy-first birthday, with a teenage thirst that'd led to a hangover the size of a Burslem Bobby, and had recently recovered from a ruptured hernia he'd had removed from his groin. A month later and he bumps into me in the garden centre where he'd been working the odd weekend as a favour to someone he'd known for donkeys, but now can never remember his name. As far as I could work out, Louis had founded Toogood Aquatics, but Selwyn had had a thirty-grand stake in it that, it'd been agreed – on a handshake and two bottles of red – would be returned with interest on his retirement, along with a small pension that Louis had supposedly set up as separate to Selwyn's piddle-pot of a council pension from his time as a gardener.

Except Louis had come to the house to ask Selwyn to not retire. Rather, he could re-invest his thirty grand back into a capsizing business to keep it afloat, this time as a partner. And, no, that thirty-grand stake had not made any interest, old boy, when austerity has had us by the nuts.

'Not because you trade in the dead niche market of pond supplies in landlocked Stoke-on-Trent,' I'd said. And I know I shouldn't have said it but I couldn't help myself. They'd been getting on my wick with all their sentimental bird droppings and whatnot, and so Louis glared at Selwyn who properly glared at me and I looked down to glare at how much rice had been spilt on the table, and we'd all got our fingers on triggers as we weighed each other up, until Selwyn buckled first and fetched out the whisky and two glasses.

'Be a poppet and get us some ice,' Louis was a sharp as a pistol and pissed. I shot him a filthy look and he slung me one back and said, 'On the rocks already, eh? Dunna yer worry yourself, duck. I prefer things neat.' It was like being cursed. He looked at me as if I had no face. I'd left them to it.

Later, as Selwyn and I cleaned our teeth at the bathroom sink, I told him that I didn't trust Louis, 'Blood brother, batman, whatever it is that bonds you, you can't put a penny between his eyes and he wears grey shoes.' Selwyn looked miffed and said he would trust him with his life, as he had done many times before, and that this was a full-blown partnership.

'But this isn't what we agreed,' I'd said. 'You promised me when I moved in that you'd retire. Time for us, you said.'

'I'm not just dabbling about here,' he'd said. 'And it's not like we have grandchildren.'

I'd said, 'If that's aimed at me, then I'm going right now.'

He'd said, 'Be fair, Ginny. A lot of my life has happened without you in it and something like this is not really your decision.'

I'd said, 'The point of being a couple is to decide together. The only couple sat at the table tonight was you and him.'

'And the closest we get to being a couple is when we clean our teeth together at this bloody bathroom sink,' he'd said. 'Because what about sleeping, Ginny? Can we decide about that?'

Only in the morning did he apologise about the grandchildren thing. 'Sorry,' he'd said. 'But I guess that's something you'll need to tell me about too.'

Selwyn treats the car park of Trentham Gardens like some race track as we hit it at fifty miles an hour on what feels like two wheels. I don't know what we're doing here when it's only a ten-minute drive from our house, but neither is this the Trentham Gardens I used to know when it's bloomed into a coach trip battleground with a Premier Inn. Apparently, Johnny Crawshaw is Head of the Pond Brief at Trentham Gardens. I have never heard of Johnny Crawshaw. I did not know there was a brief about ponds. What does the Head of the Pond Brief even do?

'Exactly what the manager of that hotel does,' Selwyn huffs, pointing over at the Premier Inn we've just driven past. 'It's hospitality management. Food. Linen. Laundry. Unwanted guests. Do you never listen to a word I say?' He gives me a look that could curdle milk.

'But what are *we* doing here?' I ask.

'I have to see Johnny,' he mutters.

'Does he know what's happened?'

He tells me I can wait in the car. It'll probably be for the best. He'll be twenty minutes, at most.

'Hang on. You've just had me leave the house at breakneck speed without packing a thing to drive us ten bloody minutes down the road and now you're telling me you'll be another twenty minutes and to wait in the car? What's going on Selwyn?'

'It's not like you to be so dramatic,' he says.

'I'm not being dramatic,' but I stop myself from causing a scene for the sake of causing a scene, tell him not to keep me waiting any longer than twenty minutes, and that he has a snag in his jumper. He seems to find this funny and says, 'Now you know how I feel,' and gives me the same look as he did when he realised the kitchen wallpaper had been pasted on upside down.

I watch him walk away from me in the wing mirror until he turns a corner and I can no longer see him. Then I get out of the car, determined to follow him, and wonder if I've become a moll.

I make it only as far as the caravan attached to us. I regard it in much the same way as I used to look at other mothers standing at the school gate: the ones who would look at me and then at Mia and think their thoughts like *slut*. A friend said they didn't think just that. Some were probably very sorry for us. 'Why on earth would they feel sorry for us?' I'd asked. 'Do you feel sorry for us?' We were no longer friends after that. I saw her occasionally with the other mothers, looking sorry, but then Mia asked me not to walk her to school any more. 'I'm not a baby,' she'd said. 'And everyone thinks you're my sister.'

The caravan does not look like it's worth as much money as Selwyn says. I don't understand what made him take it. He used to call it a desperate gimmick. A tin can albatross. He's resourceful, I'll give him that – practical and steady-minded, and he fixes things, hoards things, those natty bits and bobs that will *come in handy*, because in Selwyn's world everything will come in handy. He's like an ant carrying twice his bodyweight in other people's rag 'n' bone. And whether he's taken it, stolen it, thought himself entitled to it, attaching a caravan to a tow bar is surely no quick thing to do. I didn't even know our car had a tow bar. Did it always have a tow bar, or had he fitted one, had one fitted? Which would mean that he was always intending to take it. In which case, he must've known everything. Compensation. Recompense. Thirty thousand pounds. That dribble of ambition, *share or nothing*, one last shot. It was obvious there was only one lifebelt between them.

He did something for me at a time when no one else would, as Selwyn always says when I'm busy seeing red about him not retiring. *He still valued me, Ginny. He didn't wash me up*.

But he did, Selwyn. And it's far from poetic or just.

I stride across the car park with such a pace, I can't even keep up with myself.

I HAVE NOT BEEN to Trentham Gardens in a very long time. It used to be a courting place, back in the day, and a place you got caught when you went AWOL. Meg said they found many a broken soldier hiding out from war in the trees, and a girl, once, with a baby so peaceful it no longer cried. It was our nearest countryside, green and leafy, somewhere to fill our smoky-Stokey lungs with fresh air, and we'd stroll round in three-piece suits and best frocks. We used to come here to sit on deckchairs and eat ice cream. It was the closest we ever got to a holiday, watching the boat on the lake go up and down; us waving at the kids who could afford the ticket, while Meg sneered that it was better to look out at others than have folk look in at you. I remember the fountain mainly. Some primaeval god or other holding Medusa's head. And all those people that would ask if we were using that third deckchair. 'Can't you see someone is sitting there?' Meg would bellow, the rhododendrons triggering her allergies before hay fever was a thing.

Now, it costs £12 to get through the turnstiles. There's a woman with a zapper and a lanyard and plenty of bees in her bonnet, and she won't let me through, even though I've told her I'm not wanting to *be* in Trentham Gardens when I've *been* to Trentham Gardens, and many moons ago, and that I just want a quick word with Selwyn.

'Do you have ID on you, shug?' asks the woman with the zapper and the lanyard. 'Pensioner discount, ten pound.'

I tell her that I don't need *that* many words. And no. I don't have ID. My handbag is in the car. I see from her name badge that she is K A Y C O X, but she is far bigger than the six letters of her name.

'Who do you want to see, shug?' I'm asked again.

'Selwyn Robby,' I repeat. She's making me feel like I've been eating onions. 'Just a really quick word, that's all.' Except she breaks into such a massive smile, I fear it might tear her face.

'Oh! Is Selwyn here? How have I missed him?' She calls over to the woman manning the ticket desk. 'Selwyn's here!' she exclaims. The woman manning the desk looks up and parts the sort of hair that belongs on a Shetland pony to reveal unfashionable glasses and a face that reminds me of how skin bunches around a too-tight watchstrap.

'Is he?' she replies. 'Since when?'

'I was just saying. Not like him to walk past without saying owt.'

'Not like him at all,' the woman behind the desk says. 'I'll be having bloody words.'

'Well, that's all I want to do,' I interrupt. 'He's gone to see Johnny Crawshaw.'

They both look at me as if I've just clobbered them with a wet fish.

'Johnny?' asks Kay Cox.

'Yes, Johnny,' I repeat.

The two women look at each other in the way you can imagine two women looking at each other when they don't believe the woman in the middle of them is telling the truth. Part of me wonders if they're hiding something from me, because, let's face it, we're no longer spring chickens and they've still not cured cancer; Selwyn charms for a living and swabs his bladderwort in the backyard with cotton wool. A more sensible part assures me that Trentham Gardens, always so waterlogged with its lake and ponds, has been a client of Selwyn's for more years than he's ever let on, and, what with it being a stone's throw from where we live, he's bound to come here more regularly than I have ever thought, given that I don't ever think about Selwyn's work as a pond supplies salesman when it is ever so dull. Kay Cox comes closer.

'I'm sorry, shug,' she says, slowly. 'But Johnny's passed. Month back now. Selwyn was there.'

An image comes to mind of Selwyn in black waders and plaid shirt chucking handfuls of an old mucker into Trentham's lake. I don't remember a funeral. Or any sadness. I don't even ask what he's sold, or even where his day might have taken him, just tell him that the electricity bill needs paying and the council tax is due. The two women intently watch for my reaction.

'Didn't you know?'

I can see that this is upsetting Kay Cox. If she could clutch a Bible right now, she probably would, and read me a sermon on the afterlife. She opens and closes her mouth as if she wants to say something else but can't think what it is. I murmur something about going to wait in the car and repeat the words to both women. Kay Cox mutters how sorry she is, but I can't even thank her when I'm not sure if I should be sorry too.

The walk I take back across the car park happens without me feeling a single stride. I get back into the car. A wave of hunger comes over me and I turn to root among the empty sandwich cartons for a lone crust or a slice of damp cucumber, anything to wet my mouth and bring me back to life. That's when I realise that the blanket-covered lump on the back seat has gone too.

In the wing mirror, I see Selwyn striding across the car park pushing a wheelbarrow full of boxes. At first, I look away, which is what I always do when wondering what he sees in me. Then I open the car door and rush towards him like a startled child. I'm already talking, because he didn't leave me the keys, did he? and I needed to go to the toilet and I didn't know how long he'd be, and he'd been more than twenty minutes, and there were these women in the foyer – because when did you have to pay to get into Trentham Gardens? – and they wouldn't let me through and they knew you, like *really knew you*, and when I came back, the thing on the back seat you'd covered with blankets had gone. And if you'd just told me what we were doing here then I wouldn't have got out of the car to go to the toilet and would have minded whatever it was on the back seat because now it's gone, and that's going to be my fault, isn't it, when I've let so much slip and we've gone nowhere but just around the bloody corner? And he just stares at me as if there's something peculiar-headed crawling up my arm. And this is my least favourite tactic of the salesman: letting me talk myself into admitting something that I haven't done.

He says, 'It was a pond filter.'

'Then you should've told me it was a bloody pond filter.'

'Which I sold to Johnny.'

The words startle me. 'Selwyn,' I say. 'They told me about Johnny.'

But he's taking the boxes out of the wheelbarrow and putting them into the boot of the car. I try and see if the boxes have labels. They don't. I ask him what's in them. He tells me provisions. I ask him again – 'For what?' He tells me to stop asking him questions. I'm not letting him think.

'I don't want to lose my temper, Ginny,' he says. 'Let me think.'

'Then give me answers,' I say, with my hands on my hips, because this always seem to work for Val. 'Tell me properly what is going on.'

'You know what's going on,' he retorts, and he rests his hands flat on a box. He has his eyes closed, which stops me from asking for all the other lies – it's impossible to know how many other lies there might be, and if we are one too. He starts wringing his hands, as if they've gone numb, and when he opens his eyes again I see how scared he is. Selwyn is a frightened man.

'I'm really sorry about your friend,' I say, talking to the concrete underfoot. 'But you didn't have to lie about it.'

He takes a breath so deep it's almost stubborn. Then he slams down the car boot and heads for the driver's seat without glancing up.

'You're not listening to me, Selwyn.'

He thumps down his hand on the car roof and makes me jump.

'Actually, Ginny, I've been listening and *listening*, and the thing about listening is that you expect to be listened to back.'

'And I've been listening too,' I tell him. 'But there's a big gap between what you tell me and what you don't, so I'm not even sure how we've got here, or why you've just lied about Johnny.'

'I'm hungry,' he says.

'You're doing it again.'

He opens the car door. 'Are you getting in?' He looks at me as if he's warning me. And it makes me remember how I used to watch him, down by the canal skimming stones. Did he know I was there watching, my legs hooked around a tree branch in ankle socks? Probably. Selwyn sees the world with a fish-eye lens. He would *spin* those stones right across the canal, count their bounces as they galloped into the hedge on the other side. His whole body would be rigid. He wouldn't even move his head. And then my mother, happening to walk by, and attempting to hide herself behind a bush. 'Oh, just looking for blackberries,' she'd shout when he'd spotted her spectating. 'Just stretching the old legs.' And he was kind enough to never give me away up in the tree.

'Good,' he says, as I get into the car. 'You had me worried then that I was doing this alone.'

We might have lived next door to each other, but we knew nothing about each other. We saw each other. On the street. Over the wall between our backyards. When he queued for a pound of middle-cut bacon and two pork chops. We knew that Selwyn's mother had the night terrors – we could hear her bawling through the walls and wailing her gobbledygook. We knew that Selwyn went to work and then didn't go to work. Then he seemed to be working again, and his mother's howling quietened. We knew he was always doing something in the backyard. Out there on his hands and knees with his sleeves rolled up and dipping into tin buckets he'd have lined up against the wall. We asked him once, 'What are you doing down there?' He told us he was growing things, things that can slip through your fingers as they can just as easily pull you under. We wondered if he was a scientist. He told us no, just looking for something, and spent a long time fishing out the dead leaves.

One day, as I came home from school, he was sat waiting for me on the front step. He reached for my hand and said, 'Here.' Gave me a jam jar full of rose petals that looked melted. He said it was perfume. He gave me a sniff. As I bent down to do so, his fingers coiled in my hair. I let the moment happen and hoped my hair might leave papercuts across his knuckles.

'I know you're not her,' he'd said to me. 'But some days I think you are. How else would you be here?'

I gave him the perfume back and told him, 'No, thanks.'

Whatever was in that jar smelt rancid. Like death.

The pub is called the Swan with Two Necks and I think about this – how two heads are better than one; how swans mate for life; how my pair of mothers would sit aside of one another creaming their necks before bed. *Gondernecks,* the pair of them. There was nothing they didn't see.

Of course, Meg and the Bluebird weren't the only women living together to make ends meet and meet again in those hope-thin walls of Joiners Square, but they were women whose small minds took them nowhere. Contented women. Abandoned women. Working women. Women too busy to go in for *all that women's stuff*, as they called it, when actually, they were living it. Women who gossiped and fell out then spoke the next day as if nothing had been said. Women who got dressed in disappointment – but kept that quiet too – and never thought to lock their doors, in case someone needed a needle and thread. Women who muscled their way to the front of the queue, stuck it on the slate and worried about it later. Wise women. Knowing women. Women who put up and shut up and whipped up a cake with the cookie crumbles. Gruff women. Sick women. Women who needed no one but themselves. Meg and the Bluebird came together under a grey cloud in the middle of it all, kept the curtains shut, just in case. Children can be the cruellest of creatures, I came to find, but it was other women who became their downfall. Men would simply turn a blind eye.

I know nothing of my father – call him John for all I care – as I was once told that I was given to Meg, a child for a child so both could grow up. She would say nothing about it other than the world could be a sewer, so I never looked for him and he never looked for me, though, as the Bluebird once pointed out, there was never anything to be found.

If I ever talk about my mothers – which is not a lot, when there's not much *to* tell – Selwyn makes any number of curmudgeonly statements to stop me. It is the only time he does not treat me with kid gloves. *Your mother was a butcher who gatecrashed funerals sniffing for heirlooms,* he will say. *She carried a knife like a handbag. She stuck pictures to the wall with chewing gum. She frightened my mother to death.*

This did not, however, stop him from counting my hiccups through the wall. He tells me he would lie there listening for me at night and only slept when my hiccups stopped. I tell him that that was probably around the time when I'd discovered that eating toothpaste calmed the indigestion I suffered, because of all the meat I was served.

Don't you remember the way Meg used to look at you? I'll ask him. *She'd sparkle up like a Christmas tree!*

But no. He doesn't remember that.

The thing about salesmen, I've come to conclude, is that they start everything, finish nothing, and spin much in between. Meg used to say that it was all in the sinew and that his was twisted with pain. *You can see it in his eyes,* she would say. *They're looking but can't see what they're looking for.*

He saw me in what he called a 'thunderclap moment', and could not take his eyes off me. Said, if he didn't know any better, he'd have thought me a witch. His mother would not even let me in the house. Or she'd stop me in the street to ask me why I'd come to haunt her and reach out with long arthritic fingers to stroke my hair.

'I have told you everything I know,' Selwyn says, snapping me out of my thoughts as we carry our drinks through the pub. And no. He does not want the table by the window. Here, slap-bang in the middle of it all, is fine, and he sets about reorganising his cutlery for the left-handed diner.

I remind him that what he knows and what he tells me aren't the same thing, and is there a particular reason why he wants us to be so conspicuous in the dead-centre of the room? He takes some tablets from his jacket pocket and swills two down with his pint.

'What are they for?' I ask.

'Indigestion.' He wipes his mouth on a red paper napkin that stains his lips.

I look around the pub. It's one of those brewery-owned places with gigantic menus, mock-Tudor beams against walls the colour of banana skins, and hundreds of TVs on different channels. Selwyn spends a long time behind his menu, as if it's the most complicated set of words he's ever seen, until we realise that we must order at the bar.

The vase of wine they give me is the same price as a T-bone steak, and it gives me the courage to start asking questions again.

'Because you were partners, right? You and Louis. Reinvesting your thirty thousand meant a fifty/fifty partnership. *Share, or nothing?*'

'Not quite,' Selwyn corrects me. 'Don't forget, he owned the land.'

I screw up my face. 'You told me that you'd been made a *partner*, that was the point of reinvesting.'

He does a sort-of shrug at me and picks up a toothpick to gnaw on between nibbling his nails. 'It's never been about titles, Ginny,' he says.

I take another glug of wine. 'Then tell me this, why does one *investor* have total access to all the money to play on the fruit machines without the other one knowing?'

'It was a hedge fund.'

I don't know what that means. I ask him if he knows what that means. He just says that it was supposed to treble in value and didn't.

'And Louis put all the money in there? Your pension. His pension. Your thirty grand?'

Selwyn looks grizzled and starts to flag down a waitress to order a second pint. I remind him that he's driving.

He says, 'I've told you what I know. And yes, for the last time, please, my pension, his pension, my thirty grand and whatever the business was worth. All gone.'

He stops to beam up at the young waitress as he asks for another pint of Old Peculier. I place my hands on the table and wait for him to finish. But he says nothing and avoids my eyes.

So, I remind him about the land. 'Because he didn't invest the land, did he, Selwyn? The yard? "Why don't you sell it and move everything online?" I'd said. The price Bovis were offering for the place so they could extend the housing estate, Louis could've wound things up, retired you with your lump sum and your pension, and you'd both be bobbing about happy. But no. "It's not how we do things," you said. "That land was left to Louis by his father. I've no claim on that," you said. He has you so tightly wrapped around his little finger it's mercenary.'

'Which is why I took the caravan!' he interrupts. 'You can't stop water flowing, Ginny. But you can direct it into a pond and dam it.'

I slap my hands down on the table. Riddling is my least favourite tactic of the salesman, and we're going around in circles as it is. It makes me wonder how much Selwyn has sold me when–

'Yes, I'm the gammon,' I smile up at the waitress, though I can tell right away that it's overdone. Meg would be having kittens. Gammon is a boiling meat, she would say. Then you baste it in its juices and roast. The smell of a roasting bacon is what gets hostages talking. Selwyn has ordered the T-bone steak – the most expensive dish on the menu, but not always the best cut.

'And it's tough,' he says, pulling a ligament from his lips.

'It's probably too young,' I offer. 'The older the cow, the better she will taste.'

He carries on tucking in. I look around the pub to reassure myself that Louis is not here; there's some uncomfortable laughter and I wonder if that's him. It was his laugh that I couldn't stand. Brash and high-pitched, like women cackling under hairdryers; it made people stare and he liked that. He liked people to look at him. When he knew people were looking, he turned up the jokes until he had everyone in the palm of his hand, cracking up. *Oh, Louis,* they'd say, *you're wasted. Priceless. You should be on the stage.* I grant that he has wasted a fair proportion of his life performing, to the point that he no longer knew who he really was.

I pick up a strand of grated carrot and chew on it like cud, shift my gammon about with my fork to make a perfect right angle.

'Do we fit together?' I ask.

'What does that mean?' he spits more gristle into the red napkin.

'Like fit together. Like Alan and Val fit together. Like Meg and the Bluebird came together.' I twist my foot under the table and hear it click. 'I sometimes don't know if we're trying to be this *thing* that's just in your mind.'

He lets his cutlery clatter on to his plate. 'This *thing?*' he repeats.

'You say all these things to me, how you've waited, how there's been no one else. But there was. There was always Louis, and even now we're here because of Louis.' I pause. He's looking for my hand across the table and I hide it on my lap. 'What do you see in him?' I snap. 'What do you see that I can't?'

He wipes around his mouth with his hand and then does the same thing with a napkin. I watch his face. Wait for the confession. Brotherly love, maybe? A snatched kiss once? Two men who grew up without fathers, manning each other up into one another's heroes?

'Something binds you to him,' I carry on. 'It's unnatural.'

Selwyn looks startled by this. 'You really don't like him?'

'Are you serious? He's cheated you out of your life's earnings, yet you still treat him like you owe him your life.'

'He has saved my life more times than I deserve,' he says stoically.

'Don't paper over this. He is a liar and he is a thief.'

'And what's that out there?' he raises his voice at me and swings his arm to point out of the window towards the caravan in the car park. 'Tell me, Ginny. What is it?'

'I don't know what it is,' I fire back. 'I don't even know what you're doing with it, or where you think we're even going to go in it. All I know is that it is not your pension or your thirty-thousand-pound stake in the business.' When I stop, I see that he's looking straight into my eyes. 'What?' I ask.

'Your eyes,' he says slowly. 'They never look like they belong to you.'

I cover my face with my hands and snort. 'I'll tell you what I see, Selwyn,' I say between my fingers. 'Because when people like Val and Alan look in the mirror, they see each other. But when you and I look in the mirror, you see me and I see...' I stop. I dig my front teeth into my bottom lip. 'What I've always seen.'

I wait for him to ask me what? But he doesn't. He slices into his T-bone steak instead and, as I watch him chew, I realise that I have eaten with this man for the past ten months but have never known how he really chews his food.

'You're grinding your teeth,' says the Bluebird to Meg. 'You're eating like a pig in a trough. Take your time.'

Meg looks at me. I look down at my plate, but I don't remember what we're eating, just that it's meat. It's always meat.

I've just turned sweet sixteen. There is something stuck in my teeth and I'm taken to the dentist. He removes a piece of meat and removes the tooth too. The anaesthetic I'm given makes me dream of the sea – a sea that's a hundred miles away when we're slap bang in the middle of things in a place too north for the Midlands and too south for the north – and I'm using fried doughnuts for armbands. When I open my eyes, I hear my mother asking the dentist if he's legal. She is a butcher, and never in her life has she witnessed such butchery on the gum of a child. And though I'm woozy on the anaesthetic, she marches me out into daylight, shoving cloves into my cheeks, vowing revenge.

Later that night, my mother tells me that the anaesthetic made me say things, and not the sort of things you'd expect from a sixteen-year-old girl. I was lying on the settee with a pillow behind my head that was stuffed with a hot water bottle. My mouth was still full of cloves and my nostrils filled with Christmas. There was a stabbing throb around my jawbone so persistent that I couldn't keep my eyes open, and my gum was still bleeding. We'd run out of handkerchiefs and Meg was now mopping me up with the same serviettes she used in the butcher shop to display the meat.

'You said things,' Meg began again. 'Things you shouldn't be saying. Not ever. Do you understand? You are a child, Imogen. *A child.*' Then she turned around to the someone else in the room that wasn't the Bluebird and told them, too, that I was still a child.

And I want to be sure – sometimes when I remember this, I am very sure – that the person she turned around to address was Selwyn, and that she was banishing him for something, something he was insisting that he would not do.

'Because this is a child,' she kept on saying. 'Do you understand? She's my *child.*'

I run my tongue across the empty gap and find a little piece of meat stuck in my gum now. I look across the table at Selwyn.

You are always there, I think. You come out of nowhere, yet you've always been there. You smother me by being everywhere. In my thoughts. In my memories. In my longings. In my way.

And it was *you*. Of course, it was *you*. I dreamt about you. You'd saved me from drowning in the sea and I'd asked you to swim inside of me. *But I'm already in there,* you'd said in my dream. You were swimming inside of me with a fierce front crawl.

'What?' Selwyn says. 'What have I done now?'

But here is the waitress again, asking if everything is okay with our food.

THERE'S A ROOM TO the right of us, a conservatory, that's crammed with people wearing black. A wake, and Selwyn is absorbed. If there's one thing I do know about Selwyn Robby, it's his galactical fear of death.

A waitress is busy peeling cling film off trays of sandwiches and, for some reason, I find myself mourning the salad garnishes that will be left behind on the silver platters. A trug of chicken thighs is brought in and the people swarm. A plate of ribs next. A vegetarian is shown a cheeseboard. We start to hear a woman complaining to the waitress: she has not brought out all that was ordered. 'There should be more meat than this.'

Selwyn stares and does not blink.

The woman says it again, '*This is not enough meat!*'

Selwyn gets up from the table and lets his napkin fall from his knees. He doesn't pick it up. There's still a lot of steak left on his plate. This is not like him. He does not waste things. He does not litter. He will not owe. He pushes his chair against the table. He mutters something about needing air and loosens a couple of buttons on his shirt. He looks up at the ceiling and wonders for the watt of the light bulb above us. 'It's throwing off a lot of heat,' he says, wiping his brow with the back of his hand. 'Can't you feel it?'

He looks across at the mourners again. The woman is still dressing down the waitress who is checking a list. She is sorry, but that's all the kitchen has made, what she had ordered. I real-ise Selwyn is walking towards them, holding his plate.

I call after him– 'Selwyn, what are you doing?'

But he's already face-to-face with the woman and giving her his plate.

'Here,' he is saying. 'If that's all that's important to you, have mine.'

I am behind him holding on to his arm. 'Selwyn, come away.'

'Go on,' he instructs the woman. 'I want you to have it.'

The woman is looking at him and then at his half-eaten steak on a plate streaked with mustard and ketchup and blood. Her dress is expensive – I can tell by the darts, the way it fits her like a glove – and she wears her hair in a French pleat, with a look of acceptance that the world is this unjust. A man now, aside of her, wants to know if Selwyn has a problem. He nudges the plate into Selwyn's chest and tells him to have some respect. Selwyn says he has plenty. 'So much bloody respect.'

I pull on the back of his shirt and tell him to, 'Leave it, please,' and then apologise to the man and woman. 'It's been a really crap day,' I say, and she raises her eyebrows at me and says–

'Not that crap. You still have your husband.'

And we're all looking at each other like we want to hurt each other, and the other people about us go quiet and turn around to look at us. I start apologising again–

'I'm so sorry, so very sorry for your loss.' And I pull on Selwyn's shirt tails once more. 'Come on, Selwyn. Please. You don't know what you're doing.'

He turns to look at me, but looks straight through me, like his eyes have been glazed with honey. Then he looks back at the woman, swallows hard, looks down at his plate and says, 'I'm really sorry. But I'm grieving too.'

He walks back to our table, puts down the plate and abandons it.

THE ROOM IS DISSATISFYING and small. The door opens on to the double bed with its feeble white duvet, and there's a window above the bed, with curtains that don't meet in the middle. On the wall are two aerial photographs of when this place was all fields. Selwyn, wearing his reading glasses with the thick black rims that make him squint, is looking at them intensely.

'You should've got rid of all that lettering on the caravan,' I say, as I peer around a folding door at the en suite. The toilet is low. The wash basin would not bath a baby, and the extractor fan is lawnmower loud. I fold the door shut. 'You should do it before we start again. It makes us a laughing stock.' I pause. 'Unless, of course, you're going to return it.' I stand aside of the tiny bedside table and try the lamp. 'Perhaps enough is enough. Perhaps we don't need to go anywhere at all.' The bulb in the lamp is massive and gives the room a dirty glow.

There's an ant crawling up the lampshade. I watch it. It's so busy, so fast, so adamant in its direction. It hurries up to the top of the shade and I peer over to see what happens next. It goes down the inside, and pops up back where it started, heads in the same direction.

Behind me, Selwyn still has his nose against one of the photographs of a time when the Swan with Two Necks was a farm. Photographs like this excite him. He'll show me a grey blob in a minute and tell me it's a yesteryear pond; that agricultural drainage systems have a lot to answer for when they've slurped it up for crops. He will tell me things like, 'A natural pond is like a Turkish bird bath,' that the living organisms within them feed the flies, and that *we* need the flies to survive. He saves coffee jars to fill up when he stumbles across a manmade lake, then studies each one on the kitchen windowsill waiting for what he calls 'violent agitation'. I tell him that I am violently agitated when I find more jars in the airing cupboard, or when he scoops out my bathwater from the outside drain for skin cells to feed gnat larvae. He tells me he is saving the earth. He has a water butt in the backyard, that collects rainwater, where he's growing something alien called bladderwort, which he swabs with cotton wool. When a brook runs orange, he calls the council to inform of a bust lead pipe that will poison the voles. After the washout of the Garden Festival back in '86, he submitted a document to the Town Hall that was never read because they built on the site anyway. When we argue, he tells me it's to be expected. *I live unheard,* is what he says.

Selwyn stops looking at the photograph to fidget on the top of the bed. He takes off his glasses and closes his eyes.

'Oh, God,' he murmurs. 'That poor woman. That was unforgivable.'

He lies there with the flats of his palms over his eyes as if he cannot bear to watch what he's being reminded of. I tell myself to say nothing. Then he turns away to face the wall and from the shuddering in his shoulders, I wonder if he's crying.

He told me that, on the day I left Joiners Square, he wept so hard his mother slapped him to stop. It wasn't worth it. He told me that he stayed where he was, in case I came back. That girls chased him. That girls called and giggled on the phone. That he looked the other way because he was still looking for me. He was a year off thirty when he left for the house on the right side of Hanford, under the Queensway, and took a job gardening, up Hanley Park, where he dug, raked and found things – needles, tramps, an old tumble dryer, a carrier bag of baby clothes, once, that tore into his heart. He tamed the laburnums and planted elms, cut back the roses and battled the bamboo. Made birdboxes that got catapulted, and found one being used to deal drugs. He disagreed with *Keep off the Grass* – a public park was a public place for a public to roam – but litter hurt his feelings, and his fuchsias were often dug up. It made him awful philosophical about human nature: the willingness to destroy. When he told me all this, I felt a stirring, like a spring being unwound, but it wasn't quite enough to shed clothes.

He was let go at forty-two, owing to council reshuffles, and took part-time hours in a garden centre. He treated it like a refuge. People *wanted* his plants. He became a salesman there quite by chance: a regional manager, checking stock, overheard a sales patter he knew he needed to get his hands on. Selwyn had to confess: he'd always had a fascination with ponds. He was sent on the road by the garden centre's parent company. Up to Manchester. Down to Birmingham. Once to Blackpool. They went bust. There was no payout. He'd not long hit sixty and was having to start again. He filled out application forms – too pig-headed to sign on – and put up postcards in supermarkets advertising gardening services, when most people had concrete backyards and patios. Then, one day, a knock at the door and there's Louis with his spit of ambition, two bottles of red, and a piece of land he'd been sitting on since he'd inherited it from his father, had come up with an idea: 'Ponds, old boy. There's nothing me and you don't know about ponds. It'll be the making of us. Hobbyists pooling expertise. Then we'll retire the men we should've been.' But the only thing that was different about Selwyn Robby was the way he parted his hair.

The ant on the lampshade briefly changes direction. Stops. Looks left. Looks right. Re-joins its original path and starts again.

I put my hand on Selwyn's shoulder. He shrugs it away.

We traded our life stories in the first few days of meeting again. They were such tatty tales, so basic, so brittle – they'd barely last out a pot of tea. Selwyn said, 'Without each other, we've not amounted to much, have we?' And asked me to move in with him straightaway. 'We're just wasting more time we don't have,' he'd said, sitting on the edge of the armchair in my flat on Wellington Road. 'And I have a house, with two bedrooms. A big kitchen. It needs living in.'

He sent a man with a van to come and collect me within the week. I had barely drawn breath, barely filled that van up. I really did have nothing much. We kissed a little in the hallway, neither of us really knew what to do with our hands, and I could taste the tuna fish bap he'd had for lunch on his lips. Two hermits becoming one and trying to create something out of whatever it was we once shared; he took my hand and began to lead me. Halfway up the stairs, I'd had to confess.

'Now, don't be making a big deal out of it. It's just the way it is. And before you ask, I've seen everyone I need to see and it can happen again.'

He'd said it was me who'd got the wrong end of the stick and that he just wanted to show me the back bedroom where I would sleep; that he was happy to get me a new single or a double bed – no matter to him either way – though it could all probably do with a lick of paint and some ladylike curtains. When he held my hand, I'd expected to feel the same relief as I did when they'd counted my daughter's fingers and toes after she was born. But it wasn't relief I felt. It was fear.

'No,' I'd said. 'I have my own bed.'

He went to make us a cup of tea – still three sugars in his tea – and I remember thinking, even if it isn't love, it'll still be enough.

I do wash our sheets separately though.

I see that Selwyn has fallen asleep, and on top of the bed fully clothed with his eyes open. That's the other thing. I Googled it once. It was freaking me out. I'd think he was awake and be talking away. 'Selwyn, are you listening to me?' Nocturnal lagophthalmos, said the definition online. A phenomenon not fully understood. I'd asked my daughter about it on the Skype.

'What does it even mean?' I'd shrieked. 'Can it be cured?'

She'd asked for why it bothered me so much when we slept in separate bedrooms?

'Because his face turns to stone,' I'd said. 'He looks completely dead. But what if I get it wrong and leave him there for days in the armchair thinking he's just knackered?'

'What does Selwyn say about it?'

'I've never asked. I don't want him to know that I know because then he'll know that I've been watching him sleep.'

She used the opportunity then to talk about Anthony, something that was freaking her out, just like she always did. *Would he do this with you? Did he ever tell you? Can you remember the way he did this?*

No, I'd tell her. *We weren't actually ever really together like that...* and I'd switch off the computer. Text her later to say that the satellites must be shifting on the bottom of the world. I'd wait for her to reply as I sat on the edge of the bed watching Selwyn sleep with his eyes wide open and fearing him already dead. Would I miss what I haven't known? Sometimes, I would sit there in the darkness and tell him the dirty truth of it all. Sometimes, I would just sit. Mia would fail to text back.

I remove Selwyn's glasses as he stares up at the ceiling, take off his socks, and lie aside of him on top of the duvet, just as I have begun to do at home. Outside, the mourners from the wake in the car park shouting drunken goodnights. In here, his breath aside of mine and falling in sync. I wonder if Selwyn's having a breakdown when it happens to the most capable of people. I wonder if it was him who scattered the ashes of Johnny Crawshaw into Trentham's lake. I wonder if Louis will come looking for us and how Selwyn could've been so devoured by money. And right before sleep, Mia. Always Mia. Her radiance is why I sometimes don't sleep a wink.

Headlights swamp the room as car doors slam shut with the last of the condolences. I turn the other way. Wonder if I can sleep with my eyes open, wonder if Selwyn ever really sleeps, until I wake to the sound of the shower and I'm not sure if I've slept or not. There is something heavy in the corner of my eye, and it's my suitcase. I do want a change of clothes, to see something different out of the corner of my eye. I look at the lampshade. I cannot see the ant.

The Second Day

'Ponds are communal, highly-forgiving, hugely welcoming neighbourhoods for virtually every single major group of animals on the planet. With this philosophy, a new pond can, within less than a year, become as valuable to the ecosystem as if it had been in existence for fifty. We, as a species, could learn a lot.'

~ *The Great Necessity of Ponds*
by Selwyn Robby

WE HEAD OUT AFTER a fry up so greasy it oils all our major organs. Go left and left again.

The road winds. Fields both sides. Lime green. Bottle green. Bruise green. Nature's green. This is more green than I've ever seen in my life, and so many sorts of green I go colour-blind. Selwyn goes no faster than forty miles an hour, and the cars behind us wait for stretches of open road to overtake us. As one car does, its driver flicks us the bird, as if we've held him up, cost him his job, his affair, then his marriage and years in child maintenance. I tentatively ask Selwyn if Louis has been in touch and he starts off by saying he thought we would have had this conversation last night, as if he can only talk about it in the dark.

'Anyway, he took my phone,' he says, dropping below twenty miles an hour as we approach a roundabout.

'What do you mean, he took your phone?'

'It was a company phone,' Selwyn says, all matter-of-fact. 'He was within his rights to ask for it back.'

'And you just gave it to him?'

'We need another mirror, a better view,' he says, pointing to the wing mirror on his side. 'I can't see it all. I didn't think.'

Two miles later and we pull into a garage forecourt that's now a hand car wash manned by five pairs of blue overalls. A man greets us with a black bucket brimming with the bits and pieces that will clean us up. Selwyn opens the window and asks where the nearest garage is.

The man says, 'You want full valet?'

Selwyn says no. He thought it was a garage. One that sells convex wing mirrors to see caravans.

'We do express valet. While you wait,' the man says. He stands back to look at the size of the car. 'Forty pounds.'

He talks with clipped English, a tinge of Eastern Europe. He flashes good teeth and wears earrings in both ears. He shows Selwyn his chamois and gives it a squeeze.

'I do windscreen,' he says.

Selwyn relents. Yes. That would be good. He looks at me and shrugs. 'There's a lot of dead flies,' he says.

We get out of the car and go into the dreary innards of a navy-blue Portakabin to wait, while the man with good teeth and diamond earrings express valets the car with a Henry Hoover. Selwyn plays with the coffee machine and feeds it more coins than it needs. We share one black coffee that tastes like soap and sit on two orange plastic chairs aside of a two-bar electric fire that smells of fried insects and burnt carpet. Selwyn stands by the window with his hands on his hips. He is head to toe in thick corduroy and smelling of a good night's sleep. Then he tells me he is sorry. He should've thought this through more. He doesn't know why he failed to tell me about Johnny. 'That wake yesterday,' he says. 'It felt like mine.'

'You were so angry,' I try not to sound too relieved that he's come to his senses. 'And when we're angry we do things. Monstrous things. We become monsters—'

'I was raging,' he interrupts me. 'I'd never felt rage like it. My mother always said that it's what lives underneath. And it takes just a moment to grab hold.'

He sighs long and hard, and I wait for its full stop. When it comes, I wonder if this is when he'll tell me he's been a pillock and that he's sorry to have put me through it, and we'll go back home, laugh about it, take stock, and one of us will have to pop out for a pint of milk. We might even find out that Louis didn't invest everything and there's enough to tick us over. But all Selwyn does is stretch out his arms like Jesus and declare, 'We have set out, at least, and setting out is the biggest battle, so on we go!' Then heads outside to reprimand one of the men for taking a scourer to the bonnet.

I sink deeper into the chair in the Portakabin and hold my head in my hands.

This place reminds me of another Portakabin. The one that takes two buses to get there and sits in the dark at the back of the yard on the land Louis inherited from his father. Toogood Aquatics is full of plastic moulds and chicken wire, of contraptions that look like they've dropped from space. You'll see that he's branched out into concrete fountains and rickety troll bridges over there; that some of the ponds are now no bigger than a washing-up bowl and perfect for verandas. To the left are rolls of liners like new carpet. To the right are the metal scaffolds that house all the supplies to the trade. Above you, all the bulbs have blown in the halogen lights, so everything is sold in shadow.

Which is perhaps why Louis seemed surprised to see me. His eyes were the same blue as a second-class stamp, the touch of his skin like algae. He smelt of fancy washing powder, of stale smoke and wet chamois, and his desk was littered with papers full of numbers that weren't adding up. He was opening a bottle of wine – he is *always* opening a bottle of wine – and he couldn't find a clean glass. Or a way out. I'd noticed that he'd stopped wearing his wedding ring and had even taken down the photographs of his kids. Under the harsh fluorescent lights, I could see how he'd been peeling the skin away from his thumbs so that they were sore and bleeding, and his suit, always in a suit; it was a nice one too. Pin-striped but blotched with wine.

'For Christ's sake, Louis. What have you done?'

'Where did you even come from?' he'd said. 'How does someone like him get someone like you?'

We'd parted looking like we'd just thrown snow at each other.

I'm not sure he'd wanted to be saved.

I get up from the chair and go to the window. Selwyn and the valet man are stood shoulder to shoulder by the caravan discussing the Toogood Aquatics branding. It occurs to me that I've never asked Selwyn why a business supposedly founded by two people only ever traded under the one name. Why not Toogood & Robby, or Robby & Toogood? Though it'd probably never occurred to Selwyn to ask either. *You ask me such impossible questions,* he'll say to me. *When it's impossible for me to feel any more than I do for you. Where is it that you want to be, Ginny?*

Somewhere that is not in your head.

I go outside just as the man takes a penknife to the lettering under the caravan's kitchen window. Selwyn tells him no. It needs to be properly removed. I don't think he wants it removed at all. Then he points to the soapy gutter at my feet and asks me if I can see just how filthy it all was. He pays the man in cash. And even tips. We get back on our way.

Two miles down the road, and I start to feel carsick. I ask Selwyn to wind down all the windows. He tells me there are mint imperials in the glove box and to suck one, don't crunch.

'We need to properly talk about Louis,' I say between deep breaths. 'We still have to go back and have this out with him. It's like he's sitting on the back seat coming with us.' I pause. 'And there's the thing about him, something, I don't know what he was doing, I should tell you about it.'

But the car behind has started to flash us. 'There's something wrong,' Selwyn says. 'Without that bloody mirror I can't see anything right.' He puts on the hazards and slows us right down until we crawl to a stop in a layby. He gets out of the car.

We tell each other nothing that we should.

The village used to be known as the Three Loggerheads, or the Three Fools, before it dropped the Three and became just Loggerheads. Or, so I've been told. It has a Telford postcode and a Shropshire address, but comes under Staffordshire council. Essentially, it is everywhere and nowhere and where Meg was born.

'I've just never been here before,' I tell Selwyn, who's currently working out how to jack up the car to change the back tyre that has not fully blown but has most definitely been deflating with the weight. No, he did not weigh the caravan. He does not know the weight of the car either. He looks at me.

I say, 'Don't you dare.'

This will be one of those journeys that'll be appreciated a long time after we get back.

. . .

There is a spare and four hands would make lighter work, but Selwyn persists in working solo. Salesmen are rarely team players but very good at delegating tasks they don't want to do, and he insists it would be better if I knocked on that house over there to see if they might lend us some tools.

I point out that salesmen are better cold callers and can get inside a house better than anyone, and anyway, 'I don't understand what we need.'

He looks at me like I'm a disappointing heirloom and says we can go nowhere on three tyres.

I slap on my best smile and knock on the first door I come to, which is a chipped bright blue and has no number or letterbox. I hear a baby bawling, immediately regret it, and start to walk away when the door suddenly opens. I'm greeted by a girl thin as a shin bone with what sounds like a baby with colic in her arms. The girl looks exhausted and implausibly pale. She asks me what I want.

I try and put from my mind that she looks little more than sixteen, like she lunches on dust, that it's like looking in the mirror, and that there's so much I could tell her about what she'll come to know, but instead I point behind me at Selwyn who has managed to get the spare tyre out of the car and is rolling it on to the grass verge.

'We have a flat tyre,' I explain.

But she has no tools, not even a spanner, or an ounce of goodwill, and I'd be better off trying next door because Grogan has motorbikes. All the while she talks, the baby never stops crying.

'And don't look at me like that,' she suddenly snaps. 'I didn't have to have her, but I did.' She slams the door.

Lives and lies and lands apart, the sudden urge to hold my own daughter has me almost in tears. In fact, I want to grab hold of her shoulders and just shake and shake and shake. Then, just like that, it starts to hail.

. . .

Much later, when this journey is all over, I will remember this hailstorm more than I will remember the missed turns and dead ends that were never on the map. We were at Loggerheads, I shall tell people, and it hailed.

BARNARD GROGAN IS A generous man with a well-ordered face, the arms of a bell-ringer, and is buying another round of drinks. He wears an old rugby shirt, leather jacket, and trousers with so many pockets I wonder if he lives hand-to-whatever he finds in them. He and Selwyn are deep in conversation about a municipal pond nearby that Selwyn has never heard of, and he's flabbergasted. I sit to Selwyn's left and Barnard's right, not exactly in the middle when we're all in the middle of each other, and they're always in the middle of a conversation I don't belong in. At one point, I quip – 'Selwyn can tell the size of your pond just by looking at you' – but neither of them even look at me. I wonder how many other ponds we will happen upon that I shall lose another part of Selwyn to.

We're staying the night here in Loggerheads because the tyre is flat and so is the spare. Barnard has offered to drive Selwyn to a garage to buy two new tyres in the morning. He's also taken it upon himself to keep us company in the bar – a pub also called the Loggerheads – and Selwyn has already told him that I hail from here.

Barnard says, 'Really?'

I say, 'No, not me, my mother.'

And he asks for her name.

I tell him, 'Meg Richer, and it was a long time ago.'

He says, 'Not from the farm up Mucklestone way?'

I shrug my shoulders and tell him that I'd rather soaked off the daughter label fifty years ago and my mother was never much for a past anyway. This does not put him off, however, and next thing he's calling over Linda who looks like she knows joy and suffering in equal measures. She puts down her gin and tonic and straddles a stool. She has a lot of wicker-coloured hair that she wears hoisted up with hairspray – glamourous, garrulous, *mutton*, because she speaks as if everyone around her is stone-deaf.

'There was a family of Richers up Mucklestone way,' she immediately declares, like a tour guide. 'Farmhands mainly, treacherous lives. Cousins marrying cousins. That sort of thing. Poor souls. Common enough. No one lived beyond forty,' and she'll check the sanitorium records because most of them had TB.

I feel my pulse quicken, and flush for no reason.

Selwyn says, 'What records?'

Linda explains that she's from a generation of sisters stationed at the infirmary that was once here, when fresh air was penicillin.

'There might even be photographs,' she threatens. 'Who's asking, anyway?'

Barnard and Selwyn both point at me.

'Imogen here is a Richer,' Selwyn offers.

I glare at him. 'You watch your mouth,' I snap. 'My name is Imogen Dare.'

Now, he glares at me. In fact, the whole pub is glaring at me. Between us, Linda cocks her head and concentrates on a beermat. Barnard excuses himself to go to the gents. Selwyn looks embarrassed. He wants me to be embarrassed too, but I don't care what these people think. It'll give them something to talk about. I stare up at Selwyn as he swaps one look for another and settles on the one that always reminds me of someone who's just missed their flight. He slugs down the rest of his pint, asks Linda if he can get her a drink.

'Doing the genealogy, are you?' she asks.

My heart is hammering, though it's a sensible question. I shake my head. 'No. We have a flat tyre.'

'But stopping here?'

Selwyn tells her yes. 'Just for the night.'

'I'll bring my books tomorrow morning then,' she offers. 'Bag full, I've got. Photographs of all sorts. Might be a trip down memory lane.'

'Please don't,' I say, so quick it's rude. 'Trouble yourself.' Though I want to tell her to stuff it – I really don't care and actually things like that should really be burnt. But because Selwyn has left me alone with her and gone to the bar, I start to yawn theatrically and mutter something about my lustreless walking legs starting to ache, and even roll my Rs.

'Well, goodnight,' I say. 'It was nice to meet you.'

'Goodnight,' she says, x-raying my body language for fibs.

I take myself off to bed upstairs in a room that smells of neglect and is wary of guests.

I am starting to think that we have broken down here on purpose.

There is no species to define my mother. Meg was one of a kind. A six-foot chump with size ten feet and a heart of twenty-four carat gold – as a child, she told me she could touch the sky and pull down the clouds, and that's what made cotton wool. As for the rest of her, a natural fatness over elephant bones which she swathed in black smocks and blood-stained aprons; it was all hidden and folded away. She smelt of boot polish, of animal blood and tar, but on Sundays, of perfume – two or three squirts from an expensive bottle of something she would travel to Manchester to buy. Her hair was kept swimming-cap short and wispy about her ears, and when kids called her a man I thumped them. Jewellery. She loved jewellery, and stored it away like a magpie. She never wore any of it.

She lived in two places: the butcher shop by day, and the back kitchen by night, and both had clinical white tiled walls that she'd buff up with a nailbrush. She stopped going to bed when I was too tall to sleep aside of her, and instead snatched her sleep on an old mahogany velour armchair next to the kitchen stove. You'd think a woman of her size would have a face full of stories, but Meg was featureless. A face trained to give nothing away.

She did have four wisdom teeth that she refused to have removed, so was always chewing on cloves, which made her smell like she was constantly stewing fruit for a Christmas pudding. She talked of the deceased as if they were in the next room, and was never more than an inch away from a dead animal, which she could butcher and trim with her eyes closed. Jars of aspic fermenting on our windowsills – calf's foot jelly, she believed, cured sore throats. Though she wouldn't touch liver. Or hearts of any kind. And she'd only sell pork from a heritage pig and would even go and inspect their sties. *A pig is not dirty by nature*, she'd say. *Only nature dirties the pig.* When I was tiny, she'd hold on to my little finger in her sleep, but if I ever came in sobbing from a bicycle fall, a punched arm or bruised ego, she went into the other room and let me deal with the crisis myself.

Believe in all your lies, she used to say. *One day you'll have to explain them.*

When she cleaned, she swept the dust into a corner, just where the slightest breeze would blow it all back into the room – yet kept the butcher shop clean as a pin. She hung no pictures in any room, and certainly no photographs, but, occasionally, something pretty and bovine caught her eye and she'd stick it to the wall with chewing gum and unframed. What knick-knacks and trinkets we had on a dresser were the soils and seconds of the potbanks, collecting dust. I remember I'd have to jump from one rug to another to avoid the stone-cold floors. That our sitting room, or front parlour, as she called it, was a room we passed by on our way to the kitchen. Other than her perfume, she spent nothing on herself, only me. Dresses. She had me wearing all sorts of dresses, even bridesmaids' dresses. I have some first memory of being dressed only in christening gowns until I was two. Lace – she had an awkward love of lace, which she sometimes attached to hats like a veil. And nightgowns. The sort you imagine hysterical women wearing when institutionalised. I have no idea where she got them from, but she brought them home and dressed me in them.

Kisses. I can never remember her kissing me. Ever.

And yet the neighbours came to her for everything. To treat a wound. To mend a heart. To beg a bacon rasher for a last fried egg. A wad of lard. To *listen.*

I was ten when the Bluebird came out of nowhere. I didn't understand it all.

'Get used to it,' Meg said. 'She's not leaving.'

So, I did.

Until three became a crowd.

And then three threatened to become four.

As I toss and turn on a lumpy mattress that smells of spilt coffee and failed affairs, I try to remember if I did know anything about Loggerheads other than Meg's stock phrase that nothing was ever worse than Loggerheads.

Eet canst get any worser than the Logger'eads, she'd say, which I grew up thinking was just another one of those sayings we had that no one beyond spitting distance of Joiners Square had ever heard of. I only realised it was an actual place when given a map of the county in Geography when I was probably ten, and I spotted it on the western border, on the way to Market Drayton. And I only knew about Market Drayton because of another neighbour who'd married a gad-about from there who eventually flit back because 'his mother was such a worrier'. And then the saying went, *well, he's got more nounce than 'im from Market Drayton* – which meant he wasn't a bigot with a second family.

She was farmstock. That's all she would say. Barrel scrapings. Chicken feed. Too many mouths and not enough for their stomachs. She'd left this place behind a graveyard. *Farmhands with treacherous lives. Cousins marrying cousins. Poor souls. No one lived beyond forty.*

There's no bigger kick in the teeth than someone knowing more than you.

And then, suddenly, Anthony saunters into mind, as he always seems to do when I'm dragged back and go too far back: he walks into the butchers, Saturday morning, his trilby askew, and with another pair of re-heeled shoes for me, good as new. Meg pays him in pork loin, a couple of kidneys, goat. They are friends. I think we're friends too. I check the way I've done my hair in a silver platter from the back shelf. Remind myself to sneak brighter bulbs into the light fittings above when I can barely see if I've mascaraed both eyes. Beneath my apron, I fold over my skirt once, twice, about my waist because I'm at that age now when I'm aware I'm being looked at, and wish I could kick off the rubber boots Meg has me wearing, with their toughened soles and lard spats.

I've been practising what to say to him; how to flicker my eyelashes and bite gently down on my lip as if I've eaten too much salt. I turn around, hoping to look like I've just dropped my bath towel, but meet only with his back as he leaves the shop.

Selwyn suddenly staggers into the room claiming he's got a throb behind his left eye. He asks me to look for a cancer and if any blood vessels have burst. I ask how many pints he's had and he says three. I disagree, and have no sympathy. He goes to the bathroom and locks the door. I hear him throw up.

Eet canst get any worser than the Logger'eads.

The Third Day

'When choosing between a pond complex or multiple pools, one must consider the permanence of the pond, before concluding its area and depth, and treat each one as a single water body with its own undulating drawdown zones. To minimise future problems, it is worth contemplating how the area will be used by people and animals, because ponding is planning for the long term, rather than the aesthetics of trend.'

~ *The Great Necessity of Ponds*
by Selwyn Robby

THERE IS NOTHING IN Loggerheads but the car wash that was a garage, a Chinese restaurant that was the post office, a fire station that was a hospital wing, and so it goes in this place where things were and now are not. I'm sitting in the pub with a coffee that's making my head spin, waiting for Selwyn to come back from wherever Barnard has taken him to buy new tyres. They've been gone for so long now that I know Selwyn has somehow convinced Barnard to go and buy tyres via that municipal pond. I have not slept well, if I have slept at all, and despite a shower, a change of clothes, I still feel pestered by flies. I'm also waiting for Linda who's coming to see me with her dead sea scrolls. I've promised Selwyn to humour her.

She appears in violent purple running gear; she even sweats pure self-esteem. She'll be one of those women who likes to leave lipstick marks on everything she touches. I hold out my hand to apologise for being so brusque last night, and blame a migraine.

'It's been a very turbulent trip,' I say, but she waves me away, reties her ponytail, and places two leather-backed books on the table and some grainy looking photographs.

Go a few miles down that road and a few miles down there and that's where she thinks my mother was born, she tells me, showing me a photograph of a porcelain white cottage complete with smoking chimney.

'One of the peasant cottages,' Linda shouts at me. 'Be no more than a two-up two-down with no bathroom. Squalor really. Not fit for insects. Tough times.'

I remember our two-up two-down in Joiners Square, with two of this and two of that. Tough times too.

Underneath that photograph is another one, and this one is a photograph of this pub when it was heaving with what she calls 'logger folk', as if they spent their lives hacking down trees. Linda points at the various washed-out faces in their best frocks, dust jackets and suits, telling me who that is and who that is and who descends from who, but I start to lose track and it all becomes a blur because I'm staring at one face whose eyes I'd know even if they were worn backwards.

'The Richers,' Linda says pointing at the faces again. 'One, two, three boys.' And no, she says, she can find no mention of a daughter in the books. 'Sorry,' she says, though not all births were registered. Poor circumstances and all that. 'Some awful sad stories,' she says. 'Child pregnancies, landlord rights, rape.' She makes it sound like a shopping list. 'And I was right. Two of the brothers did die of TB.'

She delivers all this information to me like she's just on the phone to her hard-of-hearing mother asking if her cleaner's been, when this is clearly my history and the sewer Meg talked about. It makes me feel like my insides are held together with elastic bands.

'So, there you go,' Linda says. 'I knew I knew who they were. Though you don't look anything like them. Your nose looks bigger.'

I instantly cover my nose with my hand.

'I'm trying to think if anyone else might know anything,' she goes on, 'because Mucklestone was always hogs, hundreds of hogs, and the family who had the place, well, they came down from Llangollen way with a filthy reputation. And you know, when I look at these photographs and see how dead behind the eyes they were, I mean, you've got to wonder, haven't you? How they were treated.' She looks down at the photograph shaking her head, then pushes it towards me. 'Life was a shit slog.'

I smile and say it's fine. I don't want the photograph. I move it away from me.

'Heritage is important,' she says, pushing the photograph towards me again. 'Don't you have grandchildren?'

I tell her no, so no school history projects for me, and surely the photographs are better off staying together in wherever you keep them.

The look she gives me is one of someone desperate for me to take the photograph. History really isn't that frightening – but I really don't want it: 'You're being very kind, but my mother wasn't especially keen on her brothers anyway. And I never even met them,' I tell her for good measure. '*And* she's not even in the photograph either. All boys, see?'

Linda squints down at the photograph then looks back at me. 'I know they all had a crap life, but still, I'd like you to have it,' she insists, thinning her lips.

'Seriously, Linda,' I say, as kindly as I can. 'We're on the road. I'd hate to take it then lose it somewhere.'

She interlocks her fingers together over the photographs. 'You're right,' she suddenly snaps. 'History is only a beautiful creature to those who will respect it.'

And, just like that, we are properly glaring at each other. I feel this sort of antagonism in my thighs. I start laughing – 'I really am grateful, but my mother isn't even in the picture' – and she starts banging everything about like it's been a real chore and I've properly upset her, and, just as I start apologising again, here is Selwyn, thank God, and I get in such a fluster in trying to get out of the pub that I catch my shin on the table leg. I don't realise I'm bleeding from a very deep gash until Selwyn looks down at my jeans in the car.

'Ginny,' he says, 'what's that stain on your trousers?'

He gasps when I tell him, my blood.

'Why did we come here?' I shout at him. 'Did you honestly think I wanted to come here? What did you think I needed to know?'

He says, 'What are you talking about? You're bleeding.' He wants me to show him my leg in case it needs a stitch. I tell him it doesn't, I just banged it on the table leg and let's just carry on.

'You're being ridiculous,' he says. 'Why would you behave like that?'

'She was forcing a past on me that I don't want to know,' I snap.

'She was being interested, Ginny. In *you*. Your people.'

'They are not my people. They are people that I don't know. Who Meg didn't want me to know. So, if you've got any other tricks like that up your sleeve, you can turn around and take me home right now.'

'You want to go back?' he asks. 'We can go back if you want? If that's what you want?'

Loggerheads is barely behind us and already we have stopped again.

'I don't think that question is for me, is it?' I say.

He asks me what I mean by that. I look above his head at the monotony of fields behind him and wonder for bodies buried in the soil that I can suddenly smell on my fingers. I tell him that I don't mean anything other than what I said.

'You're answering all your own questions,' I tell him. 'Going where you want to go, doing what you want to do.'

He studies his fingernails on his right hand as if he can smell the buried bodies too.

'We had a flat tyre and the spare was flat,' he says. 'But now we have all good tyres, and a spare, I'd like to know what *you* want to do.'

This is another sales tactic I have never warmed to: putting all the onus on the buyer. The seller can't make that decision for you, he can only tell you the *facts*.

'Is there something you're not telling me?' I ask. 'Because you haven't just taken the caravan for compensation, or for a holiday, or to work out what to do now you're completely broke. This is about something else, isn't it? Something about *me*.'

He goes to say something, then looks out of the window and thinks better of it. 'It's hard,' he mutters. 'But no, no—'

'Because there's a lot of things you don't know about me,' I interrupt. 'There's a lot of things I don't know about you.'

He tells me that he can't think straight; that he thought, if he just got on the road, things might slot into place.

'But we keep on stopping!' I yell.

'Well, let's keep on going.' And he starts the car before saying once again, 'If that's what you want.'

Men. That's what I start thinking about as the fields streak past. All the men that were never in my life. *Don't give them a second thought*, Meg used to say. *And never a second chance. In some species, the father comes back to eat his own.*

I'd believe her because it was slim-pickings back then, saddling yourself with a husband from just around the corner and living your mother's life, and when I start going down this road, I go cavorting across the playing fields to where the gipsies would come and set up camp once a year. I was always three rows back, my lips parted nonetheless, and I'd copy the older girls watching the boys groom their horses; the boys watching the girls watching them, and everyone hot under the collar, until, this one time, a horse cut loose and galloped straight for Edie Cartwright and took her legs right from under her. It confined her to a wheelchair so heavy only men could push her about. I learnt a lot from that. She'd been clever enough for university.

'You're deep in thought,' Selwyn says, peering under the visor at a road sign up ahead.

'I was thinking that you never talk about your father,' I say. 'You could tell me about him, pass the time.'

But Selwyn is concentrating on something I've not seen.

'I knew it wasn't far,' he replies jubilantly, as he flicks up the indicator to go right. 'And here we are.'

Though it was once home to a twelfth century Norman castle, only the sixteenth century Tudor mansion house remains, which is now a restaurant, currently catering for a daytrip from the Black Country with enough walking sticks to erect a garden fence. In the late nineteenth century, a neo-Elizabethan house was built on the warmer and less damp side of the valley, and it's been the home of the Heber-Percy family since the 1960s. The gardens were the dream-child of Brigadier A. G. W. Heber-Percy, who set out to create a union between the older grounds surrounding the earlier mansion and the newer gardens of the house that remains today. He'd constructed dykes, dammed the stream and created a chain of pools, which now animate the gardens.

I read all this from the little glossy booklet we've been given as we paid our full entrance fee, since both of us left any form of pensioner identification in the car and couldn't be bothered to trudge the mile back. Selwyn nods his head furiously and agrees with everything I've just said.

'Yes,' he says. 'I can see exactly what he did with the channelling right there, because of the downstream confluence.'

We've been in Hodnet Hall Gardens for the best part of two hours. Selwyn has been in his element and found a new lease of life, while I've been walking on the side of my sole because of the gash on my shin which is chafing under my jeans. Selwyn takes my hand and says it's a shame that it's not June because the geraniums around the ponds must be stunning. He spends a long time analysing the lily pads, as if he's contemplating crossing to the other side, and wonders for otters, because what he's just spotted is definitely not manmade.

I look at the ruck of sticks and stones he's pointing at and try and see the organisation that he does. I think about how he likes his knife and fork to be an inch away from his table mat and set for the left hand, with a butter knife for bread rolls. How we have conflabs over what's a breakfast cereal bowl and what's a pudding dish, and how it needles me when he takes a knife to decapitate his boiled egg as if it were a spirit level.

'Shall we have a spot of lunch?' he asks, checking his watch. 'Then I'd like to walk around the gardens again with fresh eyes. I feel like I'm missing things.'

It seems that we have stopped again.

The woman who takes our order at the café till recognises Selwyn from the garden centre. She says, 'I know it was long ago, but I know you,' and Selwyn looks proud as punch and says, 'It was a long time ago, but I know you,' and they grasp at one another's hands.

She's a string bean in black, with casserole-brown eyes, and does he remember what he sold her? There's not a day goes by that she isn't thankful for meeting him, and he tells her that he's glad that she's still ponding. She tells him that she's more than just ponding. She's now part of some project that's looking to exceed a million ponds, and that they're always looking for guest speakers and donations. Selwyn looks interested and asks where would he speak, and suddenly the details seem less interesting because that would mean going backwards. So, he apologises, and tells her, 'We're off up to Wales,' and she gives him a sour look and I give him a little smile, because I'm glad that he's remembered that we're still meant to be going somewhere. To further his apology, he pays for our lunch, gives her a five-pound tip and adds a twenty-pound donation to the million-pond project.

'Tell me something,' I begin, as we sit waiting for our sandwiches and quiche to arrive. 'Are you really flat broke?'

He adjusts his knife and fork against the table mat and asks me what I'm getting at.

I find a pen in my handbag and start a long addition on my napkin:

£47.57 for Swan with Two Necks meal
£50 for B&B at Swan with Two Necks
£40 unnecessary express car valet + whatever tip he gave
£2.75 air freshener
£45 room rate at the Loggerheads
£30 meal at the Loggerheads (+ drinks with Barnard)
£168 for two new tyres
£16 admission fee to Hodnet Hall and Gardens
£23.15 for lunch at Hodnet Hall Gardens café
£25 tip + million-pond project donation

'You've spent almost five hundred quid,' I gasp.

'What's your point, Ginny?'

'You've paid for everything in cash. You're walking around like it grows on trees.'

He puts up a thumb. 'One, I sold a pond filter back at Trentham. Two,' he says, adding his forefinger, 'I can't begin to tell you what I've been through to get here. Three—' middle finger goes up, 'I'm working this out as I go along and when the opportunities arise. Four—' wedding-ring finger, still bare, 'you have no idea for that man's life and what he's endured to do what he's having to do, which is wash cars. He could be a doctor, for all we know. Five—' he waves his left little finger, 'I have always wanted to come here and today I didn't need to just drive past thinking one day I will come.' He puts both hands in his lap. 'And I took the petty cash tin.'

My head is in my hands.

When I look up, he's looking around the café as if he's been asked to quote for a re-plaster. I rap my knuckles on the table to grab his attention. He looks at me stonily, and says, 'What?'

'I thought we were going somewhere,' I say. 'Like a specific destination.'

'We are,' he agrees. 'But we can get there when we want.'

'And what about Louis?' I ask. His name lodges in my throat like a stuck lozenge.

'What about him?' Then he follows it up quickly with, 'What do you want me to say, Ginny? He did what he did, and we've hardly left the country.'

'Perhaps, if we had, I'd be clearer about what it is we're doing and not feel such an accomplice.'

He looks at me like I've just pushed him nettles.

'You're being a coward,' I say. 'And Louis is cleverer than you think—'

But here's pond woman with our order and she starts up another conversation with Selwyn about the maturing of her pond water, which she is hoping to stock with koi. I take in her shoes, which are little black school pumps and she really does have around size two feet. I look up at her and then back down at her feet and cannot work out the maths.

'Have you dropped something?' she asks, and she is looking down at the floor too.

'Just my napkin,' I say, which is still on the table underneath my knife and fork. And then because I've been caught out, 'Do you do wine?' because that suddenly seems like a really good idea. 'Anything white? I'm not fussy. Sauvignon? Chardonnay?'

'Only on special occasions,' she says. 'It's a license thing, I'm afraid.'

I clap my hands. 'Well, this *is* a special occasion,' I smile, and even bare my teeth. 'Right, Selwyn? Long-lost customers and us on holiday. Does that count?'

Selwyn looks at me as if I've barked out every word.

'I'm sorry,' the woman says to Selwyn, and she starts to laugh all shrill and it bugs me. Neither of us know what's so funny. She says, 'It's funny. I was just thinking to myself, I could tell you all about the acidity in a dew pond, but not the difference between a sauvignon or chardonnay for your wife.'

And the bastard goes, 'Oh, she's not my wife.'

I kick him in the ankle under the table. He winces and glares. I glare back. She sashays her way back to the counter, beaming like a butcher's stripe.

'Don't do that,' he snaps at me.

'I fancy a glass of wine,' I snap back.

'You're looking her up and down,' he says.

'Because she has the feet of a child yet the crush of a widow.'

'She was being friendly.'

'She was flirting.'

He starts on his plate of food with such gusto that he barely chews. I don't know what's worse – Selwyn being right there in front of me, or Selwyn not being there at all.

'What?' he goes. 'Why are you watching me eat?' He looks like a fish with a rock stuck in its mouth.

'I used to think you'd clipped my wings,' I say, out of nowhere. 'But actually, you've clipped one wing, which is worse.'

He rubs at his mouth with his napkin and does that thing he does where he pinches his nostrils together and sniffs. He says, 'You want us to tie our shoelaces together so you know where I am all the time?'

'That's not what I'm saying,' I say. 'To be honest, I don't know what I'm saying.' I shake my head in case it puts all my thoughts in order.

He says, 'Sometimes, Ginny, I'd rather you didn't say anything at all.'

To that, I jolt forwards in my seat and even point a finger.

'But before you get your hackles up,' he carries on quickly, 'I'm just saying that sometimes it's best to let things pass.'

The muscles at the back of my throat contract. 'So, I'm to let you flirt and only speak when spoken to?'

'That's not what *I* said either. I'm just saying that sometimes,' but he stops. Sighs. Sighs again, and even sneaks in a third for good measure. 'I don't know what I'm saying either,' he eventually says. 'So, let's both of us not say anything and just enjoy our dinners.'

The smile he gives me is half-baked and crumbles quickly, but it will do. For now.

We leave the café to a thunder rumble. We both look up. Blue sky above us, but rain coming in from over the hills. 'This *will* be interesting,' Selwyn says. 'There might be sturgeon.'

I roll my eyes and zip up my jacket. He may as well be speaking a foreign language. 'Please don't make me walk around those ponds again,' I say. 'Especially if it's going to rain.'

'Anyone would think you didn't have feet for how little you actually travel,' he said. 'You've got to keep the blood pumping, Ginny. What do you do all day while I'm at work?'

He had no intention of listening to my reply. Too busy waterproofing himself and looking for carrier bags. A second thunder rumble, a little closer than the first, but he heads off into the wilderness all the same.

I lay down on the back seat of the car stewing and grinding my teeth.

What do I do all day?

The arrogance of *What do I do all day?*

What do *you* do all day?

Because all I know is that *you* leave the house on the dot and come back on the dot, come in through the front door and head straight out the back door where you do things in the yard with your bloody tin buckets and your back to me. *Have you touched them?* you'll sometimes accuse. *The water looks jellied.* I tell you that I've not paid them any attention. *I've been busy,* I say. But you don't look at me, just back down at your watery little allotment with its slippery fish-fingers of algae and other bits of green that smell of the sea.

I say, *Selwyn? Would you like to eat?* And though I've set the table, cooked a meal, tidied your house, *you* eat it lukewarm on a tray on your knee in the front room with the big light on like we're the local takeaway, and pay attention to the telly like it's a vital organ.

Selwyn, I sometimes say, *don't you want to talk?*

And you give me that serious smile you save for moments like this, and say, *Sorry, Ginny. I'm so used to being alone, I forget you're there.*

What do I do all day?

I'll bloody give you what do I do all day because I think that's the first time you've asked.

Pointless. That's how I *feel* all day. Waiting for you to point me in the right direction.

What do I do all day?

What *do* I do all day?

I think.

I give it some more thought.

When friends drift away and you can't call them back.

When your daughter heads off to the other side of the world and the house is clinically clean.

When you open your purse and think enough for a fancy loaf, half a pound of back bacon, a dozen eggs, and bleach. He always needs bleach.

When you think of the time when you had no time and wished you had all the time in the world to do nothing. And then you have it, all that time, and you realise you've been so busy working, treading water, keeping afloat, that you can't remember what it feels like to catch your breath. And then it comes, that time – the time to ourselves, for ourselves – and you don't know what else it is you do; where it is all the other old women go. I'd been travelling at a hundred miles an hour in a single direction. The world has passed me by in a smudge.

What do I do all day?

Charity shops, he'd said. *They're always looking for volunteers. You could talk until your mouth ran dry.* I thought about an exercise class. Spent the day swatting flies and felt energised enough. I dusted the figurines. I recognised some. From when he and his mother lived next door in Joiners Square – hassling every shelf, nook and cranny. I cleaned out the kitchen cupboards and found out-of-date tins. I made a list of things I knew how to cook. Made another list of things I'd like to cook. Cooked none of them. I took down the curtains in every room, washed them, dried them, and pressed them into pleats. I picked fluff off the rugs until I had a small ball of wool. I thought about learning to knit with it. Knit and natter. I'd heard about that. I went to the library, but got stage fright and never went in. I doodled in the margins of the free newspapers and found my fingers hovering over the telephone numbers in adverts telling me to solve the hangover of life with a call to God. I cut up old bed sheets for dusters. I looked out of the bedroom window and hoped for exciting strangers walking past. If the postman ever rang the doorbell it was a big deal. I kept the telly on. I began to have conversations with it. Then I got sick of the telly's backchat and turned on the radio. Listened to a documentary one day about *The Little Mermaid*. Fairy tales and once upon a time, and my mind had wandered to circa 1958 when I'd told Mrs Galley that I didn't need to come to school any more because I was going to be a mermaid. A divine and beautiful underwater goddess. Mrs Galley was a woman of much patience and vocabulary, and told me that there was a big difference between ambition and Stoke-on-Trent. I left the classroom accepting my position in the world and vowing not to jump in the canal just to check I didn't have gills. I turned off the radio. It was exhausting listening to all those things I didn't know. I began to understand the meaning of the elephant in the room. It was me.

What do I do all day?

I did a lot of things, Selwyn Robby. Then I moved in with you and you gave me nothing to do.

I must've fallen asleep, because I'm woken by Selwyn knocking on the windscreen and rustling his carrier bags at me as if he's found treasure.

'Did you hear that thunder crack?' he shouts through the glass. 'Sturgeon, Ginny. Right on the ripples. I could've kissed them.' He blows out his cheeks to show me how blown away he is. 'The ecosystem here is out of this world.'

I get out of the car and immediately start up, 'You were out of order. You let that woman shame me. You never, ever stand up for me.'

He cocks his head to one side, as if my words have whipped his cheek. 'Why won't you marry me?' he says, bending down to untie the laces on his walking boots and kicking off the mud.

I roll my eyes. 'You're lucky I even got in the car.'

He looks hurt. 'Don't you remember anything about us?'

'We're here now,' I say flatly. 'Hanging out in stately homes like other old couples.'

He's putting on his clean shoes like someone without thumbs. 'Why can't you make the most of things right now?' he says.

I glare at him. 'What? Happen upon places and hope they have a pond? What happens when you run out of things to sell?' I pause. 'In fact, what do you even keep on selling?'

He seems to be swilling his mouth with his own saliva. 'Okay,' he says. 'The reason I've been gone for so long is because I've been discussing some work.'

I suck in my breath as if pushing his words through a sieve. 'Okay.'

'How do you feel about staying here for the rest of the week?' He goes on to say that that woman – Rachael – has propositioned him. She'd like him to talk at their Spring Fayre on Saturday. Something along the lines of the great necessity of ponds, she'd suggested. To encourage the creation of a million ponds. And one of their gardener's has gone down with a vomiting bug.

I feel the colour draining from my face. 'Did you plan this?'

'Perhaps I was meant to be here, such is the nuance of fate,' Selwyn says, thoughtfully. He is using words now that I've never heard him use before. If the carp started talking, I would simply reply, 'Yes, thank you. I'm fine,' and appreciate the sane conversation.

'I'll get paid,' he tells me. 'Rachael says the Lord is very generous.'

'We're here now because of the fucking Lord?'

'For God's sake, keep your voice down,' he seethes. 'I'll be talking about the necessity of ponds, not the Garden of bloody Eden.'

I hold up my hands and feel my whole body start to vibrate. 'I don't know *what* is happening,' I stammer out. 'You're sending me demented. I don't know what we're doing here. I feel like I can't breathe.'

He just smirks. 'Well, only the good Lord will know that for sure.' But I can tell by the rest of his face that what he's really asking is for me to start believing in us.

The Fourth Day, and then the Fifth

'Freshwater habitats are within reach of most of us. In many ways, they are, like us, interdependent on one another and will do what they can to reach out and merge, creating a larger pool from which life can evolve.'

~ *The Great Necessity of Ponds*
by Selwyn Robby

WE ARE STAYING IN the Piggery. A cottage that's hidden away from the rest of the world, in the undergrowth of Hodnet Hall Gardens' damp valley, that's not so much spick and span but sparse and sparing on natural light. The walls are the colour of an old two-tone cardigan, the bed is almost in the kitchen, and there's one armchair, which we fight over. The smallness of the bathroom intimidates me and all the curtains are tangerine. If this is what woodworm smells like, then this is what woodworm smells like, yet people actually part with money to stay here and call it a 'retreat'. Precious quiet, they say. The sort of quiet only a new mother would pay for.

I think of that young mum back in Loggerheads and wonder if her baby is still crying; how Meg used to say that the squeal from a dying pig is not for her life but for her piglets to run.

Last night, Selwyn met the Lord and 'took sherry' – the Lady is in Fuerteventura on a walking holiday – leaving me to get things straight in here, as he likes to say, as if I enjoy playing house and putting things in straight lines. He hauled my suitcase into the Piggery's oblong bedroom and said, 'Perhaps you could see if you do have everything you need in here?' I looked at the double bed and asked him why I couldn't take sherry? He tapped his nose and said, 'Business, Ginny. Pond stuff. It's a serious negotiation.' He'd sounded like a megalomaniac.

He ambled in, flushed and rambling, around eleven o'clock, with his pockets full of seeds. He'd been gone for the best part of three hours – 'So forgive me,' I said, 'if your seeds aren't very interesting.' He slumped into the armchair, his head in his hands and asked for a bucket.

I'd said, 'Carry on drinking like you are doing and you'll be kicking the bloody bucket. That's two nights on the trot.'

I went to bed and listened to him dry heave.

Swearing he's not hungover but perhaps a little carsick, when towing a caravan takes such intense concentration, Selwyn is now reading to me from his notes for his talk on Saturday. He is very nervous. He keeps stopping to change a word. He reads to me like I'm five. I have long zoned out, and he sips his coffee, carries on reading aloud at me, and occasionally looks up in between sentences for nods of encouragement. I offer him the same nod of encouragement I used to offer people in the laundrette when they struggled to identify the correct slot for the washing powder. Back when we worked with wicker baskets that were perfect cribs, and Mia was not even crawling. It amazed me how many people tried to drown receipts and bank statements, losing betting slips, and in one pocket I found a suicide note. Later, I would sit in that laundrette just to kill time. There was something soothing about the smell, the tumbling around of clothes, and I'd imagine the stains and the scuff marks floating away like fairy dust. Clean clothes. Dissolved mistakes.

'I might move this part on enzymes to earlier on,' Selwyn says. 'What do you think?'

I nod with encouragement. He carries on. As did I, as young mothers alone must do, because, after the laundrette, I took on a housemaid's position in a downtrodden B&B with velvet wallpaper that used to smell of men coming home with sick on their shoes. I'd find forks in the bedsheets. Underwear. Dead insects. A bag of screws. They were kind enough to give me a key to room thirty-one, in the attic, with a black and white TV, when our poky little Fenton flat, with its glistening slug-lines on concrete floors, had mice. Mia and I both cried when we were told we could go home. It was the busyness of the B&B that we liked. The comings and goings and the losing of ourselves in other people's lives: the warmth. Then my little girl went to school.

'Will you pass me a pen?' Selwyn asks. 'I'm repeating on myself like cod liver oil.'

I look for a pen.

Like I'd stand on the other side of the school railings looking, wishing my daughter had been born a boy. Boys seemed to sort things out with a ball. Girls were catty. One another's downfall. They left her out. *This is a two-person game*, they'd say. *It's a game for us, not you.* I'd tell her, *It won't always be this black and white,* and I'd will the world to change quicker. She still punctured herself with a compass one day to prove that she, too, bled red.

I hand Selwyn a Biro that I've found idling in a fruit bowl, where he's also left the caravan key.

'I don't know why I agreed to do this,' he says. 'Who's interested in what I have to say? I'm boring myself.' He scratches at his forehead and leaves dents, pops another two pills – that makes four this morning – and pulls at the grey hairs around his mouth. He has stopped shaving.

I carried on putting one foot in front of the other and found myself in shoe shops. Measuring little feet and finding perfect fits to go off and conquer the world – I had a knack for reading lives from the feet up. Lived my own on the basis that a lie can travel around the world while the truth is putting on its shoes.

'I'm not going to do it,' Selwyn says. 'It's ridiculous. No one will come anyway.'

Mia's tenth birthday and only three children came. *Do not let them see you cry. You must never let them see you cry.*

Mia's sixteenth birthday – drunk on Martini at someone else's party and brought home by someone's father like a wilted flower. Being told, 'She came with it in a flask.'

Mia's eighteenth birthday – a map of the world and a box of drawing pins. 'Go and adventure,' I'd said. 'Anywhere and everywhere and far away from here.'

And she did. Straight down the A14 to its Ipswich tip, where she trained to become a nurse. Three years later, she came back up the A14 and had the gall to tell me that I hadn't moved an inch.

Being a mother. That was what *I* did. Clothing her. Feeding her. Keeping her warm. Consoling her. Arguing with her. Explaining her. Sticking around for her. *Paying* for her.

'No fool like an old fool,' Selwyn mutters from the armchair. 'Who am I trying to kid? Who's going to sit there and listen to me?'

All those things I did, and she never listened to a word I said.

I know you're afraid to depend, Mother, my daughter's voice. *But you can't be my father as well.*

My girl in a photograph; an image on a screen. Her voice dipping in and out with failed satellite connections. *What's that, Mother? I didn't hear you.* My little bird. My little bluebird fluttering away to the other side of the world to a man she so desperately wants to be her dad. *Let me just know what it's like in the time that we have.*

'No, I'm going to start again,' Selwyn declares. 'Approach it differently. There's small fish in big ponds, and then there's minnows. I'm going around in circles. I need it to bite.'

'Yes,' I say, without thinking. 'It could've all been so different if it'd been the other way around.'

Selwyn drops his eyebrows, reminds me why he's doing this and what he's going to be paid. 'This wasn't planned,' he tells me. 'To be honest with you, Ginny, I didn't plan for any of it.'

'So you keep saying. Yet here we are.'

He gets up from the armchair and comes towards me. Grips my shoulders like he likes to do when he needs the upper hand. He tries to get me to look at him. 'Look,' he murmurs into my hair. 'We're only here till Saturday. In the scheme of things, that's no time at all.'

I carry on looking down at the carpet and see where two pieces have been botched near the skirting board. Cut from the same cloth, yet when seamed together they look odd.

'It's just that I've done all these things yet never have anything to offer,' I say, my forehead resting against his chin. 'Nothing to show for what *I've* done.'

He plasters on a smile for me. 'Then who is Mia?' he asks.

'I just can't help thinking that if you'd put that money down on the shoe shop…'

His hands go up as they always go up when we have this conversation. 'Not this again.'

'Yes, this again. We would've had something to fall back on.'

His head sinks into his shoulders, tells me it wouldn't've made any difference. 'And we'd have a mortgage,' he says. 'At our age.'

'It was a good business that had found its feet,' I shout. 'We had some really loyal customers. Everyone needs shoes. Not everyone wants a pond.'

'And what it is now, Ginny? Remind me. What is it *now*?' He always does this. He can't help himself. Salesmen love one-upmanship. It's the mallet of their trade. 'That's where your loyalty would've got you,' he says. 'Bankrupt.'

I start to laugh. 'Your loyalty has got *you* bankrupt,' I shout a bit louder. 'I needed a thirty-grand down payment to secure that loan. Instead, you gave that money back to Louis.'

'Oh, I see.' He slumps down into the armchair. 'You moved in because you thought I had money to give to you.'

'Don't you dare twist this! That was the circumstances when we met.' And I reel it all off again as I strut up and down – if not to reassure him, to reassure me – because to catch a fish you need to start with a fish and, a month before we'd met, the Parkinson's had got so ugly that Caro – for whom I'd worked for almost twenty years – could no longer bend down to tie a bow. I went to the bank. They called me an unsuitable candidate. I had no collateral and no credit rating. I'd pointed out that I'd always lived well within my means, however meagre; always had a job, never not worked, and paid in my stamp and that's why I couldn't be found on any blacklist.

'I've never had a mortgage, credit card, or passport,' I'd announced proudly. 'Never went to university. Never taken out a loan. Neither lender nor borrower be.'

The bank said that without evidence of previous repayment schedules they had nothing to advise me on my suitability and sustainability. I was also knocking on the door of sixty-seven and dealing with the fallout of Mia's divorce. I called her from a phone box on the street and said, '*My Daughter's Shoes* has a nice ring to it. What do you think? New start for us both.'

She said, 'I'm a nurse, Mother, and money is not why I do it.'

So, Caro's sister-in-law bought it, and the last time we walked past it was a charity shop.

'If she could have given it to me, she would've done,' I finish, thinking of all those women's voices telling me their stories as they tried on new shoes – all those stories that weren't mine to own but I did anyway when so much had never happened to me. 'It was a solid little business. It knew what it was. Why couldn't you see that?'

He says, 'I'm not the enemy here, Ginny. And I'm not your husband either.'

I grab the caravan key from the fruit bowl and flounce out of the room.

I SPEND SOME TIME feeling the cold metal panels of the caravan's exterior with the flat palms of my hands to simmer down, occasionally stopping to rub over the nuts and bolts that hold it all together, as if feeling for its bones. I did the same thing when I first went inside Selwyn's house under the Queensway, hoping that my fingerprints would spell something out that would assure me I'd come home. Because it was an exact replica of his house in Joiners Square. In measurement. In smell. In its *lack*. Only breadcrumbs on the breadboard gave away that someone lived there. And a pair of trousers slung over the radiator to dry. What I could smell most was moss. And the tomato plants on the living room windowsill. In the dining room, the same table and four chairs in the darkest wood, and his mother's lace tablecloth browning across the top. I'd told him I remembered the tablecloth and the dining chairs. And some of the porcelain knick-knacks too. He'd put his arms around my waist from behind and asked if I remembered him enough to forgive the old skin. And that perhaps I'd like to redecorate.

I go inside the caravan.

. . .

The main thing about living under the Queensway flyover is that it reminds you every day of where you are not going.

Louis had bought the caravan to take on the road. Expand the business, he said. Think global. Exhibitions. Festivals. Rudyard Lake. School fetes. Laybys. He'd park it anywhere he could to flog a pond pump.

And then the phone ringing, late at night. The jangle of car keys. Selwyn putting on his coat. Louis had got the caravan wedged against a wall; he'd misjudged a corner; drank that second bottle of wine; been clamped in a layby that forbade overnights. *He needs me to tow it back to the yard,* Selwyn would say. *I said I'd go and get him.*

I should answer when Selwyn tells me things, but when he tells me things like this, I have nothing I want to say. At least, I've remembered that Selwyn had had a tow bar fitted to his car all along.

I park up on one of the screwed-down leather bar stools and see that each of the four optics are full. Smirnoff. Plymouth Gin. Jim Beam. Courvoisier. A fridge, to the underside of the bar is fully stocked with mixers and six bottles of white wine. On the shelf at the back, a basket of complimentary salted nuts. A stainless-steel sink as big as a man's hand. It's a burnished mahogany bar, bespoke and expensive. The two settee beds have been reupholstered with an emerald-green leather to resemble Chesterfields, and are punctured with gold studs. Two single mattresses live under these beds, which come together with a single zip. There's a smell that reminds me of horse trailers. Behind me is the restroom with a porcelain toilet bowl with wooden seat. A washbasin – its pedestal a rectangular fish tank full of tropical rainbowfish, which still swim.

. . .

Sometimes, when I watch the traffic up on the Queensway flyover, I think of all those people who'd missed their turn and had to go all the way down the dual carriageway to go all the way around the roundabout to come back the way they came. I liked to pass the time imagining the arguments they were having.

The constant thrum of traffic on the flyover can sound just like the sea.

I kneel down on the caravan floor aside of the washbasin and count how many tropical rainbowfish swim in the pedestal tank underneath. Selwyn once told me that they were worth a hundred pounds each. I'd said, 'It's so cruel. Can they even properly breathe in there?'

Sometimes there are accidents on the Queensway flyover. Someone driving too fast. Someone cutting up another. The gleam of the sun. A wet road. Too many idiots driving their cars like tanks. Some days, I hold my heart in my mouth until I hear Selwyn's car park up outside the house. But when I come to put my heart back where it should be, it no longer fits.

I turn around to open the four floor-to-ceiling built-in cupboards in the caravan and find meticulous packing and starched shirts on coat-hangers. I open another door and wish I hadn't. Open another, close that too. I return to my bar stool and stare at the cupboard doors as if they're about to ignite.

Selwyn has stolen *a lot*.

He is suddenly behind me. I can smell him. Selwyn does not smell like anyone else. I tell him things like this when we stand aside of each other at the bathroom sink brushing our teeth.

You have this smell, I will say. *Something mausoleum.* He spits, I spit. He uses mouthwash. Spits that out too. I say other things, like, *We could do a drinks thing, you know. With the neighbours. Like Val and Alan. So they don't think anything untoward. She still thinks I'm your cleaner.* He will say, *Ginny. Let tomorrow be tomorrow and us get used to us.* He swills out the sink then, with a mixture of hot and cold water, like it's his job to do that. Like I don't do it right.

Now, he says, 'I give you any more time in this caravan without me and you will leave me for sure.' He's wearing his fishing garb, his waders, his wellies, and I think what I always think – *where have your hands just been?*

'I guess you needed to do what you needed to do,' I say, pointing at the open cupboard doors. 'Now I need to do something else.'

'I don't regret it,' he murmurs. 'But don't leave me because of this when I'm owed.'

I gesture wildly at all the stolen pond equipment in front of me then tell him that I want to go home. 'But it's not even my home, is it? Not my trip, not my home. Everything is *yours*.'

'Then we will keep on going until we find what is ours,' he says, resting his hand on my shoulder.

'But you're a thief,' I carry on muttering, as if my voice has been anaesthetised. 'And a liar.'

'Was it you?' he suddenly asks.

'Was what me?'

'Who he was doing it with. Doing it for. Was it you?'

I glare at him.

He glares at me.

We glare.

Like we have never glared before.

'How dare you!'

'Was it you?' he asks again. 'Because there was someone, Ginny. There was someone else he was doing it all for.'

And he's in my face and I can smell how much this matters to him. Because it is me, it is always me, and here I am again, being me.

'No,' I say, flatly. 'It was not me.'

WE SIT ON THE bar stools side by side, our thighs bristling with static. Selwyn is showing me some spreadsheets. He has plenty of them. His mouth keeps moving, like he's blowing bubbles. There are words, but I'm not hearing them. He's telling me all he has worked out and has been working out. This multiplied by this. This divided by that. What he knew. What he didn't. Everything is top-drawer in pond equipment. Stately homes, Hodnet Hall Gardens. A prototype pond filter from Trentham Gardens.

'And a buyer,' he ends, 'on Anglesey.'

'I see,' I say.

'Do you?' and he assures me again that Rachael was a bolt out of the blue and he's not going to turn his nose up at three hundred quid, cash in hand, for what he can do with his eyes closed.

'This much preparation,' I say. 'You've known all along, haven't you?'

He nods.

'And the caravan. Louis gave it to you, didn't he?'

He twists his lips. Cocks his head to one side. 'He didn't stand in my way,' he says.

I sigh. Then sigh again because the first one wasn't enough.

He holds up his hands, and says, 'I have nothing more to declare.'

I find myself wishing he had.

'Don't leave me,' he says again. 'You're all I have left.'

He reaches for my hand and I let him steal it too. Then I ask for the fish in the washbasin pedestal. What is he going to do with them? He tells me he doesn't know yet – their value goes up and down – but the Candy Basslet should, if he cares for it well enough, go for over a grand to the right collector.

'The Candy what?'

'Come see.'

He leads me into the toilet and we both crouch down in the tiny space. Selwyn presses his nose against the tank and points to what he calls the holy grail of marine aquarium fish. 'I have the strangest feeling that it might be pregnant too,' he says of what looks like a goldfish with a few sketched purple stripes from back to belly. 'We'd double our money then.' I try to see what he sees as he explains something about dorsal to anal fin. I burst out laughing. He says, 'It's not funny, Ginny. I'm being serious. That fish is our capital.'

I stand up before my knees lock. 'I've got to hand it to you, Selwyn.'

'Except they're not fully responding to the food I'm giving them,' he carries on, pricking the bubble. 'I'm wondering if they've got used to something else. A different kind of flake.' He peers into the tank again. 'Do you see? Where the water clouds in clumps? That's congealed food. They're not even fighting for it.' He shakes his head as he starts to get up. 'I'll have to see Judd,' he tells me. 'He'll know what to do.'

'Who?'

His smile is the size of a wheelbarrow, and he even looks tearful, but I have no skills when it comes to tearful men. So, I make a quip about our fish making us chips, and he cups my face and stares into my eyes for so long my eyes start watering too.

We make our way back to the Piggery for our last night, holding hands. We don't talk. Just look straight ahead. Like we know where we are going, and me, following him.

The Sixth Day and the Sixth Night

'Although some flagellates have clear affinities with the animal kingdom when they feed upon one another, it is worth noting that if too submerged in the pond, and kept in the dark, they will not survive.'

~ *The Great Necessity of Ponds*
by Selwyn Robby

I SELLOTAPE RAFFLE TICKETS to tins and cans, fish hooks, and bottles of cheap plonk for the Spring Fayre's tombola. Rachael, who is never half a foot away from Selwyn, shows him the glossy leaflet she's had produced, as if *The Great Necessity of Ponds* is about to be launched as a global bestseller. I notice that she has started wearing lipstick and her skirts are rising above her knees. She catches an earring on his jumper and there's a kerfuffle between them. I peer over their joined shoulders to look at the photographs, mostly of Selwyn standing looking overcast and across Hodnet Hall Gardens' many pools deep in thought. Here, Selwyn stands aside of the Lord convincing him to handover the best part of a grand for a Pond Jet Floating Fountain with twenty metres of waterproof cabling. Here, Selwyn wistfully lifts the weeping willow from his eyes to show the Lord what a gleaming pool that two-hundred-and-fifty-pound filter has produced. I don't know when these photographs were taken, or why he looks so handsome all of a sudden. But he does.

Rachael is intending to sell these leaflets at five pounds a pop, and is wondering what royalties he would like. Selwyn gushes. It's been his pleasure, and for some reason this propels Rachael into talking about the swans. She tells Selwyn – not me, though I am here too – that there used to be a pair in the grounds, and they had one clutch of cygnets, five if she remembers right. But then came the terrible freeze of 2011 and the hen didn't make it. They have never found her body. And because the cob has never found her body, he won't stop looking for her until the day he dies.

'We tried to introduce a new mate, but he'd already found his,' Rachael says, tearfully. 'So, he carries on looking for her. And that's all he will do for the rest of his life.'

Selwyn sniffs as if this is the saddest story he has ever heard. 'Astonishing,' he says, shaking his head. 'We certainly do live in their world.' Then he looks at me as if the story is about us.

I rip some Sellotape off with my teeth and pull some skin off my top lip. I wince. There is blood. But no one notices. I realise I am a different species entirely. So, I look down at Rachael's shoes, which today are neat silver plimsolls with black leather bows and already scuffed around the toes. She must've seen me looking because she asks, 'Why are you always looking at my shoes?'

'I used to work in a shoe shop that should've been mine,' I tell her. 'It was a little goldmine, truth be told, so I can't quite quit the habit of seeing a woman from her feet up.'

Selwyn pretends he hasn't heard us squabbling and instead starts up a conversation about cows. Something he once read to do with a couple of bulls who slept with their heads resting on each other's shoulders.

'We cannot not be a pair,' Rachael tells him earnestly, her fingertips briefly brushing his sleeve. 'And nature's daughter at best.'

'Except one ends up in the abattoir,' I suggest, with a beaming smile that neither of them reciprocates. 'Daughter of a celibate butcher,' I specifically tell Rachael, tapping my nose. 'So, I know a lot about hard faced cows.' Then I lick the blood from my lip and ask if anyone would like a cup of tea.

Except while I stare at the kettle waiting for it to boil, Rachael comes to stand aside of me and asks me outright if I want him.

'It's just that you don't wear the look of being the luckiest woman in the world,' she says. 'And you are. Selwyn Robby is one of nature's saints.'

THERE ARE STALLS AND people grinning as if they're having the time of their lives. A lot of pushchairs. Cake. It's one pound for this, and you get three goes on that, and Selwyn's talk on *The Great Necessity of Ponds* is on at three o'clock. I watch a child take a mallet to a coconut rat coming down a drainpipe. An ice-cream van has a long queue. Rachael had already set out the room with rows of hardbacked plastic chairs, and has been dusting some, wiping down others with a damp cloth. Occasionally, I take one away claiming to even things up. Selwyn is to stand at the front to give his talk, behind a lectern that he and Rachael carried in together, and I notice he is wearing cufflinks. Brassy-looking and probably hooking through the buttonholes with fish bones. He's fiddling with them as his mouth tots up the forty empty seats when it's only ten past two. I consider taking away another couple of chairs to make him feel better. Perhaps less *watched*.

I have never seen him do anything like this. I'm not even sure I want to see him do this.

'You mustn't be nervous,' Rachael suddenly says, striding towards him. 'This is *your* second nature.' She has a hand on his shoulder as he looks at her sheepishly. 'I absolutely assure you,' she carries on. 'Everyone is coming because they're interested in what *you* have to say.'

I should be saying this to him.

'Just think of them in water,' she says. 'Don't look at them. Look into them. That way, they will come to the surface to investigate you.'

Why don't I have words to say like that? It makes me want to slap off her smile with a fish slice. Her lips are so red they look full of blood. Nourished. She is someone who nourishes.

'Thank you,' he says. 'I needed that.'

She moves away and there's a space for me. I tap him on the shoulder and go to say something encouraging, but he tells me right away that I don't have to be here if I don't want to be. I could go do things, perhaps get myself something nice. He has seen a stall selling shawls.

'Oh,' I say. 'Would you prefer it if I wasn't here?'

He fiddles with his tie and does that thing he does with his nostrils and sniffs. Then he reaches into his wallet and hands me a twenty-pound note.

I walk as far from the fayre as I can, until I'm not sure what is bustle and what is birdsong.

THERE IS A POND. THERE is always a pond. When there is not a pond, Selwyn fashions one. Then he will bore me silly with the burgeoning ecosystem of plankton in a rainwater butt. *Ginny*, he'll say. *Come see. It's fascinating. Just look at the way it's flagellating.* To show willing, I'll put on my glasses in the hope of witnessing some gnat larvae whipping another with its lashing hairs, but no. It's just a pool of muddy dishwater on the manhole and Selwyn's dirty finger poking about. Then he'll suck on his finger and tell me, *Moss. Already. Astonishing,* and stir up whirlpools in the puddle. Showing me his world within the walls of our backyard in his sensible shoes. I'll say to him, *Why didn't you live somewhere with a garden? Where you could have had your own pond.* He looks at me as if the idea has never crossed his mind. *The house is council,* he says. *Was* council, and now there's a landlord I've never met. *You've earnt money, Selwyn. You could've owned your own place. Dug out your own pond.*

Again, *that* look. I exasperate him for not understanding. And he disappears behind his words: *Stagnant water is a breeding ground for parasites. They worm into the intestines. Have you ever watched a drowning hedgehog in pond scum, Ginny? Algae is an iceberg without an irrigation outlet, a fifty-foot phosphorous buffer, a sewage pipe. It'll resist treatment and spawn. It gets into your very pores.*

Then why are you so obsessed with them if you think them so dirty? I'll ask.

And he'll back away from me, as if he's about to fall apart.

I am taking off my shoes and socks and edging closer to where the water laps against the banks of this stately pond with its bulrush verges and lily pads the size of hearth rugs. There is glitter on this pond. It's like a magnet. It even winks.

After the kippers and the fishman, Meg and I knocked on the door of number twenty-four, Joiners Square, to greet our new neighbours properly.

'As fresh and fat from the fields as if I'd shot 'em myself,' Meg had declared, offering up a silver platter of sirloins to a horror-struck Sarah Robby and the man who came to count my hiccups through the walls. I don't remember the rest of the conversation – if anything else was even said – just that Sarah Robby, with her flaming red hair and black-grape eyes, looked straight through Meg and bore into me. 'You still live,' she'd yelled. I'll never forget it. She'd looked as if she was about to sink her teeth into me. 'What do you want? What is it that I didn't do right by you?'

Selwyn was aside of her, soothing her, like she'd tumbled over the handlebars of her bicycle. He brushed her hair away from her face.

'You are very kind,' he'd said to Meg. 'But my mother is not herself today, the little winged-thing.' And he'd shut the door.

'Like slammed that door in my face!' Meg came to wail at the Bluebird, as we returned home with the two steaks that Meg then declared no fit for a dog. 'Any closer, an' he'd have taken off my nose!'

'Oh, Meg,' the Bluebird's turn to soothe. 'She was just a child.'

'Aren't we all?' Meg's retort and sulking then. As much as she didn't need people, she still wanted them to like her. It was like being mothered by a toddler.

My right foot dangles into the pond water below. I'm surprised for how sticky it feels. How warm.

'There is a great necessity to create ponds in our lifetime for the generations we will never meet,' is how Selwyn's talk begins. 'Our country needs them. A pond is the most diverse source of life. It begins with no history and focuses only on its future self.'

My right ankle is deeper inside the pond. It calls to my left. *Come in! The water's lovely!*

I feel like I am entering his world.

I'm standing in the pond shin-deep. I try not to think about the two thousand odd species Selwyn tells me can live in a single pond. Species that are alien to me. Things that would make me squirm and gag and probably scream at the top of my voice. But why didn't he want me there? Is there something he doesn't want me to hear? I can listen. I can support. I can be proud. I won't laugh. I might even have learnt something.

Jesus! What was that? Selwyn says that grass snakes sip from ponds just like cows.

He'll have to explain you though, when you can't even explain yourself.

The pennies dropping are like rockfall, and the water seeps into my skin. I concentrate on what's above me. Magpies, being awful playful. I count six for gold and cannot feel my toes. There is nothing else around me, only what I'm ignorant of. Yet, I am wading, further and further in, and, as I wade, I sway, as if in a dress made of silk and not a pair of burgundy cords and an unravelling navy sweater that is raining cheap pearls. I can hear them plop into the water as the stitching comes loose. *Plip. Plop.* Like hail, and just before it thunders down. The water is finding the corduroy ribs and using them as channels, making streams. Selwyn is right. Water does flow both ways. The feeling is enveloping. I am breathing like a fish.

I turn to look back towards the bank. Look for where I have left my shoes and socks and real life. I can see just two black spots that don't even look like shoes any more. Specks of me. That's all. I'm in deeper than I thought and I cannot swim a stroke.

My daughter was married to an architect ten years her senior. It outlasted all my expectations. He was forever renovating their rooms and giving them new labels. His work was never finished. Rooms never stayed put. Stand still long enough and you'd be given a lick of paint. 'He's never satisfied,' Mia came to complain. 'He's either colouring me in, or washing me out.'

They tried for children half-heartedly, and never with any success. 'Don't be too disappointed, Mother,' Mia once said to me. 'I'm not. And I'm sure, if you had your time over, you'd have chosen otherwise.'

'Oh, Mia,' I'd replied. 'I have wanted my life to be exactly how it was.'

She would visit me. Once every couple of months maybe. I'd make her bed up on the settee and she would *treat me*, as she called it, to pub lunches up Endon way, or we'd walk around Finney Gardens remembering the peacocks. Sometimes, Stoke Market – taking her arm in the drizzle as we rummaged, and relishing in the few seconds she allowed me to keep my arm linked in hers. I've dedicated my life to you, I'd be thinking, as soon as she pulled away to– *Oh, will you look at that? I've been looking for an old-fashioned sink plunger.* Me left on one side of the market. Her on the other side and holding back.

She's ashamed of me too.

My hands are in the water now and spinning whirlpools, like little doorways, in the scum.

Mia would send an envelope of train tickets to make me visit her. *For a change,* she'd say. *It's like you've shrink-washed your world. Where's all that confidence you used to have?* I found the journeys long and tiresome; the weekend breaks, as she called them, unlovely. Silence wallpapered every room we sat in, while her husband redesigned other rooms. I dreaded the words, *I've booked us a table for seven thirty.* We had more to say to each other on the phone.

I have never known water to be this alluring. I could walk for miles.

It began with noticing things. Just small things, but still. They were quarrelling a lot, Mia said. Her and her husband. And not just about rooms. Nit-picking, she called it. That she cooked for him and slept aside of him, but everything else they did was done in separate rooms. When she told him it was over, he wasn't a bit surprised. A week later, a *Thank You* card in the post from him to me. Which was all it said. *Thank you.* And his name, signed, as if he was signing off on a project he was glad to be shot of.

Our bodies are more water than blood, Selwyn says. We are as ruled by the moon as is the sea. It's why we howl. Why we bicker and bloat. At full moon, in a pond, creatures will suddenly change direction as if, all this time, they've been going the wrong way.

After she left her husband, Mia came to stay with me – three or four days was all – and lay sleepless on my settee mulling it all over. By the time I properly knew about Anthony, there was nothing I could do or say to dissuade her. She'd been planning it for years – nothing can be hidden any more; everyone can be found – then talking to him for months on the phone – her noon, his midnight; her midnight, his noon – and, eventually, his invitation to enter his world down under.

'The thing is, Mia,' I'd tried to say. 'There was more to it, and certainly to that day.'

But she was already at boiling point and using the word 'jealous' – 'Are you jealous because it was meant to be your journey?'

It took me a very long time to answer that question. And when I did, all I said to her was, 'It is your journey. Not mine.'

So much water under the bridge, we collapsed.

Then I hear it, in the distance: the applause. It cuts across the sky like a jet. Not just dull clapping, but a standing ovation for a man reborn, and I am not there to see it.

I am guilty of devotion. I devoted my life to my daughter who then left me behind. I am guilty of parking my life up and putting the rest of me to one side so my daughter would never know doubt. But when she left home for the places where she blended in, I lost sight of her. Some days, I couldn't even remember her voice when it is all a mother usually hears. By the time I'd rallied myself enough to jangle the car keys once again, the clamps had been on for so long, I'd neither the desire nor inclination to start again and move on. Then I looked in my purse and realised that I couldn't afford the petrol either.

It's not what's in the pond now, but what *began* the pond that Selwyn wants to understand: those things that are there, but we can't see. Then he and I can start to love each other in the simplest of ways.

I don't turn away from the water. I don't even want to leave it. Ponds are complicated. We are complicated. But we can learn this living and loving together. Sometimes, it's better not knowing what's just nipped at your ankle bone and slid around your shin. Especially when it's already slipped away.

I back out of the water, thanking it, and slowly. So much I will never understand even when this pond is as clear as day and as warm as toast.

I'M COUNTING OUT SELWYN'S wages by the light of the glovebox. 'So, three hundred for your work and talk, and what did you get for the fountain and filter?'

'Grand and twenty-five.'

I do the sums. Recount the twenties again, just to check.

He says, 'You found things to do then?'

I tell him I took a walk. I did not tell him that I waded into the pond and right up to my waist where the pondweed underneath turned into step ladders going down. That there was something in that water that called to me and seemed to make a lot of sense. But I did tell him that I heard the applause.

'See,' I say. 'What you do *does* matter.'

'To fifty people,' he says.

'Which is fifty more than have ever listened to me,' and then just like that, I tell him about Rachael and what she said to me in the kitchen. *How* she said it, as if asking me if I'd like it hot or cold, with chips or mash. 'Do you want him?' she'd asked. 'It's just that you don't wear the look of being the luckiest woman in the world.'

I watch his face as closely as I can in this dim light. I want to notice everything about it and see it change. But it doesn't. Nothing does.

He just says, 'That's quite a hair shirt to wear,' and does that thing where he pinches his nostrils together and sniffs. This is the self-deprecating veneer of the salesman. Underneath his skin, he is singing and still lost in the adulation of fifty-odd people clapping his talk.

'There's been a lot of Rachaels in your world, hasn't there?' I say.

He clips in his seatbelt and clears his throat. His mouth curves, but he avoids smiling. 'But no particular Rachael,' he replies.

I close the glove box and look out of the car window thinking of this last Rachael; how I'd told her that this was the furthest I'd ever been from all I've only known. That I'd spent the past sixty-seven years lost in the same place, going around in circles, living in squares, neither here nor there or even changing my hair, just hoping to get by unnoticed.

'So, I thanked her for seeing me,' I tell him, looking down at my hands on my lap that still smell of my pond dipping, like damp pine and wet sand. 'Because even if she couldn't see me with you, she still saw *me*.'

But he's muttering about the lack of mirror again and that everything behind him is a blur.

'IS THIS US ON our way to Wales now?'

We have been driving for over an hour, but now Selwyn is slowing down to peer over the steering wheel like we're lost. It's not just night but the depths of night. I ask him what he's looking for and he says, 'Nothing.' He's not looking for anything.

'Then why have you slowed down?'

He is adamant he hasn't and, to prove his point, speeds up again. I feel the pull of the caravan behind like a magnet pushing away from us. Perhaps it's the caravan that's slowed down, and not Selwyn.

'Are we going somewhere else before Wales?' I mutter at him. He's concentrating so hard the blood vessels in his neck are protruding. He starts to indicate, thinks better of it, flicks the indicator off. So, I tell him that I was listening to the radio the other day and that on this programme they were talking about getting lost and this guy came on, some psychologist or doctor, and, apparently, we spend almost two weeks of our life completely lost. That if you add up all the times you take a wrong turn, or find yourself somewhere you don't want to be, it equates to fourteen days of essentially being missing.

'But it hasn't been two weeks,' he says. 'It's only Saturday.'

'I'm not talking about now. I'm talking about in the whole of our lives.'

He's thinking about what to say to me. 'People get lost for a reason, Ginny,' he begins. 'We no longer live in a world where you can be lost. There are signposts everywhere. GPS tracking and electronic chips.'

I clench my fists and look out of the passenger window and see it's started to rain. I glance at the outline of Selwyn's face and wonder if I'm just his shadow and that's why I can't ever leave. Then it occurs to me that everything we've done since he came home with the caravan on Monday has been agreed on glances and brief nods alone. It occurs to me that I have not been the one delivering the glances. I don't ever remember nodding my head. Yet, here I am. Somewhere. With him – deliverer of glances and brief nods – and with curious consent.

'There it is!' Selwyn announces, and he flicks up the indicator again to take us down some potholed waste-bucket of a lane, where we swerve more than once into the hedgerows as if we're driving on thin ice. It is absolutely pitch black.

'What are we doing down here? This isn't even a road.'

'There!'

I look out of the windscreen. Selwyn swears it is there – he cannot understand why I can't see it – but, even as we edge closer to what he says is there, I still can't see the faint dot of light he tells me we're heading towards.

The dot turned out to be a single outside light, on a house somewhere so nowhere it clearly does not want to be found. While it occurred to me that a house this nowhere could only be found by those in the know, who had been here before, Selwyn had stopped the car and got out. Two figures were there. Like *there.* Small figures. Hunched figures. I swear they were cloaked. Selwyn *knew* these figures. He threw himself on to them. They embraced him like he was something magnificent. They were all crying. Loud crying. I started thinking, are his parents still alive?

I got out of the car. I wanted to be part of this. Something was happening. But in the brief moment it took me to get out of the car, Selwyn and one of the figures disappeared. Like *disappeared.* I checked for my stomach. I felt like it'd dropped through the floor.

Now, there is only one figure left and it does not embrace me. I move closer. It seems to be of womanly shape, and it speaks.

'Come with me.'

She has the voice of a small child, but what to do but follow her when all I have done is follow? And we are walking on gravel that crunches so loud I wonder if it's a path of bones. I keep asking who she is and where we are and, 'I'm sorry. But how do you know Selwyn?' and when she doesn't answer me, I remember my manners and say, 'Please. I don't understand where I am.' I also state the obvious: 'It's very dark.' And then, 'Bloody hell. This is proper dark. How do you even see anything?' And, 'Do you actually live out here? It's the arse-end of nowhere!' And I'm blinking wildly in case I can see something before it sees me. At one point, I come out with, 'Are you Selwyn's mother?' Because some long lives defy science. And there is nothing to tell me the time.

I realise that I'm frustrated, rather than scared. Selwyn tells me that frustrated people make other people frustrated because frustration, he says, when it detonates, becomes panic. And when people panic, he says, because of the things they don't think are happening, they try and make it happen and spoil it. And that just means more frustration, because it's not how they imagined it to be. Salesmen are very adept at creating vicious circles, I find.

Eventually, she opens a door and finally there's light, from a washing line of dangling bare bulbs of all different watts in a kitchen of exposed brick and it's cold, really bloody cold. There's an old Rayburn in the chimney recess with a large tin kettle hanging above it, and a rabbit, skinned and hanging from its ears. Over there, in that far left-hand corner, is a bucket full of enamel plates still mid-meal on a cracked stone floor. But then in the other corner, where the bulb is so dim, I can't make out what's in the sink and if it's a crack or really does crawl. So, I start to tell her that when you skin a rabbit you take out its legs first, which makes it far easier to yank the fur from over the neck, and that it's also worth cutting off its feet, though you don't have to. 'You don't even need a knife. Just your finger.'

But she's not at all interested, like I wasn't interested in Meg's bleak butchering advice, back when I just wanted erotic: a boy with a knife.

This is how my mother's life had been. She had lived like this. Selwyn has brought me here for a reason.

I introduce myself again. 'My name is Imogen and it's lovely to meet you.'

She turns to look at me, to tell me her name is Maisie, and as she turns, and so slowly with such effort, I see that inside all that brown draping she wears – and it really does make her look like a medicine bottle – is an old, old woman, peeping around the corner of the next life, if some part of her hadn't crossed over already. Brittle. Delicate. I could snap her in half.

She turns back towards the stove – a sheet of hair as white as a snowdrift cloaks her back – and how she lifts that kettle off the enormous butcher's hook to put down on the stove begs belief. I move forward to offer to help, but she looks at me alarmed. 'I don't need,' she begins. I back away. This is a woman so private, so withdrawn from everything she once knew, that talking has become too strenuous to even finish sentences.

She heads for the bucket and roots about, brings out a cup and a saucer, which she takes to another bucket and dunks them both in. It's like watching an ant carry about a tarantula.

'You know, I'm not really a tea drinker at night,' I say, because there are flies flying out of the bucket. Dirty creatures – Meg didn't so much swat flies as punch them dead mid-flight. 'And I really have no idea why we should be putting you to all this inconvenience, and so late, too.'

She stares at me as if I've insulted her. They are eccentrics, I think. Recluses. However does Selwyn even know these people? And where the hell did he go? The wind picks up and rattles the window – it reminds me of the whistling classrooms we sat in at school and the lines I got given for wearing skirts as short as dishcloths. *I am not yet a woman. I am not a woman yet.* Then going home to admire the beauty of my backside in a baking tray. Meg did not believe in mirrors.

'We must sit,' Maisie suddenly says, in such a shadowy voice I'm convinced that this is not just the end but the absolute of ends and that this woman has been sent to fetch me. I wonder if we've crashed the car, or if I'm still in the pond back in Hodnet Hall Gardens and have actually begun to drown. And I'm royally pissed off that Meg could not find it in her heart to come and get me herself.

'I am going to sit,' she says again, and smiles a little smile.

She has me follow her out of the kitchen and down a stone-floored corridor lit only by the kitchen lights behind us, and opens a door into what must be their sitting room.

A cluttered place of bare concrete walls where stacks of old newspapers make tables. Upon them, stuff – a paperweight, a candle in a jam jar, what might be a vase or a pot for pens; the things we find by accident but keep all the same. Above me, a rusting brass chandelier hanging so low it could scalp you, with two missing bulbs out of five. Wires sprout from plug sockets, the painting of the ceiling is unfinished. This place is a hovel. War-torn. The loneliest place on earth. She takes to a battered armchair and perches on it like a bird. She has forgotten about the tea she was making because she suddenly asks, 'Was I making tea?' and says that she didn't know about me else she would've made up the spare room.

'Please don't worry about the tea. You really don't need to go to any trouble on my account,' and I wonder if they're reli-gious. Those that give up their possessions so they've nothing left to lose.

'We have not seen Selwyn in so long,' she says. 'Hugh thought we never would again.' And that little smile again, like a fingernail of moon: she seems to drift in and out from one world to the next.

'Who is Hugh?'

Her reply is that they've gone to the pond.

'They've gone fishing? Now?'

She says, 'Do you know where you are? Why he has come?'

I shake my head. 'We're on our way to Wales,' I tell her. 'Feels like we've been driving for days.'

'You don't know where you are, do you?' she says again. This time, she gets up, holds out her hand and gestures for me to follow. She takes me to another room across the corridor and disappears into its darkness. Reappears when she's illuminated herself by the lights of a massive cabinet tank that fills so much of the room you could quite believe you were in it yourself and the fish were looking at you.

'Jesus Christ!' I yelp. 'Is that legal?' I clutch at my chest as my heart beats anti-clockwise.

'Six hundred and fourteen fish,' she murmurs, tapping at the glass with the rings on her fingers that slip up and down. 'I like to watch them spawn, mostly. I'd show you, but I had to kill the last one Hugh impregnated. He experiments, you see, and I don't agree. The gold was always in carp.'

'I see.' I don't know what else to say. She makes me feel like I've lived my life with my eyes closed. I have never seen fish like it. Some of them are the size of small shoes. And their colours are luminous, glow-in-the-dark, like highlighter pens, fins like rosettes, and some look as if they wear beaks. They swim in an underwater woodland that ruffles and bubbles, and all across the pebbles at the bottom of the tank, fairy-tale castles, troll bridges, and mermaids.

'Do you know about fish?' she asks.

'No.' I watch the tank like a television screen.

She looks disappointed. 'I'm not even sure where to put you when I've had no notice,' she says, looking around the room as if she's lost something. 'I suppose I could get you a blanket and you could sleep in the chair.'

'I'm fine in the caravan,' I tell her. 'Though we've not actually slept in it yet.' I give a small laugh that echoes and bounces off the walls. 'We came with a caravan and sleep everywhere but. Do you think I should wait for Selwyn to come back?'

'You won't see them till morning,' she sniffs, tapping at the tank. 'But I'm afraid that it's just been far too long.'

She turns to look at me and it's as if I've just told her that summer's a wash-out and we might even get snow in July.

'Imogen,' she cocks her head to one side and seems pleased to have remembered my name. 'Yes. I can see what Sarah saw.'

'Sarah?' A jolt of ice shoots down my spine. 'But you said you didn't know about me.'

She stretches out her fingers on her right hand to shuffle her rings back into place. Then straightens the lid of the tank and pats it. 'She'd rattle them up, those boys,' she starts to tell me. 'Always wanted things to happen quicker than they did.'

I look around the rest of the room. It's clean. Lived-in. White plastered walls. Like something has been covered up. Painted over. No curtains mind, but rugs, thin and musty and filled with old-fashioned patterns – she has them spread across the quarry tiles like stepping stones – and what looks like a large pouffe cinched in a dirty pink velour with lilac buttons. This room is looked after. It feels like a shrine. And it's all done to please those six hundred and fourteen fish.

I start to feel uneasy.

'You know what?' I say. 'I'll sleep in the caravan. I'm absolutely fine in the caravan. And it's really late.'

I make to leave the room, but she stops me. Her hand reaches for my arm and those gold rings have tiny diamonds set inside them; little riches she wants to keep secret.

'He still looks, doesn't he?' she says, that childlike voice verging on sinister. 'Even after all this time. He can't help but look.'

I tell her very quietly that I'm not sure what he's looking for.

She turns over my right hand so that she may rest her fingers on the flat of my palm. I start to bend my knees because I'm towering over her, like I could crush her; she is no taller than where my heart beats.

'I used to be able to do this,' she tells me, tracing her forefinger along my palm. 'Not any more. Even knowing what will come cannot stop it.' She curls my fingers over my palm, then cups my fist with her own hands. 'No soldier ever forgets,' she says. 'But we learn too late that what we battle in ourselves is only because of what we think we have done.' She releases my hand and leaves it stone cold. Wanders back towards the fish tank and taps against the glass again. 'Watch,' she mutters, as two fish change direction to swim towards her fingertips on the other side of the tank. 'This one is curious. This one is acting upon a memory it has no recollection of.' She keeps on tapping. 'Does it really matter? It's just something else happening. That is all. And then they will forget about it.'

I don't know how long I stand there in the corner of the room, so very still, like I'm frozen in ice. I'm entranced by her fingers stroking the side of the tank. Never have I seen someone so comfortable in their skin that they feel absolutely no need to explain themselves. She has the measure of me without even looking at me.

'You're sulking,' she murmurs at the tank. 'Because it's just as you remember and you thought people change.'

I haven't the heart or the energy to argue with her. Besides, she is right. I have been sulking. And playing dead.

I watch her say goodnight to every single one of those fish, as if they are children. I count those goodnights until I lose count. I wait for her to say goodnight to me. But she has forgotten I am there.

And on the Seventh Day...

God finished His work that He had done, and He rested.

'Nymphs are not normally active creatures unless alarmed. In general, they remain quietly among water plants waiting for their prey.'

~ *The Great Necessity of Ponds*
by Selwyn Robby

I AM NOT PART of all of Selwyn's past, and he is not part of mine. We did not have anything to salvage, reclaim, or return to. No life lived together, or a love enjoyed. So much he should know. So much I should say. It has never occurred to me to think the same of him.

Selwyn knocks on the passenger window to wake me. Despite the grin, the fresh set of clothes, the comb to his hair, he looks like he hasn't slept a wink, and I'm loathe to open the car door because I can't be held responsible for either my use of words or the swing of my feet towards his shins. 'Where the hell have you been?' I yell. 'You left me. Again.'

'I thought you'd sleep in the house,' he says, gesturing behind him. 'Why would you not sleep in the house?' I let my eyes adjust to the blush of daylight and see all that I didn't see last night.

'Oh, my God. It's a bloody mansion,' I say.

And it is.

It's been someone's stately home. Far less stately than it used to be, but rustic and ruddy with lattice windows and acorn-brown stone draped in a laburnum yet to flower. There are four bedroom windows, all in a row, and pillars outside the front door. It is majestic. It is wild. It's housed civilised life and perhaps some gentry, but now it is full of woe. When I look up at the roof, it has dipped, like something heavy has landed upon it, and two of the chimneys have crumbled apart.

'I said I would sleep in the car,' I mutter at Selwyn who's watching me gape at the place. 'She didn't seem too pleased—' and I stop. Maisie with Hugh, out of the corner of my eye, and I see them coming into focus as a single shape. She, as she was last night, still in that brown drapery and all that hair that almost reaches her waist. But he is the crippled one, bent so far over that he can barely raise his neck. He holds on to her so tightly, the rhythms of their bodies fuse. I find myself checking that their shoelaces aren't tied together. And then my throat tightens. This is us, I think, with a brief glance towards Selwyn who is offering his arms to both of them. This is the future us, and right before we must part for good.

'Good morning, everybody,' I say cheerily. 'How were the fish?'

But nobody speaks. Maisie and Hugh look away. Everyone is sobbing. Selwyn tells me to get back in the car.

'ARE WE GOING TO talk about it?'

Selwyn is yet to speak to me. He's making me feel like we are irretrievable.

'I don't know what I've done, Selwyn. Why won't you speak to me?'

He is putting his foot down to move us into the fast lane of this dual carriageway, and more than he needs to, and I feel the caravan behind us start to sway. It is weighing us down, I think, that caravan, swaying left to right behind us. It is a dead weight carting about memories neither of us want to keep or even make.

'Selwyn, pull over, please. I don't know what's going on.'

He changes down in gear as the caravan struggles against a small incline.

'Please, Selwyn. I don't want to go any further. Not like this.'

He slows down – starts to indicate, pulls over into a lay-by and sighs. He won't look at me. He just murmurs, 'Why do we leave things too late, Ginny? What is it that we keep on waiting for?'

I think about what to say and how to say it, but mainly of all the things I want to say that I shouldn't say. I think of him and me and what we are, and look down at my hands expecting to see sores from where we hold on to ourselves; wounds that will not heal. I think of the past ten months and how the word 'reunited' belongs on a grave. *Me and you, we have a story,* Selwyn always says, yet this is his story and not mine. I'm just his passenger. The anonymous one who got in the car.

I look out of the window and have no idea for where we are, or why we're here, and if I want to go any further. I feel as far away as I can possibly be and yet closer to what I can't quite put my finger on. I look at him. At Selwyn. This man who loves me as I should love him. Do I have any questions for you, old man? I think. Do I really want to know any more?

'I thought it was still like it was and it wasn't,' he suddenly tells me. His chin buckles. He is trying to hide his face with his shoulders and rubbing his eyes. He has not shaved in a while, but it suits him, this rugged jaw – he positively reeks of the doomed hero.

'Why would it be?' he carries on. 'Why did I expect it to be the same? Why do I expect you to be the same? That everything should stay the same?'

I tell him he's making no sense. None of it is making any sense.

'You left me,' I say. 'Just disappeared. And there was this enormous fish tank where they were breeding all these fish.'

He slaps the steering wheel. 'Goddamnit, Ginny! Not everywhere is about you.'

'That's not what I'm saying. You left me with a woman who was a hundred, if a day. She could barely remember herself let alone wonder for me. Put yourself in my position. I *am* in this car with you!'

'Are you?' he asks. 'Are you really sat there aside of me?'

I take my time to answer this, because physically I am sat here, but no one else knows I am here, not really, not even Mia. Anyone who might see me sitting here will see me only as a stranger and someone they will not ever see again. It will not cross their minds to think that I might not want to be sitting here when I am in the car. They will just assume that I'm going somewhere and, more importantly, want to go there. I am a fish in a moving glass tank having my eyes opened.

Carry on like this and I will start talking about myself as an obituary.

'You are making this about me,' I say, eventually, 'when this is all about you. Where *you* want to go. You have planned it and you have been planning it, I can see that now, and I will come with you, Selwyn. I said I would, and I'm here, right here. But you said we were going to Wales. A holiday in Wales. You can't keep driving to places and not telling me why we're there! I still don't even know who those people were last night.'

'I left it too long,' he is raising his voice at me. 'They thought I'd forgotten them and I thought it was still the commune and it wasn't.' He makes it sound like a diagnosis.

'Commune? What commune? It was the middle of nowhere!'

'That was its point. You don't just drop out, Ginny. You drop off the face of the earth.'

'So, why were we there?'

'Because it's where we went before...then after...but Mother...it wasn't for Mother and we left. I thought it'd be like it was. That we could stay. Have some time.' He isn't looking at me. He's telling it all to the windscreen. 'But I couldn't. I couldn't stay. How can I stay?'

'I don't know what you're telling me,' I say quietly. 'Are you saying that's where we were headed? This thing we're doing. That you wanted us to live there?'

He doesn't speak. Just stares straight ahead.

'Selwyn!' I shout. 'You have to talk to me!'

'I've just told you!' he shouts back. 'That's it. End of story. And on we go.'

'I've just about had enough of this,' and I'm unplugging my seatbelt and I'm out of the car.

Except I have nowhere to go. There is a ruddy great hedge in front of me and the only option I have is to head straight down the dual carriageway.

So, I do.

SELWYN KERB-CRAWLS ME all the way with the hazards on. For once, he is following me and I start to think that this is it. We have parted. He will carry on and I will carry on as we have always done. Because that's what we do, me and Selwyn Robby. He asked me to move in and I moved in, but he carried on with his life, as if he didn't know what to do with me, and I carried on being there in case he started to change. But Selwyn doesn't change. Do I even know enough to know if he has changed? Can change? So, I will walk home. That'll be the story. The day I walked home down a dual carriageway. And he will carry on going to wherever it is he's going because Selwyn is going somewhere and I am not.

I think of my phone on the bed back at home, like a body between lives, and if there are any missed calls. People who miss me, people I will miss. Have I gone nowhere because I didn't want to miss him? Has my life really been about *just in case he comes around the corner?*

It isn't that big old house that's lonely and falling apart. It's *me*.

There is a band of rain, gunpowder clouds: they make the fields below look filthy, and I take it all in – this unfamiliar outside world I've never seen before; the furthest away I have ever been – and think myself braver than I am.

Maisie was right. I have been sulking. I have been a child.

Then I think of Mia.

I say her name as if she can hear me. For a minute, I think I do hear her – her voice travelling by cloud, telling me she's okay, she's always been okay, as I have always been fine. It's all we ever say. I'm fine. I'm okay. Easier to say that than say we are not. Only when I put the phone down do I blow a gasket. I expect she does too.

I look down at my feet and wonder how far they could take me right now. I'm wearing these silly blue canvas plimsolls and they are giving me a blister. Selwyn is ahead of me now. Picked up speed and over-taken me. He pulls over on to the hard shoulder and the caravan's hazards are flashing me.

Get in. They say.

Walk past. They say.

Get in the car, Ginny. I need you to get in the car.

He'd asked me to get in the car and I got in the car. We get out of the car and then we get back in. It's not like he's begging me to get in the car. I only have to be asked once.

Yet, I roll up my sleeves as if there is about to be a fight. I roll up my sleeves exactly as I do when I'm about to wash up or unblock the drains of Selwyn's ruddy bladderwort. It's started to rain hard. Rain that hurts and splits the skin. I remember the hailstorm as if it was yesterday. Bladderwort. Why does Selwyn grow bladderwort in our drains? I have no money. Just silly blue canvas plimsolls that are starting to stain my feet. I will have blue feet. And I've no coat. Did I even bring a coat with me? I do everything without thinking. I never think. I just do. My daughter is on the other side of the world with a man she thinks is her father – and he could be; he could be not. And, then again, of course, he is. I think of the pebbledash photograph that Linda tried to give me back in Loggerheads: was it really Meg, or was it not? All farmhands, those Richers, and three boys. The sort of poverty you can't get your head around. What does it matter, I think? Do I even care? I've spent fifty years nibbling on deadly nightshade, yet seem to have the stomach for it. *Life is an ice cube*, as Meg would say. *It melts.*

Selwyn has got out of the car. He is waiting for me. He has always waited for me. He waits and he waits and still I say *no. No, Selwyn. I will not marry you.* Because he wants us to be something that we cannot be when those two people we were have gone. And yet, we have always been looking for each other. Spent our lives waiting for each other. *You've let no one come near you for fifty years,* he says. *And neither have you, Selwyn. Neither have you.*

I went to see a doctor once. I'd kissed a man who'd said it was like kissing porcelain and that there was something very wrong with me. The doctor sent me to a specialist who sent me to a therapist who sat me in a room on a circle of chairs with six others who shared my problem. I never went again. I thought they were inventing words to create problems that weren't problems; to make you think that things were wrong and get you addicted to pills. I remember the therapist saying to think of it as a choice, if it helped. A biological choice that our bodies had made of their own accord. She was there to help us live with that choice. But I'd made a choice that gave me a child, and then it was no longer about choosing. I had a daughter to raise. I couldn't be complicating her life any more than it already was. The therapist asked me of my birthing experience. Was it very traumatic? But that was something else I'd boxed away, and so deep I couldn't remember it. She suggested hypnotherapy to relive the miracle. I burst out laughing and left the room.

When my daughter became a nurse, she took to leaving leaflets in places where I would find them. In the bread bin. On the grill pan. In my apron pocket. I put them in the bin or burnt them on the bars of gas fires. She'd said, 'Stop treating it like it's just a case of bad breath. It's a serious problem, Mother. You're absolving yourself for no reason.' I disagreed. Though I'd had to look up absolve in the dictionary. She'd got that bit right, but women like us, we just got on with it. I didn't have the time to be worrying about all that didn't work when I had to go to work. 'Besides, no-one else got hurt.' I'd said, after another leaflet dropped out of the TV guide. 'Would you have preferred it if I'd worn a habit?' She still accused me of lying through my teeth. 'Chastity is a choice, Mother. This is something else.' 'You're right,' I'd said. 'It is, and because after you left my body, Mia, I let it seal, for nothing and no one to come between us.'

I came out with it to Selwyn on the stairs. I wasn't planning on saying it, and so soon – I wasn't even sure if I'd said it out loud – 'I don't work like that. I don't know why. I just don't.' He'd led me back down the stairs and said, 'It's not all that love is, you know. Not everyone learns to swim either. But that doesn't stop them going near the water.'

Sometimes, I would climb into his bed. He would wake and shuffle over. Lift the blankets to offer me a warm pod where I might curl up aside of him. Like a cat. Like my daughter would do, and probably for longer than she should. The space always felt like a deep bath, and I was fine within that space until he began to touch.

Sometimes, I would try to touch too. Mostly, I didn't.

I have stopped crawling into that space. I just sit on the end of the bed, watching him sleep with his eyes fixed on the ceiling, and telling him sin after sin after sin when actually there was no sin. Just two bodies, and then three.

'Here,' I lift up my nightdress to show him, as he sleeps, where I have drawn on myself with a series of dashes across my midriff and right along my caesarean scars; the same as Meg would draw on pig skin to determine between shoulders and thighs and best back bacon. 'This is where my body divided on that day and then opened up on that other day. It has never come back together you see. There is this part and there is this part and I don't know how or if it will ever work as one body, do you see, Selwyn? Do you understand what I'm trying to say?'

His eyes fixed on the ceiling like two marbles, his body with its slow breaths. It's like un-fathoming the meaning of life with a man in a coma.

Now, as Selwyn comes towards me with the traffic thundering past, I see there *is* something different about him. Something that didn't live under the flyover. This Selwyn swaggers and doesn't shave. This Selwyn could light fires with his fingertips and rustle up dinner from roadkill. His shirt is more unbuttoned than normal. Has he done something different with his hair? As he breathes out, dragon-smoke. As he breathes in, me; always me. And I will it, I really do. I *will it*. I wish I knew what to do.

'Ravish me,' I murmur.

But it is me who runs into his arms.

SELWYN TELLS ME THAT Wroxeter is the most Roman place on the planet.

'What? More roman than Rome?'

We're staying the night in Shrewsbury, in a weary looking mediaeval B&B hidden within the black and white timber-frames of an old crooked house that is full of candles and the sort of loud-mouthed businessmen I'd thought the internet had eaten alive. Selwyn thinks it will do us good to gather ourselves, as if we have scattered our limbs on the A49 and cannot find which belongs to me and which belongs to him. We're up in the Gods, in the servant's quarters, and I will forgive the smell of damp washing, the black boot-mark on the back of the door, the bleak little en suite with its sliver of green soap on the basin, for the bed linen is lovely and, after last night's sleep in the car, I feel like we've arrived somewhere lavish.

Selwyn is reading from some tourist magazine he's found, and telling me something about how some of the buildings out in Wroxeter would be up to six storeys high.

'Practically skyscrapers,' he's telling me. 'And all to prevent people from coming. Smoke would billow out from the sixth storey – there was a chimney, you see, right through the middle of the building – and so people coming down what is now the A49, between the Caradoc and Cardingmill Valley—'

'What do you mean people?'

'Enemies, really. They would see the smoke and think, that's some powerful city over there. If they can build that, then I've got to watch my step.' He pauses to tap his nose. I am always wary when he taps his nose. He makes me feel like I look at history through wooden eyes.

'That's what they thought?' I'm straightening the coasters on the bedside table. They are very plain.

'A city belching smoke was a signal of power and industry.' He is being smug now. He likes knowing more than me. 'And primitive man was awful territorial,' he says this bit as if it is something I should still appreciate. 'I should have taken you there, really, for you to see it for yourself. There's lots of things I should've done for you, Ginny.' He pauses. His face brightens. He is cheery all of sudden. 'We could go back home,' he suggests. 'Plan it all out. Together.'

'You should have told me where we were last night,' I snap, looking for the switch for the bedside light, which, I find, is an oblong brick in the maroon velour headboard. 'You should tell me if we are actually going to Wales.'

I watch him arrange his lips into a scowl and start to think of him as my enemy. The man who built a six-storey house with as many bricks as he could find. I think of women stuck up towers for their beauty and masterful kings. I think of territories and borders; of the walls we build and the lines we draw to join and make squares. I wonder where we are all going. I wonder if we really have moved on, and if all this exists underwater. I wonder how much smoke I could make compared to Selwyn. If my fire would be bigger than his. I think of the fire that he and Louis made when trapped in a thunderstorm in a fisherman's hut. Did something happen between them that night that only happens when you think your life's about to end? Another road I shouldn't go down. I think of all the roads he has been down and how many without me. Salesmen know roads like the back of their hands. And every shortcut known to man.

I've never heard of the A49 but am going to remember it in case this is another trick. Tomorrow, I'm going to buy my own map. Own my own. And a big red felt-tip pen. Draw my own roads. Find my own places. *Live* without dashes on my skin.

He's about to shower so wears no shirt or socks and has unbuckled his belt. His chest is wide, anointed with grey hair and liver spots, old scars from ill-shot jabs and the barely there lines of an eagle tattooed on his right bicep, from another time he will not speak of, during a stint of National Service that I only found out about through mistaking a brown envelope for me. 'No soldier ever forgets,' Maisie has said. A dirty green ink stain now, with smudged edges; it reminds me of mould on a bread crust.

He lies back on the bed covering his face with his hands. I look at his skin and how it stipples around his shoulder blades. There are still muscles in his arms, but they are old now and worn out. He still thinks he can lift heavy things because he desires to lift them, and high above his head to prove that he's not broken. No other woman has touched that skin: that's what he tells me, assures me, promises me. There has been no one else, just *you*, *Ginny*. I used to believe this. Now, I don't.

'You should've married,' I find I am saying. 'You would've made a good husband. A good father.'

He leans away from me to flip the switch on the wall behind him. We're left in the dusky oblong lamplight. He is trying to start something between us, and he gives a little quirk of the lip and holds out his hands.

'I have,' he says. 'To you.'

'And what are you imagining right now?' I move towards him, sticking with the thought of the masterful king.

'Holding your hand,' he says, quietly. 'Listening to you breathe.'

He is offering his hands up to me. I take one. Then the other. And sit on the bed. His hands move to my waist as he tries to lower me down on to the bed aside of him. I spot a sweet wrapper under the bedside table. He isn't pushing me, but he is trying, ever-so-gently, to get me to lie down. But that sweet wrapper is bothering me. It reminds me that someone has been in here before us. Using the bed. Doing things in the bed. Tossing about sweet wrappers without a care in the world. I pull away to reach under the cabinet to retrieve the sweet wrapper. It's pink foil, the sort that covers fudge in Quality Street. I crumple it in my hand and go back into the bathroom to put it in the bin. I close the door.

We sit looking at each other by candlelight, the candle so big I have to look around it. Selwyn wears a black linen shirt that creases around his armpits. He picks up a fork, puts it down, picks up another fork, then picks up the previous fork and measures them against each other.

'They're the same size,' he says, and I know he is stalling because he knows he's got to tell me properly, including whatever else there is to tell, or I will go no further. 'It is not an ultimatum,' I had said, as we sat down at the table. 'But the secrets have to stop.' He shuffles his napkin into his lap and begins where he always begins. 'There's a pond,' he says.

'And that's where you and Hugh went?' I ask. 'To a pond?'

He nods and swabs at his neck with his napkin as if having a hot flush.

'It was pitch black.' I also remind him that he came back in the morning with no fish.

'I wasn't fishing,' he says. 'I didn't go there to fish.'

I tell him about the fish tank. The size of it. The amount of fish. The way Maisie spoke to them and spoke of them. It was creepy. But the wine is here and the waiter asks if we want to taste it. Selwyn instructs him to just pour and the waiter straightens as if he's proud to be pouring wine he is too young to drink. When I look at the glass, I realise the wine is the wrong colour.

'It's red,' I hiss at Selwyn. 'We ordered white.'

'Does it matter? You drink red too, don't you?'

'Yes. But it's not what we ordered.'

'And what did you order, Ginny?'

It comes out so quickly I feel slapped. I pick up my wineglass and drink half of it. 'It's fine,' I say, though it's cheap and sweet. 'It's very good.'

He stares at me, yet he is gone from behind his eyes, off somewhere else where I am not. And he is blushing. And not from the wine.

'You obviously don't think it too bad,' I say, watching him pour himself a second glass.

'I'm just thirsty,' he says. 'It's been a long day.'

'It's been a long trip,' I say, knotting my hands in my lap. 'And yet we've not even been away a week.'

This is a shock to him. He had thought it longer. 'Really?' he says. 'Not even a week?'

'Not even a week,' I repeat. 'We left on Monday, and today is Sunday.'

He rubs his chin with the heal of his hand and appears to be counting on his fingers under the table.

'Look,' he begins, 'we went to live there, at the Corbet Hall, when it was a commune. Maisie and Hugh's commune. Maybe about ten, twelve people.' He squints with one eye.

'I don't know how many lived there. There were always a lot of people, just coming and going. And we had this little place, out back, away from the main house. For about four years, as it was.' He pauses again to drink and finishes the second glass. 'I thought it was paradise. But then Mother—' He pauses. 'It just wasn't somewhere she thought she could be. No privacy, she said. So, we left.'

He puts his elbows on the table and plays with the forks again. The waiter is here with our food and there is more fussing about sauces, condiments, and the waiter tops up our glasses until the bottle is empty, and yes, says Selwyn, why not? And the waiter trots off for a second bottle.

'Your father,' I begin. I am drawing the outline of a fish with my knife on the table as I say it. 'He didn't come with you to Joiners Square.'

'No.'

I put two and two together and make five – once I caught a fish alive. 'You weren't expecting to see him, were you?'

He sighs. 'My father died a long time ago. You know that.'

'Then why did he not come with you to Joiners Square?'

'What's your point, Ginny?' he demands.

'My point?' I am angry with him. 'You never ever talk of your past and now you are. I'm interested to know.'

He looks at me with very round eyes. *A good salesman*, Selwyn always says, *maintains eye contact by concentrating on the bridge of the nose so that even his lies are sincere.*

'Father didn't come with us,' he murmurs. 'He had his reasons. He stayed.'

By rights, I should be far more inquisitive, but I slug my wine and look away because I don't think I do want to know. If I know more about him, he'll use it to know more about me, and we once agreed, call it a pact if you like, that what we didn't know shouldn't matter. Not everything needs to be sewn together to make a past. We don't always need to know everything about each other. We found each other again. Let that be enough.

'But we're going around in circles,' I say. 'You and me, this trip, there's no A to B.'

'There never was any A to B,' he says, slicing into his steak. 'Why do you need to keep working everything out? Why can't you just enjoy the journey? Like a magical mystery tour!'

My knife and fork clatter on to my plate of their own accord. '*A magical mystery tour?*' I start to laugh. 'Is that what you call it?'

I beam up at the returning waiter, that moment when they come and ask if everything is alright. 'Thank you, thank you. It's lovely. No, we can pour it ourselves, thank you.' I trip over my words until I am flat on my face, pick up half a buttered potato with my fingers and shove it into my mouth.

'You need to start again,' I tell him.

'There's really very little to say.' Selwyn straightens himself in the chair. 'We lived at the Corbet Hall for four years. That was all. And it was four of the happiest years of my life. I thought we'd be there forever and leaving was a wrench. I've thought a lot about going back – I even tried once, but then the years passed – and we were heading that way and I just thought…' He pauses to drink more. 'There was absolutely nothing more to it than that.'

I can see a small bone protruding from the cod loin. I pick it out and realise that I'm always picking bones, picking fights.

'They're good people,' he tells me. 'Salt of the earth. So, I gave them some money.'

I swallow hard. 'That was kind of you. How much money did you give them?'

He tells me what he made at Hodnet. I swallow hard.

'All that money? You just handed it over? For what?'

'You saw the state of the place. My father would have done the same.'

'It's completely on its knees! And what are they both, a hundred? What money will help them now?'

He puts down his knife and fork and pushes his plate away. 'You don't get it, do you?' he snipes at me. 'It's a way of life, Ginny. A sense of sharing, family, and that was the life he wanted. Because him and Hugh…' he wipes his mouth with his napkin and makes to get up from the table.

'Your father was gay?'

The look Selwyn gives me could catch fire. 'You are talking about my father, Ginny.'

'But he wanted to be with Hugh. That's what you've just said.'

'That is not what I said at all.'

'But he stayed behind.'

'It's where he wanted to be.'

'Why are you being such a gnarly old oak tree with me? I never knew my father. Christ, what do I even know about fathers? Stop punishing me for being interested.'

'Then don't make him out to be the monster here. Goddamn you, Ginny. That is *not* what happened!'

'But what does it really matter when it's a life long gone, and you have nothing to be ashamed about. For goodness sake! Where are you going? Selwyn! You've not finished your food…' But in the time my fork takes to drop to my plate in frustration, Selwyn has disappeared.

She was always going to ask, my daughter. You hope the questions won't come, but they do, and they came home from school like a dirty lunchbox. Everyone else had one. Why didn't she?

'Look,' I'd said. 'They aren't always necessary, and you've been lucky in other ways.'

Another time: 'That's the way it goes, sweetheart, and it never bothered me.'

And another time: 'Yes, I know you know about the birds and the bees, but he really was just an irrelevant sperm.'

Then later, Mia had a different set of questions: 'Does he know about me? Why doesn't he want to know me? Someone must be out there thinking about me. What do you mean you don't know, when it was '70s Stoke-on-Trent?'

Mia is twenty and she's nursing so she knows about records now, how to acquire birth certificates, death certificates, so I may as well tell her my version at least. I tell her: he was almost thirty and a cobbler by trade who became a ten-pound pom. He re-heeled my shoes and Meg paid him in goat. He set about me like tying up a pair of temperamental bootlaces and it was such a bloody nuisance for it to be that one and only time.

'And that's it,' I'd said. 'That really is it.'

I can see the disappointment in her face even now.

In times so far away they've grown rind:

Me to Meg: 'Do I have grandparents? Where are they?'

Meg to me: 'Ask the Bluebird. She'll tell you.'

Me to Meg: 'She's not here.'

Meg to me: 'Yes, she is. She's standing right beside you. And don't look at me like that. Everyone's dead.'

I once had a friend who went through her husband's wallet on a daily basis. It wasn't because she didn't trust him, she said. But because it made her trust him more. I've known other women for whom their husband's bulging wallet is something they like to leave on the side for me to see. As if it had secret powers. Meg kept her money in a drawstring bag made of cowhide that she kept under the sink. I've never had a husband, and, until that moment, when a lumbering light cracked through the curtain slits, I have never taken Selwyn's wallet into the bathroom to check its contents for explosions.

I laid out everything in a line on the bathroom floor while he slept in the next room. I then sat back on my haunches puzzling over how I'd ordered it and asking myself all sorts of little questions. A bank card. A library card. A National Trust membership card. A coffee shop loyalty card. There were receipts. One for the tyres. Another for petrol, where he'd also bought mint imperials and a jar of coffee. There was a slip of paper with a telephone number on. I recognised that number. It was his. There was a button, its holes still filled with a dark brown thread that seemed to be concealing something, so I pulled it all out and put the thread in the bin. The button was naked, but it still told me nothing. There was money. Almost two hundred pounds in twenties and tens, and then an old five-pound note folded up into a small square that he'd pushed deep into a section of his wallet, which made me think other things – when that five-pound note was of another time. Why had he not spent *that* five-pound note so specifically? And then there were the business cards.

– Selwyn Robby, Sales Executive –

– Selwyn Robby, Sales Manager –

– Selwyn Robby, Commercial Sales Director –

– Selwyn Robby, Co-Partner Toogood Aquatics –

Flimsy little slips of paper really; they could barely stand on their own two feet.

I put everything back in the wallet as I'd found it, then folded the old five-pound note back up, but this time with the button inside of it. I wanted him to know that I'd seen something. Then I went downstairs to call Mia on the lobby phone. I called again. And then another three times, just to make sure I wasn't being ignored.

Status. He has craved status. And when it came, it broke him into a thousand little pieces that we have slowly begun gluing back together.

The Eighth Day

'True water plants, or hydrophytes, when taken from water become limp, weak and pale. They are quite unable to support themselves. They lack the tough fibres which enable them to grow upwards, towards the light.'

~ *The Great Necessity of Ponds*
by Selwyn Robby

AT BREAKFAST, OVER SCRAMBLED eggs, he says, 'I'm sorry for storming off to bed. I hadn't really slept the night before. It was a lot to take in, you know? A lot that was asked.' He pauses. He looks like he hasn't slept at all. 'Did you sleep okay?' he asks.

'Not really. I tried to call Mia, but there was no answer.'

He fiddles with his cutlery. Something is agitating him. 'I mean, where would you start?' he begins. 'There's no central heating. No gas. The place has just been left to crumble. And you can't blame them. No.' He shakes his head at me and starts to butter a piece of toast. 'Sometimes, you have to let things go to earth.' And he's nodding at me as if he's agreeing with *me*. 'Yes. I was right to say no.'

I put down my knife and fork. 'Okay,' I say. 'You're having a conversation with yourself here.'

'I mean, there is no one else. They've not seen anyone else. It's been years. No one knows where anyone is to ask if they'd even consider it. So it's only right they asked. I don't blame them for asking. But when you are asked, and it's not like I've not thought about it, but it's not right, is it? It wouldn't be right. Not even legally.'

'Again. This is not a conversation you are having with me.'

He narrows his eyes. Dislodges a piece of toast he has stuck in his teeth. 'It's not really inherited, you see,' he carries on. 'There's no deeds, no paperwork, no rightful owner as it were. And those rights, what they were then, well, I don't think they count now.'

I wipe my mouth with my napkin and then slap it down on the table. 'Are you telling me what I think you're telling me?'

'You'd hate it,' he says. 'You did hate it. You were horrified.'

'Okay,' I put up my hands defensively. 'You need to use actual words, Selwyn. Talk to *me*.' I thump my chest as I say it. 'I'm here. Talk to me.'

He swallows hard. 'They asked if I wanted it. And if I did then they would will it to me. But that would mean legalities and—' he holds out his hands and bites down on his bottom lip. 'It took me by surprise.'

'Okay.' Now, I swallow hard.

A waiter hovers over us with a coffee pot and refills both our cups even though we've both been drinking tea. But it doesn't matter. We wouldn't notice the difference anyway.

'Is it worth anything?' I have to ask the question. 'I mean, it doesn't even have a compass direction.'

He shrugs at me. 'It's whether it's worth *it*,' he says, lowering his voice. 'It would take years to rebuild. Would I have enough time to do it and see it rebuilt? And could we cope with the rebuilding when rebuilding anyway?' He shakes his head as if bothered by a sound that only he can hear. 'No. I'm going to have some bacon. Do you want some bacon with your eggs?' He flags down a waiter as if landing a plane.

A young girl heads over and we have to repeat to her twice that I don't want bacon but Selwyn does and we are drinking tea, not coffee, so might we have new cups, please? And Selwyn would also like two slices of white bread and they can come on the same plate as the bacon, save the washing up.

'Is it really that complicated?' I say to Selwyn after she flusters off. 'At the end of the day, we're just asking for bacon and bread.'

He says, 'Please let's not start the day on the backfoot.'

'Then let's stop going sideways,' I say.

His reply is to take out forty pounds from his wallet and tell me to treat myself to some decent shoes.

'Why would you be telling me to buy shoes?'

'Because you need some decent shoes,' he says, securing the two twenty-pound notes to the tablecloth with a fork.

'What I need is for you to stop telling me what to do and tell me exactly what happened at the Corbet Hall.'

'I see.'

'No, you don't. You don't even have the right mirror *to see.*'

He gives me his mother's broken-winged bird look then, tells me that there's a hardware store nearby that he's been recommended and it's likely that they'll stock convex wing mirrors. Not having one is weighing heavy on his mind, and he's worried about the tow-bar too. The dirt track back at the Corbet Hall might have damaged something. He had felt a curling, like the caravan was resisting him. But I've already left the table by then. And left his forty pounds on the table too. I don't want his money. It has never been about the money. Then I think better of it, and walk back to the table.

'Why are we here, Selwyn?' I am trying not to raise my voice. 'In Shrewsbury. Is something going to happen *here*?'

He looks at me as if I've just asked him what the capital of Bolivia is, wipes his mouth on his napkin and tells me he's going to find this hardware store and how long do I need?

'For what?'

'To buy shoes,' he says.

I snatch the forty pounds from his hand – tell him that this time, he can wait for me.

I head right away from him, as far as I can, and up a winding hill that takes me into the town centre. I walk into shops not knowing what shops they are. I browse paperbacks then underwear; wander through clothes aisles and try on hats; spray various perfumes on my wrists until they all bleed into one. The two twenty-pound notes burrow deeper into my pocket until I can't remember if I've been here before, because not looking is what I do best and then I'm so lost I'm easily found.

A sign for a café calling itself 'quirky' and I head towards it, ask for a table for one.

I am not, however, led to a table for one, because this is a community café and customers are encouraged to share tables.

'And no mobile phones,' says a girl with wild red hair and a strange looking jewel on her upper lip. 'We want you to chat and make noise in the old-fashioned way.' She laughs like she doesn't care whether I find her funny or not.

I think, we had nothing, this lot have everything, now they don't want any of it and that makes them quirky – but I'm also distracted by a woman sat alone in a pale-blue duster jacket with buttons as big as her eyes. I might be lost, but she is absolutely lost without whomever it was she'd just lost. She gestures towards a chair and shows me a little line of baby teeth that slot neatly behind her lips. I realise how I've been sat at a table with Selwyn who hasn't been looking at me either, and that, one day, one of us really will be looking across the table at an empty chair. The buttons on her coat are very tightly stitched.

'Thank goodness,' she says, as I sit down. 'I can't read the menu. I've left my glasses in the car.' And out of the corner of my eye, I see that's a foam-based heel on those burgundy slip-ons she's wearing and not the leather uppers she's been sold.

As I read from the menu, she tells me that the broccoli and salmon quiche is always nice and she's up for sharing a pot of tea. Then she starts to tell me about her life, which is one of those stories about a woman who once lived, did some things like teaching and mothering, then found an abscess under her tongue. It is this that takes up the bulk of our conversation, because the abscess, though nothing sinister, is very uncomfortable and certain foods – which she spends a long time listing – make it sting.

I eventually realise that I've drank all my tea and eaten the quiche and not been asked a single question, other than where are you staying, and yet I have so much that I want to tell someone. So, I do. I start to tell her.

'Eight days ago,' I begin, 'I was told to get in the car – our car that was towing a caravan that Selwyn thinks is worth what he's lost – and that we were going to Wales. For a holiday. And we haven't got there, because we keep going to these other places and all these things keep happening and right under my nose, but I don't see it happening and he can't really explain why it's happening because he's so afraid of me thinking that he might be someone else to the someone I once knew. And now, just this morning, it turns out that he's being willed some rundown stately home in the middle of butt-fuck nowhere, but it's somehow my fault that he doesn't want it.' I pull my coat around my shoulders then take one of the twenty-pound notes out of my pocket. 'So, I'm really sorry about your abscess and all those things you can't eat. But at least that makes sense. That's normal life.'

The woman looks down at the money on the table then breaks into an enormous smile. 'Oh, how kind,' she says. 'I didn't expect you to buy me lunch. That is so lovely of you. Thank you.' Then she reaches down to take a pair of glasses out of her handbag along with a pen and paper. 'You said you were staying down Wyle Cop?' she checks. 'Right then, let me draw you a map back so you don't lose your way.'

Meg used to take me to a lot of funerals when I was little. Not because she knew a lot of dead people, but because she seemed to know which dead people were disappearing without a trace. I've stood aside of her – and I mean just me and her – more times than I can remember, watching a coffin be lowered into the ground with absolutely no idea for who was inside. Occasionally, they'd be distant relatives Meg would suddenly claim to know, or a neighbour from the Square, and then she'd pretend a friendship that went way back, and we'd be invited to someone's house somewhere to mourn a bit more because the dead, said Meg, helped us to live.

Other stock phrases Meg used at funerals:

1. *For your soul to have to work this hard in this life, you're not telling me that it doesn't go on somewhere better.*

2. *The dead can't hurt you. It's the living.*

3. *No one's ever lonely in death. It's life that takes everyone away.*

4. *It doesn't matter who you are at a funeral. People are just grateful for you coming.*

I make my way back to the B&B feeling like I've just turned a very curvaceous corner, and find Selwyn sitting in the lobby with a box on his lap and reading a glossy caravan magazine.

'How long have you been sat there?' I ask.

'As long as you needed me to be,' he says, and that he's settled us up. 'You didn't buy shoes then?' he asks, looking down at my feet and then at my empty hands.

'No. I bought someone lunch.'

He briefly raises his eyebrows, but I don't know what to tell him when I'm not sure who felt most sorry for who.

'Selwyn,' I say. 'Are we lost?'

He folds his hands over the top of the box and looks me straight in the eye. It's not for long though, and he shakes his head.

'No, Ginny. We are not lost.'

He also has the mirror he wanted. 'And would you look at this?' He passes me the magazine and shows me an advert. 'Trade fair. One day only,' he starts to shake his head as if he cannot believe it. 'Today. Of all days.' He smiles. Laughs.

I cannot believe it either.

Selwyn sets about attaching the convex wing mirror to the actual wing mirror on the driver's side of the car, so that one mirror reflection reflects into the other mirror reflection. I sit in the passenger seat and pull down the visor as it's suddenly sunny, and there's another mirror reflecting what all the other mirrors are reflecting, as if I need to be reminded three times. We have also lost a Y somewhere. So what used to say, *For your pond life and beyond*, on the side of the caravan, now says, *For our pond life and beyond*. I wonder if Selwyn has removed the Y on purpose, so I no longer think this journey is just *his*.

I close my eyes and start to tell Selwyn about the woman I ate my lunch to in the café. How it was a community café where you *had* to share a table with someone and talk like it was something just invented; how this woman had practically guilted me into sitting with her and had pretended she couldn't read the menu when her glasses were in her bag all along.

'She never took her coat off,' I say. 'It was like the world was only about her.'

Selwyn is doing something with a screwdriver and cusses it.

'Do you know what coddiwomple means?' I ask.

'Nope.'

'It's what the woman in the café said of her life. It means to travel in a purposeful manner towards a vague destination.'

I hear him stop doing whatever it was he was doing with the screwdriver. My eyes are still closed, but I don't need all these mirrors to know that he's looking at me and smiling, because he knows, despite everything, that the one thing I can do very well is go it alone. And that, finally, I am choosing not to.

I open my eyes. Selwyn says I've been sleeping and that we are here. I automatically assume Wales, but no. We're at the trade fair – somewhere else – except it is *not* quite a trade fair but a social for caravanners, and they are everywhere. White tin squares over there, white tin oblongs over here, airstreams and motorhomes and straightjacketed in rows like one great big milking parlour all hooked up. We are asked if we are caravanning, or caravanners, by a man in a hi-vis jacket and gleaming veneers, because if we're caravanning then we should have pre-paid. I don't know what this means, but Selwyn has his wallet out and is taking things out of it: a business card and a sheet of paper that definitely wasn't in there last night, and I can see he has signed it as well. At least four or five twenties pass hands, and the man pats the roof of the car and starts telling Selwyn where to go.

'We haven't just happened here, have we?' I say, as we make our way through the tin-can alleys, and Selwyn pats my right thigh and says, no, not exactly, but we might have made it into paradise all the same.

I smell fried chicken and candyfloss. And despair.

I make two gin and tonics from the caravan's optics to take outside while I take it all in. Selwyn has gone somewhere behind the caravan to hook us up to something and told me he'll be back in five minutes, because he's not sure if a fuse has blown or if he's using the right cable. I sit on the caravan step and look over at the backsides of the caravans parked in front of us. How sheets of welded metal and jolly looking backlights can make a person feel so at home.

We've been shoved up in a corner and next to a motorhome so enormous it makes our caravan look like its cub. I sit in shadow among the hawthorn bushes to our right, yet a woman still approaches me, in a red dress busy with blue flowers, and green wellies fill up her legs. There's a gravy-brown cardigan and the rest of her looks made with gelatine. There's something abnormally stiff about her hair.

'Are you flogging, or snooping?' she asks, in a voice as thick as her midriff, and she's Welsh. 'I don't recognise the van.'

But before I can reply, Selwyn comes around the corner with such large strides I wonder for the health of his groin.

'Ilma?'

She gasps so hard it seems to take up all her breath.

'Selwyn? Oh, my Lord!' Her cheeks flush, her knees buckle, and she cups his face with two fat hands. 'Selwyn Robby! For crying out loud! Selwyn Robby!' – and the hug they give each other is terrifying.

'Never in a million years,' he gushes. 'I mean really, Ilma, what in God's name are you doing here?'

'What am I doing here? What are *you* doing here?'

Though neither of them actually tells each other what they're doing here because Selwyn is reaching for the two gin and tonics I've just made and parked up on the caravan step. He hands one to her and says, 'The Highlands are what you want,' and she laughs like it's just the funniest thing and chinks his glass and says, 'The highlands are what *we* want,' and it's as if I've just been erased. And I'm here again, faced with someone he knows but has never heard of me.

'Talk about following your nose,' Selwyn says. They're still holding hands. 'Honestly, Ilma, what *are* you doing here?'

She starts to tell him about Duncan. You know, Duncan? He doesn't know Duncan, and I don't know why he's looking at me because I don't know Duncan either. 'Duncan,' she keeps on saying. 'My son.'

'You had a son?' Selwyn looks gobsmacked.

'1974, Ruthin village hall?' And Selwyn clamps a hand over his mouth and goes, 'Noooo!'

'Afraid so,' she tells him. 'But you know me, Selwyn. Never could keep the bedroom window shut.'

Selwyn wags his finger then shakes his head like he couldn't be any prouder.

'Everything built up from dust,' Ilma announces, with her arms wide. 'As far as the eye can see.' Selwyn looks around him as if he's just seen it for the first time and is possibly inheriting it too. 'Always said my Duncan had it in him,' she carries on. 'Caravan mad, all his life. Obsessed!'

'I'd love to see him,' Selwyn mutters, which makes me wonder if he knows Duncan more than he is letting on. 'Is he here? Can I see him?'

Ilma's hand arrives on top of Selwyn's, though I'm not sure their hands have ever parted.

'He'd love to see you.' And something fizzles between them.

I stand up and thrust out my hand. 'Ginny,' I say, unnecessarily loud. 'It's nice to meet you.'

They both look at me, as if astounded that I've stuck around, then look back at each other. Something else passes between them – something I can't put my finger on when it's all in the blink of their eyes – and Ilma eventually pulls away to shake my hand. She looks at Selwyn, and says, 'Married?' as if she can't quite believe it, then drops my hand quickly. Even her handshake felt disappointed by me.

'Oh, no, no,' Selwyn tells his feet. 'But yes, this is Ginny and, Ginny, this is Ilma Cheadle. A *very* old friend, who I cannot believe is actually here!'

I go to say something, but Ilma is already talking about dinner – she's making veal pie, figgy crumble – 'You don't still make figgy crumble?' – 'Of course I still make figgy crumble! About seven?'

She has a bungalow. And then they're suddenly mid-gas about pond lining, because it's only idling about the yard. 'Carrier-bag thin, won't hold spit,' Ilma says. 'But take it, please.' Selwyn winks and tells her that moulds do little more than shape the ground; it's the lining that brings a pond to life. To which Ilma grips on to him again, and says, 'Sometimes, old friend, what we don't know keeps us going.' And then they're hugging again, like *hugging again,* and oh, I could've caused a scene. Said things. Done things. Thrown a glass. Stomped off behind the caravan and dramatically unhooked us and demanded Selwyn to remember me. I am here too. And *we* are going to Wales. That's how it should've played out.

I could've said that I was going to take a nap and listened to their *figgy* reminiscing from behind the caravan walls. Don't mind me, I could've said. Pretend I'm not here. No one knows I'm here anyway.

Instead, I tell them that I think I'll go take a look around. 'Let you two catch up.'

Ilma smiles. Though it is the same smile I would give Meg when she'd tell me to set the table for three.

Caravans, caravans everywhere and not a place to think. Mobile homes and home from homes. I mooch about browsing accessories and gimmicks for storage solutions; one veteran asks me if I'd like the 'touch-feel-see' experience, but I tell him I'm fine, thank you. I contemplate buying a lipstick at twice the price and perhaps a pair of green leather gloves. So, Selwyn has friends, I think. He always talks of friends, but I never meet them. They are people he meets when he's on the road. *I saw Jim, today. I ran into Reg Collingwood.* Someone he knows. Someone who knows him. Kay Cox. Rachael. Women who act as if he's been missing in action. There are his neighbours, of course: Val and Alan next-door, Tony and Rose from across the way, and we stop for a chat and chew the fat – the weather is terrible, the bus is late, will they ever finish whatever they're doing to that flyover? And Louis. The BIG friend.

When I left Joiners Square and found myself elsewhere, I realised that I'd been so used to neighbours just being there that I didn't know how to make friends. I'd chat to my new neighbours – to Lizzy and Freda, to Jack and Betty Smalls – and I'd borrow things and enquire of things, and there were people I worked with and liked. People I worked with and didn't like. I lived in places where you wouldn't ever want to answer the door. Had neighbours who never wanted to know more. Another place. Another flat. Caro took me on at the shoe shop and I guess she was a friend. We never went anywhere as friends, but I told her a lot.

Eventually, I wander back to the caravan and find that Selwyn is talking to a man with savage eyebrows and a cheap grey suit.

As I walk towards them, I hear this man offer Selwyn thirty thousand pounds, cash in hand, for the caravan. Selwyn is sitting on the caravan step in his shirtsleeves and smoking. He thumps the side of the van and says the metal alone is worth that. I do not know when Selwyn started smoking, but he does so like he's done it before and with dignity. The man asks for the reconditioning papers. Selwyn says he has them inside – he does nothing that isn't above board – and then looks away. The man shifts from one foot to the next and peers over Selwyn's head into the caravan. Selwyn moves slightly so the man can get a better view, though I can tell that the man has seen inside already, that this has been a long conversation and Selwyn has run out of tricks. He says something about the fish in the pedestal in the toilet that I can't quite hear. Selwyn tells him firmly they are not for sale. The man says, 'But you are selling, right?'

'Perhaps,' Selwyn says. 'Eventually.'

He makes no eye contact and the man gives him a card. 'That's me,' he says. 'When you're ready.'

Selwyn nods. No deal. The man walks away. He doesn't seem to see me either.

Selwyn drags on the roll-up and blows smoke in my direction.

'You're smoking,' I say. He looks at the roll-up.

'Yes,' he says. 'I am.' He drags on it again. Even blows a smoke ring.

'Does Ilma smoke?' I say it very cruelly.

He raises his eyebrows at me, lowers his chin into his neck, and goes, 'Really?' Like it's all very boring for him. 'We're going over there for dinner, Ginny. That's all.'

'That's not what I asked.'

'And what you're asking is what you're thinking, which isn't true,' he pauses to take the last drag on the roll-up. 'Ask her what you like. She'll tell you. She's nothing to hide.' He rubs the roll-up out under his boot and gets up to go into the caravan. I call after him.

'Why didn't you take his money?'

He shrugs, shoves his hands into his pockets, does that thing with his nostrils and sniffs.

'It wasn't enough,' he says.

'Thirty thousand pounds *isn't* enough?'

He shakes his head. 'Not at the moment, no.'

He turns his back on me again and heads into the caravan. I follow and raise my voice.

'Take his money,' I demand slapping my hand down on the bar. 'Then let's just go home.'

He glares at me.

I glare back.

We glare.

We've got good at glaring.

And then that smile. Like a half-risen moon. Like a shield.

'We're not even halfway and you already want to go home,' he says. 'But if you want us to go home, then we will go home.'

A cold tunnel of wind passes between us. Words form, but make no sense. My eyes glass over until waterlogged. My arms go limp as his strengthen around my neck. He holds me. Coils himself around me. Holds me until he checks his watch behind my head. Tells me it's ten to seven and he'd just like us to have a meal with an old friend. That is all.

I pull away, wipe my face with my sleeve. 'Is he your son?'

Selwyn shakes his head and only half of that smile appears. But it is enough.

'We all make mistakes, Ginny,' turning away from me. 'But no. He's not my son.'

'I know everything about you and nothing at all,' Ilma says to me, as she bustles us both into her bungalow barefoot. 'Come in and tell me everything!' But she immediately starts talking to Selwyn. *Where has he been?* as we walk through the hallway. *Why hasn't she known?* as she leads us into the kitchen. *All this time, yet it feels like no time at all.* Stirring something on the stove. I lean against the kitchen wall of her bungalow, waiting to be told what to do when never a visitor but hardly visited. I notice the ceilings are very low when she is very tall, and she's partial to cheap gold frames for photographs. The absence of Duncan's father is notable. I wonder if I should take off my shoes.

I can smell the veal roasting in bone broth and sage. Selwyn had told me that Ilma was farmstock, and she cooks on Aga hotplates with heavy-iron pans; that her largeness is Swedish blood. As we weaved through the caravans to get here, Selwyn filled in a gap: they'd known each other as children, that's all, and she was one of ten. He talked of her father's farm as if it existed in the last century. He and one of her brothers liked fishing and she'd trail after them carrying the maggots. I butted in with, 'Why haven't you told me this before?' His reply was, 'It was just a farm under a very big sky.'

Ilma forks a potato then drains the water into a larger pan. The boiling water slips over her fingers but she doesn't wince once. She reminds me of an old grandfather who hoards pencils. She instructs Selwyn to pour wine and loosen his tie, asks him to start at the beginning because she's struggling to believe he's been where he's been all this time.

'We're talking almost fifty years,' she says; half a slab of butter and starts to mash. 'You in a house, in a city, and on the road,' she clicks her tongue. 'It's just not you.'

Selwyn fills three glasses with a deep red wine, a claret, she's already said. He hands one to Ilma, swigs from his, asks her why she's counting, then gestures that the one on the table is for me.

'Because you never kept in touch,' she snaps. 'Dropped us all like flies. We all thought you dead.'

Selwyn concentrates on what Ilma is doing, which is mashing the potatoes with only a fork and she's starting to sweat. She looks over at me – I'm trying to blend in with her wallpaper that's a blue and white stripe – points her fork and says, 'I'd blame you entirely, though it's hardly your fault.' Then she turns the fork on Selwyn. 'You really do have some explaining to do,' she demands, and I take a sip of my wine and allow myself a small smile.

'Yes,' I agree. 'He does.'

She has set the table for four. Duncan is coming. But then Duncan calls to say he's not coming. He'll do coffee in the morning, Selwyn is told, and Ilma looks disappointed. He's more than the apple of her eye, and for the next five minutes she slats stuff about: the hospitality a chore, and she forgets to offer me peas. We're all drinking quickly so another bottle is opened. I ask for water. She points and says, 'There's the tap.'

While I'm at the sink, with my back to them, I hear her ask Selwyn if I know.

He says, 'No, and please don't,' and Ilma digs the knife into the pie so hard it clinks the plate beneath. I swill out the glass twice in case something else is said, but she starts up a conversation in Welsh. And Selwyn answers her. I almost drop the glass in the sink.

'You speak Welsh?'

Selwyn bites his lip and shrugs. 'It's been a long time,' he says, though he's looking at Ilma to remind her to *please don't,* and Ilma says something else in Welsh before looking across at me and saying, 'Tell me about you.'

I fold my arms – I'm quick off the mark – and I tell it all to Selwyn. 'Oh, Potteries born and bred, this is as far away as I've been. And yes, we were next-door neighbours for a year, perhaps not even that. That was fifty years ago. Then I left. I had a baby. Lived some other places. Amounted not to much. Never married. Had some chances.' I pause. I've had too much wine. Even my full stops are drunk. 'What about you?'

Ilma stares at me, wets her lips, and even rolls up the sleeves of her cardigan. The only feminine thing about her are her eyelashes, which flutter, like she's dust in her eye, and she inhales, as if about to deliver a long-winded life speech, but then says, 'Farmer's daughter. Farmer's wife. Widowed at fifty. Did you enjoy the veal?'

'Veal always feels too young, to be fair,' I reply. 'But then what else to do with bull calves not bred to mate?' I take a sip of wine. Tell her that my mother was a great advocate of veal. 'She used to say that a short happy life knowing only good was better than a long sad one knowing only want. "The calf is full of wonder," she used to say. It's why you can taste it in the meat.'

Ilma looks vaguely anguished, then slaps her hands down on the table so hard it makes me jump. Then she slaps me on the shoulder. We have bonded over meat and she asks if I want a smoke as if we're a pair of cowboys seeing the funny side after a shootout. She pulls a leather pouch out of her pocket and begins to lay all the paraphernalia on the table like a crack addict. She takes what she needs then pushes it towards Selwyn who does the same.

'Can I roll you one, Ginny?' she asks, pinching tobacco from a tin.

I fear they're going to go outside without me so I nod and say, 'Why not?'

Selwyn laughs. 'You don't smoke,' he says, licking a paper. 'She doesn't smoke,' he says to Ilma, who ignores him and sets about making me one anyway. 'Why are you smoking?' He carries on with the statements, as Ilma hands me the roll-up and then pushes the candle towards me to light my cigarette. 'You really don't need to smoke,' Selwyn says.

'You don't know what I need,' I reply, as I hold my hair back and lean into the flame. Then I drag as only smokers know how. I blow smoke across the table as Ilma lights hers then pushes the candle towards Selwyn. It's clandestine, what we're doing, finding all these things out, and by candlelight – I'm not even sure the bungalow has electricity – and Selwyn ices the cake by saying something in Welsh that only Ilma can understand. Then she looks at me and says, 'What love is, eh? And how it waits.'

But then she turns on Selwyn again, and there's more Welsh, and it's aggressive. He answers her with a lot of hand gestures. Then she lowers her voice and speaks to him like he's a cat curled up on her lap. I watch this all from behind the third wine bottle, until I press my fingers in my ears and shout for them to, 'STOP!'

They both look at me.

They carry on looking at me.

But what to say? Stop leaving me out? Stop talking in *your* language? Stop all this past without me in it?

Selwyn gets up and asks for the bathroom. I reach across for the wine bottle and pour what's left of it in my glass. Ilma lets me, like she expects it of me. Then she sets about rolling us cigarettes again, even though I haven't finished mine, and I watch how she does it like it's an art. How she pulls out two papers and shapes two thin snakes of tobacco; how she tells me that she married a snake, and that the worst thing about marrying a snake is that you never know whether their coiling around you is to work out the size of you in order to digest you. She seals the papers around the tobacco and pushes one towards me.

'For later,' she says. Then she blows smoke across the table and says she's going to just say this. That when we get to Sioned, the water will be clear. And that she likes me. 'You're not what I expected at all,' she says. 'But I do. I like you very much.'

I bite my lip and play with the burning cigarette between my fingers.

'Did he know you were here?' I murmur. The smoking is giving me a sandpaper throat.

'He knows where he's going,' she replies. 'And he's taking you with him. Remember that.'

'But I don't know where that is,' I whisper, and I start to say something about Meg. How her broken-mirrored take on the world would have her tear up the maps so I knew nowhere else. 'Every day is a foreign place,' I say. 'And he drifts further and further out of sight.'

At that, Selwyn slouches back into the room, hunkered in drink, and stops me from saying any more. Ilma slaps her hands back down on the table. She's forgotten about the crumble. It'll need half an hour in the oven. Selwyn tells her not to get up, to stop apologising, and there's something in Welsh again, their voices kept low and below the candleflame. Ilma nods – she understands – and he leans over to kiss the top of her head. Then she holds her hand out to me and I take it, though this time the handshake is strong and full of sympathy.

'So you've lost a daughter too,' she says, slowly. 'I'm so sorry.'

I snatch my hand away and look over at Selwyn who stares down at the table.

'No, no. She's not lost. She's in New Zealand.'

Ilma turns to look at Selwyn who meets her gaze. Something else in Welsh, and something Welsh spills from him too.

'Even so,' Ilma says, looking at me again. 'The wrench I'm sure you'll understand.'

Something is happening. Something is not being said.

'No. I don't understand,' I say, my temper heating up. 'You keep talking in Welsh and I don't understand Welsh. I didn't even know that Selwyn understood or spoke Welsh, but he does and so do you. Which means both of you understand each other, but not me, you have your own language, you have this…this… I don't even know what *this* is between you!'

'Time to go.' And Selwyn has somehow manoeuvred himself to be behind me with his hands on my shoulders, my coat under his arm. I shrug him off and reach over for the bottle of wine again. I am laughing. It's all so funny. I pour what's left into my glass and drain it so petulantly the bitterness overwhelms and starts a coughing fit. Ilma looks over at me and then up at Selwyn above me. She says his name as if it's made with ice-cream and sensitive on her teeth, then she looks across at me, and says, 'I understand you, Ginny. Think what you like, but I understand you more than you think.'

She fetches me a glass of water and orders me to drink it straight down to calm the inflammation in my throat. And then silence between us. Him and her and me. Wherever we go, we are three; never this couple he keeps banging on about.

'It is never just us,' I tell the table. 'Is it, Selwyn? Even when there is no one, there is someone always there.'

But I am drunk and he is lifting me up. He steers me into the hallway – one foot in front of the other – and out into the night.

The Ninth Day

'Bacteria and fungi are nature's great agency for bringing about decay and decomposition. Without them, the world would be piled up with dead bodies and stinking.'

~ *The Great Necessity of Ponds*
by Selwyn Robby

WE ACTUALLY SLEPT IN the caravan last night. We pulled the mattresses out in silence, zipped them together, and shook out the duvet. I'd expected mustiness and married women, but they smelt brand new.

Selwyn fetched the pillows from the top shelf of the cupboard and we took it in turns to clean our teeth at the bathroom sink, like strangers in a public toilet. We undressed and put on jumpers. Neither of us said goodnight. I don't know who fell asleep first.

Selwyn isn't there when I wake up. Coffee, I assume. Duncan. No doubt all speaking a language I will never understand. I wonder why he is so keen to meet him, the son that isn't his, but my head hurts. I am parched. It's been a long time since I've drunk that much wine so quickly, but I suppose that's what old friends do.

I look out of the caravan window. It's raining this morning, and the raindrops wriggling across the glass remind me of tadpoles – lives just starting out. I search for aspirin and hear a phone ring. I scurry about to find it before remembering we don't have one, presume it is someone's in the motorhome next door. I look at the optics on the caravan wall and think about hair of the dog. The caravan door opens and Selwyn strides in, buoyant as you like, carrying a great big roll of pond lining. I can smell liver and onions on his breath and he is still wearing last night's shirt.

He stands very tall in front of me, proud as a woodcock, like he is about to announce something. There are beads of sweat on his forehead and I wonder if this is when he will tell me that he does have that terminal disease after all; that Duncan is his – the resemblance is uncanny – and he and Ilma have rekindled their flame.

'You're finally up then?' he says, rolling the pond lining underneath the bar.

'Is there something you want to tell me?' I strain to keep my voice in a straight line.

'You knew I was going for breakfast.' He runs both hands through his hair. 'What?'

'It's just that there seems to have been an awful lot of women in your life.' I say it as if accusing him of putting a black sock in with a white wash. He squints at me, as if the light in the caravan is too much pressure for his eyes, and he even shields his face.

'They keep turning up,' I carry on. 'Without explanation.'

'And there is only one woman I've wanted to share my life with, Ginny, and if you don't know by now that it is you, then I don't know what we're doing here.'

'You brought us here!' I shout back. 'And here was Ilma! We go to Hodnet, and there is Rachael!'

'And here could've been a man, not so different to myself, that you could be swearing to me meant nothing at all.'

I lay my head on the cold leather of one of the barstools and ask him, as nicely as I can manage, to stop shouting at me. My head is pounding.

'Why aren't you suffering?' I groan childishly. 'Why is it only me?'

'Suffering?' he repeats. 'Why aren't *I* suffering?' And suddenly, he's pulling me up from the bar stool and holding on to my shoulders with fingers like pincers. 'Suffering?' he says to me again, as if he's just understood the word. 'You have no idea, Ginny. No fucking idea what suffering really is.'

And I gasp, because Selwyn never swears. And if my mind didn't feel like it'd cut all ties as a blood relation, I may have had something coherent to say. But whatever it was, it is over before it's started, and he is sorry about it. He tells me that he's going outside to hook us back up to the caravan, so I might feel a jolt or two, and then we can be on our way.

Another dual carriageway. A straight road ahead. A lot of silence. Until Selwyn suddenly says, 'I needed to get the caravan valued. That's why we went there.'

I carry on looking out of the window. I feel his eyes weighing heavy on my shoulders.

'Duncan Cheadle is someone Louis told me about. Said he might give me a clear idea of what I could do with it. The metal is decent, you see.' He pauses. 'I didn't put two and two together until I saw Ilma.' He pauses again. Comes down in the gears as we approach a roundabout. Makes another decision without me and goes straight across it. 'It was lovely to see her. I mean, never in a million years did I expect to run into her.' He makes it sound like an epitaph. 'Look, you can't be like this. You have to appreciate that I had a life before you, and, yes, there are things I'd like to do, to see again, but it's not some great plan I have that I've not been telling you about.'

I point out of the windscreen. 'Is this you going back home then? Is that what this is all about? Did you think I wouldn't want to come, because I know nowhere else?'

But he's leaning against the door of the car and the steering wheel seems to be moving by itself. He's altered the new convex mirror to improve his view in the wing mirror and perhaps it's too heavy for the wing mirror to carry. Perhaps he hasn't followed the instructions correctly or fitted the right screw. I start to wonder if convex-mirror fitting is like shoe fitting and that width is as important as length. I wonder if we were sabotaged at the trade fair by some envious caravanners looking *in*. He also seems to have dropped further down in his seat and is leaning to the right. He doesn't seem to have the strength to keep us in a straight line.

'Christ, Selwyn! What's happening?'

He is shaking his head in time with the sway of the car. His face is a knot of clenched eyebrows, sucked-in cheeks and gritted teeth. I panic he's having a stroke, but he says it's not him, it's the caravan. He's holding on to the steering wheel so tightly his knuckles have gone white. He pushes his foot down hard on the brake and I'm thrown slightly.

'Put on the hazards! Put on the hazards!' he shouts.

I press the button with its little red triangle and listen to the faint tick-tock-tick-tock-tick-tock as Selwyn slows right down and makes to drive the caravan to the side of the road, where he lifts up the handbrake with two hands and turns off the car. He looks at me. He is pale. He had, for a moment, lost control. We both breathe heavily.

'Must be the coupling head,' he says gravely. 'Something's amiss.'

He checks in his mirrors, looking, I assume, for a gap in the traffic when he can get out of the car. I get out too. He asks me what I'm doing.

'I'm not staying in the car if you're not in the car,' I say.

For once he doesn't argue with me. Instead, he comes around to my side of the car and gets down on his hands and knees to look underneath. I wonder if I should do the same. I realise I have never looked under a car before, so get down on all fours to do so.

'I don't need you down here too,' he says crossly. 'You're casting a shadow.'

'I've never seen under a car before,' I tell him.

'You don't know what you're looking at,' he snaps back. 'Get up.'

'Do you know what you're looking at?' I haven't got up but am settled back on my haunches with my hands flat on my thighs. 'And the coupling is there, by the caravan, not under here.'

He turns to give me a dirty look.

'I'm not the unhitched head,' I tell him. 'So you can stop looking at me like I am.'

He tells me to get back into the car. I tell him I will not. If a lorry comes around that bend, and the driver loses his grip on the steering wheel and ploughs into us, I will die and he will not because he is out of the car. Selwyn stands up and shakes his head at me.

'Don't be clever,' he says, heading towards the axle.

'Then don't be smart,' I call after him. 'Where are we anyway?'

He pretends he hasn't heard me over the traffic. He doesn't know either.

He does, however, eventually agree with me that the coupling has not unhitched and the convex mirror is not too heavy either. We are not out of petrol. He dipped the dipstick and this seemed fine too, though I didn't feel at all comfortable with that being the way that you checked the oil. 'Is that really all you have to do?' And if I told him once, I told him six or seven times to check inside the caravan, which he eventually did. And it would be *my* box that caused the problem, wouldn't it?

It had dislodged, fallen from the cupboard above the bar, where Selwyn had stashed it when we left home, and had obviously been sliding around the floor until it had worked itself under a barstool. As Selwyn reminded me, 'I told you it would only take a tin opener.'

'What the hell is in there, anyway?' he asks.

I help myself to a squirt of vodka from the optics.

'I mean,' he says, 'is it absolutely necessary?'

'It's the only thing I have in this caravan that I want with me,' I say sternly. He glares at me. 'Don't be ridiculous, Selwyn, I'm talking possessions, not you.' I remind him there's all that pond liner Ilma gave to him. 'What do you intend to do with that?'

'Even so,' he says, placing the box in front of me. 'It could've killed us.'

I start to laugh. 'For goodness sake, Selwyn. Compared to what you have stashed away in this caravan, that box is small fry. It'll take a lot more than that to drive us off the road.'

'It upset the balance,' he is raising his voice at me. 'That time we were lucky.'

I start to gape. 'Are you being serious?'

'Of course I'm being serious,' he carries on shouting. 'We almost unhitched!'

By now, I'm incredulous. 'You're being completely ridiculous!' I tell him. 'Whatever's a matter with you? Have you actually lost your mind?'

He is staring down at the box with his lips pursed, and clawing at his jaw.

'Oh, no,' I say. 'It comes with me.'

'Then we'll need to negotiate its contents to regain the balance,' he says stiffly.

'What *are* you talking about? Selwyn, for goodness sake! It's just a box of silly stuff—'

He interrupts me, 'A box that's unbalancing the weight. It drove us off the road!'

'You are not getting rid of that box.' I make it sound like the statement it is meant and even slap my hand down on a barstool. 'There's a lot more in this caravan that's weighing us down and what's in that box is of no consequence. No consequence at all. Whatever is wrong with you? I don't understand why you're being so stupid! This is crazy!'

He keeps on shaking his head at me like he's appalled, disgusted, and the air between us is clammy. 'Then we can't go on,' he says. 'That's it. Journey over.' He stands away from the box with his arms folded, like a sulking child too young for a gobstopper. He says, 'Safety first, Ginny.'

I burst out laughing again, but he is absolutely deadly serious, which makes me more incensed. 'You have pulled some stunts on me on this trip, Selwyn Robby, but this? This takes the biscuit when you have all that heavy bloody pond equipment and those fish, for fuck's sake! Those fucking fish! This is absurd. And entirely unreasonable! What on earth has got into you?'

But he is steadfast. Sets himself in breezeblocks again and folds his arms tighter. I have never seen him like this before. He's behaving like a blunt pencil. He gestures again at the box with his head. He will have no other view on this.

'Well, then it's over,' he says. 'That's as far as we go.'

And he slams the caravan door on his way back out on to the road.

I STAND ON THE roadside with my box at my feet. This is a fast road. Even faster than the dual carriageway on the flyover that I have lived below. The traffic keeps on coming, as I should have seen this coming. An articulated lorry drives so close that it almost clips the new convex mirror and whips it off. I imagine my face in the smashed glass down there on the tarmac. How my veins have started to look like roads to North Wales, South Wales, and all those mountains in the middle. How I can see what's happening – my eyes feel as wide open as this road – and I can hear what he tells me, but I don't seem to be able to connect it with my body to do anything about it. I'm aside of him but on the side, and that girl I was – all blurry to me – is running to catch up with us when I'm already right here.

A motorcyclist. A trade van for a drainage company. A mini bus. Three silver cars in a row, and I try not to be superstitious. I think of what I must look like to the passing traffic. A woman. On the side of the road. Abandoned. A car to the side with a now completely unhitched caravan. I wonder why no one stops.

In a blind moment of insanity, I stick out my thumb, urged on by the sudden desire to be in a car with someone else. But every car that passes me ignores me. Then a car starts to indicate and slows down. He is stopping. Then he isn't stopping. He's indicated not for me but for something else. His journey carries on. Perhaps I didn't look troubled enough. Or too old.

Then a van starts to slow. A tidy-looking small black van driven by a man in a shirt and tie. Professional. Business-like. I can smell his aftershave from here. He is grinning like he knows – *he knew* – we wouldn't make it. He's surprised we've made it this far. His hair is different, less grey, more unruly, and he's been following us all this time.

He indicates. My feet are rooted like horntails in a pond, though the rest of me floats above them. The van is suddenly aside of me. The passenger window is wound down. The man is bent towards the passenger seat and I can hear the rustle of papers, things he is moving to empty the seat for me. He calls out. 'You okay there?' His voice is rich with his own downfall. 'Where are you going?' he asks. 'Can I help?'

I will never forget that man's face. Or his thoughtfulness. I thank him over and over. Not for stopping, but for not being Louis. I tell him that I'm waiting for petrol. That we'd misjudged how far we had come. The man drives away. I look down at the box at my feet and start to shift it slightly – further and further and out into the road, so that it is in the way of everything that drives past. A lorry is coming towards me flashing its lights, but only I step out of the way, and I start to walk in the direction of the traffic. I need to find Selwyn. Behind me, I hear the lorry hit the box.

Before you can get anywhere you have to remember where you've been, and I find Selwyn in one of those roadside diners you see marooned in laybys, a jog trot from where he'd abandoned me. All corrugated iron and welded metal sheets – *It's the Snax!* it says, on the outside panels in black gloss paint – a container of sorts, given a new lease of life. I wonder who towed it here to this very spot and applied the brakes. *Here*, they might've said. Here is good enough. Perhaps why it smells of fried eggs and spilt milk, of unfinished arguments and tea, the colour of woodchip, in Styrofoam cups. Meg often dreamt of selling hot dogs from a roadside van. She said she would appreciate the calm.

I go inside and Selwyn is sitting at a single white plastic table and sipping from what looks like a bowl of hot milk. He doesn't look at me, yet I am the only other person here, other than the owner who bristles when he sees me – as if I'm spoiling things – and asks if he can get me something. He has skin like leftover sauce brought to the boil for a second time. His hair is slick, black, well-cut, and he wears a tie under his apron, as if he can't sweep aside who he used to be. I look back at Selwyn and see that he is also wearing a tie. I can't predict him any more. Be careful what you wish for, as they say. This one's a livewire.

I ask for coffee, as it comes, and help myself to the seat opposite Selwyn.

'You look terrible,' I tell him. 'Are you feeling alright?'

'And you're surprised by that?' he snaps. 'It's not as if you're looking your best either.'

My hands instantly reach for my face. 'You're right,' I say. 'But then I've stopped looking at myself. In fact,' I pause and screw my eyes up, 'I can't remember the last time I looked in a mirror.' I think briefly of the convex wing mirror and the view it has given Selwyn. 'It's like I'm only ever looking at you.'

The owner comes over to the table with my coffee. He asks where we're off to. I tell him Wales, then look down at his bright white trainers slippery with grease. This is not a place where anyone lingers, and neither does he. He goes back behind his counter to check his phone.

'Another stranger from a strange land,' I say, turning my cup around. 'Do you know him too?'

'Anthony.' Selwyn spits it out and it startles me.

'His name is Anthony?'

'Anthony Cadman.' Selwyn is now practically spitting on the table. 'The cobbler. You did it with the cobbler?'

'Oh. I see.' I turn my cup around again, in case it will turn back the clock. *Cobblers* was what Meg called the leftovers. We had it when the larder was bare. 'That's what this has all been about. You looked in my box.'

He puts his mug down and stares into it. 'Is it the truth? Did you and Anthony really...?' He pauses, grimaces, pulls back his eyebrows. 'For crying out loud, Ginny. Do I put nothing past you?'

'What do you want to be the truth?' I lock my hands together on the table as I say it and perch my chin upon them.

He looks at me. Then looks away. Looks at me again. He shakes his head. Then lowers it. 'Jesus, Ginny. He was twice your age.'

'And I was sixteen, and it was one time. He promised me things a sixteen-year-old bored out of her mind wants to hear, and I fell for it. Hook, line and sunk very deeply.'

'Did I not make those promises?' he leans towards me. 'Did I not love you enough?'

I bite my lip and look away. There's a calendar on the wall. Cheap paper with white blocks for days crossed out with a red pen. There is a date I will always remember, and my suitcase had looked so little out there on the street. So full of hope, there was barely anything in it. It was like something you'd pack for a doll. I'd used it as a step, in the end, to peer into the window of where he cobbled and shone shoes when no one had answered the door. 'Come before six,' Anthony had said, after he'd rolled off me. And I did. At ten to six, and he'd already left. No note. No ticket. Nothing. I went home, hid my suitcase under the bed, took off my coat, and no one was any wiser since I'd told no one I was even going.

'And I don't know why, I've thought and thought about why until I've almost thrown myself in the bloody canal, but I needed to get out – I couldn't be in that house any more, in Joiners Square, it was so crowded all the time, no privacy, and yet I was so alone. And there was your mother out front scrubbing the step and she said you were upstairs. "He's upstairs, if you want him," she said. So, I went upstairs.' I pause. Drink some coffee. Feel sick. Wish there was a different version. 'For some, it's a bed of roses and the promise of being a wife. For me, it was twice in one day.' I look over at the calendar again. 'So now you know. And you don't need to be disgusted. I've been so disgusted with myself that I've torn myself to shreds until there's not a part of me left to like. I know I devastated lives, but Mia has had a good life, I've held it all together on shoestrings and have never been ashamed of her. Not for one second. You need to know that, Selwyn. She's been the love of my life.'

He keeps his head low. Sighs like he does when phoning a customer services hotline. He spends a long time turning his mug around. He makes to get up from his chair, then thinks better of it. Judders instead. Makes a retching sound. I wonder if he's going to throw up. He looks down into his mug again. He's working out if he still has enough love for me.

'This is about me and you, though, Selwyn. Not her,' I say it really quickly, as if brushing away the decades with the crumbs on the plastic table.

'There are still two birth certificates in that box,' he hisses at me. 'One of them has my name on.'

'And the other has Anthony's name on.'

'To hedge your bets? Heads she's his, tails she's mine?'

I shrug.

'How did you even get *two* birth certificates?'

I suck in my lips and make myself small. 'Maybe I didn't want someone else. Maybe I just wanted to do it on my own. Maybe I wanted it to be both of you. Maybe I cut my body in half. Maybe I wanted her to choose. Maybe I can't give you a straight answer.' I take another gulp of my coffee and find, this time, it scalds the roof of my mouth. 'But *you* dislodged that box to come between us, Selwyn. Not me.' I run my tongue across the roof of my mouth and feel the blister, the tag of skin coming away. I watch Selwyn's face and try to read it. A man this broken can do stupid things. 'I don't know why you've never put two and two together and asked me before,' I carry on. 'You've seen her in photographs, met her on the computer. I thought you'd just worked it out. And I would've told you if you'd asked.'

He makes a noise, like an owl tearing up prey, then starts to murmur very slowly, 'I have loved you from the moment I set eyes on you. Why won't you love me? Why haven't you let me love her?'

We look at each other. I concentrate on the bridge of his nose, which makes him think that I'm looking at him – a sales tactic I have learnt from him – and I think of him as that twenty-year-old man who moved in next door with his mother and his buckets, and complicated everything.

'What would you have done, Selwyn? Would you have been able to love her?'

He closes his eyes. I know he understands the question. I know how much it asks of him.

I think about the box, caught under the lorry's wheel and how it should be the end of everything. No father. No claim. No past lives to remind us of what we did and who we once were. 'Getting on that boat with Anthony was the only way

I could see of getting out. I had no talent. No looks. A mother who was scared of her own shadow. I was factory fodder. Pigswill. A butcher's girl. Meg would take me to market and I'd look at the cows in their pens and think, that's my life. Except it's not even that because no one looks twice at me.'

'I was right there in front of you!' he shouts.

'No, you weren't,' I say quietly. 'You were behind your mother's back.'

Now he does get up from the table.

'Where are you going?'

But he doesn't tell me. And when we get back to the roadside, the box has completely gone.

'THE TROUBLE WITH CHILDREN is that you want them to have everything you haven't,' I shout above the traffic. 'You want them to do everything you don't, be everything you're not. The problem with my everything is that it's been nothing. And the trouble with Mia is that she is me. She only knows how to keep going. And that's what you have to do to get anywhere. You have to keep going. Selwyn. Please. Stop!'

He's marching just feet ahead of me. We're marching on the grass verge away from the caravan, the traffic floundering towards us like it doesn't expect two people to be arguing in its path.

This is no place for an argument, but we are arguing all the same.

'But you didn't have to keep going,' he is shouting back at me. 'I would've looked after you. Both of you. I *wanted* to look after you.'

'And I didn't want to be looked after!' I cry over the traffic. 'You look after, or you're looked after, and when you're looked after that's the end of it. Finished. Don't you see? I wanted the world!'

He pulls me into the hedgerow as a lorry practically scalps us. 'Goddamn you, Ginny!' he shouts in my face, as he holds on to me tight. 'I would've given you the world!'

'You would've kept me, Selwyn. Right there. In Joiners Square. Like you keep me now. In a box. Going nowhere.' I am yelling, trying to free myself from his grip. 'Look at you,' I flip my hand on his shoulder. 'Look at what's happened to you! You're not even a hundred miles away from your own backyard going to where you came from, and you are completely lost!'

'You have never gone anywhere either!' he shouts. 'You're panicking at every bloody road sign we pass. I am trying to make us a new life. A right life. One that *is* going somewhere.'

'But it's not your place to put things right,' I shout back. 'My wrongs are not yours. Your wrongs are not mine. And I know there was a dream. Of me. Of money. Whatever else it was that made you agree to that stupid bloody gamble with what little you had when it wasn't needed, Selwyn. I didn't want it.'

He grabs on to me again and tighter. 'I did it for you,' he says, digging in his fingernails. 'To keep you. For us.'

I pull away from him. He knows what he's said – his body pulses with the words – but I remind him anyway. 'There it is,' I say, calmly. 'There it is.'

'There is what, Ginny?' he snaps. 'There is what?'

But I cannot say it again.

When we get back to the caravan, him now behind me, there is something else missing. The F has now gone. *For our pond lie and beyond*, it says. I point it out to Selwyn.

'We've lost the F from our life,' I say, tracing my fingertips over the empty space. 'Or we've been found out.'

He looks at me.

I look at him.

He said.

She said.

Is there really anything more we should say?

'Ginny,' he begins.

But my mouth on his means nothing more is said, and we start to kiss in a way we never have, as I never thought I could: our mouths glued so tightly that when we pull apart, our lips rip.

We sit side by side in the caravan as still as statues. For a moment, I wonder if Selwyn is still breathing and fight the urge to check his pulse. I have my arms folded and my legs crossed: I could not be more caught up with myself, so astonished by myself that, if I don't say it now, it will never be said by the woman who has just performed a personal miracle. I am all in with everything lost and nothing to lose, right here as we are in this caravan, unhitched on the side of a dual carriageway, and somewhere between England and Wales where the borders start to blur.

So, I begin. And it begins where I always begin.

With Meg.

And shoes.

I never had new shoes, but shoes that were forgotten, or left behind by someone with so many shoes they'd lost count. Anthony Cadman was the thick-necked leather-skinned cobbler who came to see Meg to buy goat. An English mother. A Jamaican father. He was the most exotic thing I'd ever seen. He'd tell Meg his stories while I'd be hosing down the butcher's yard out back. Stories she lapped up as she mangled and minced; stories I wanted to be part of. He'd say, *the lifespan of a shoe depends upon the kindness to the hind.* The bull was a rich animal to him, to Meg. He could twist a chicken neck with two fingers. He talked of blackness, of whiteness, and where he put his dreams in between. I didn't want Meg to have him.

He gave me shoes. Three months he'd give a customer to come back for what he'd cobbled and fixed, and, when they didn't come, he gave them to me. My feet didn't grow like the rest of me. He'd say, *If the shoe fits*. I thought I was Queen Bee.

He used to call me a fidget. He said I couldn't sit still. 'The world won't be big enough for you,' he said. 'Yet you'll race through it without looking at it at all.'

He wore a three-piece suit with a tie and a leather apron, and you'll remember his bowler hat, won't you? With the feather. So smart it was arrogant. He took it out and stroked me with it as if he'd picked me out from the crowd. 'Well, ain't that a thing. I've turned you into ice,' he'd said.

I told him I was older. He said I couldn't be. Meg had told him I was sixteen. I reminded him my mother was still older than me. The younger the calf; mutton dressed as lamb. God, I served myself up on a plate! And Meg forgets things, I'd said. Makes stuff up when her life isn't exciting enough. Ask the Bluebird. She'll tell you the truth. He'd said, 'Who?' So, I told him, and he started to laugh. We both laughed. 'That's actually very sad,' he'd said. 'Don't you think?'

I'd seen his ticket. Pinned up on the noticeboard behind the spanners and the drill. He said that ticket was glued on his soul and he was going no matter what. I asked him how much it would cost me to go with him. He said, 'I only want to take my wife.' I thought he meant me.

I remember the telephone ringing all the time we were upstairs. Someone was trying to get hold of him. I often wonder who she was. I found out that there was a girl – much older than me, and wearing his engagement ring; Anthony has since told all this to Mia – but she failed to turn up at the dock.

He said he'd stopped because he wanted to stop. It wasn't right. I was beautiful. But it wasn't right. But like someone who has witnessed a head-on collision of two cars travelling at the same speed. You don't know whose fault it was.

I felt nothing when it was happening. There was something happening to him that wasn't happening to me. I told myself I was in love, this is love, and tried, ever so hard, to unlock myself, to feel what you were supposed to feel – the fireworks, the light switch, the stars – I thought *hammer and saw,* isn't that how this works? But all I felt was a dead weight. I don't even think he looked at me once. Then he stopped and covered himself with a bedsheet and started to sob. Told me to go away. To get out.

I still went back to him, with my suitcase, and he wasn't there. I told myself it was me, because of me, because of what I didn't feel – like a pair of those left-behind shoes, worn only once and never broken in, I didn't fit him. I was so angry, so revolted, so empty, so rubbished. That suitcase I dragged back home was solid with rage, a monstrous rage, and I hid it back under the bed and started to panic. This can't be it. *This cannot be it! This world won't be big enough for me!* I ran back outside and there was your mother scrubbing the step. She looked up at me and she smiled. For the first time ever, she'd smiled at me – a mother's smile, a proud one – and she ordered me to go to you. 'He's upstairs if you want him.' It's exactly what she said to me. *He's upstairs if you want him.* Because that's as far as I needed to go, up the stairs and right under my nose; when I wanted to find you hundreds of miles away in a somewhere else that was so far off I couldn't picture it. Not next door where I felt it all – heat surges, electricity, firework after firework, and then this voice. I remember thinking, is Meg in the room? The Bluebird? Who is telling me that everything will just be as it was? And you asked me to marry you, remember? Straight after. You called me Imogen Dare, and said, *marry me.* And I wanted to tell you what I'd just done was not because I wanted you, but because I wanted to hurt *him*. Except it was the other way around, wasn't it? The devastation of three lives because of me. And I knew you'd never forgive me.

'The thing is,' I come to end. 'When all is said and done. I just wanted to see the world.'

At this, Selwyn stands up so assertively I wonder if he's cracked vertebrae doing so.

'Then we go no further until me and you work out exactly what it is you want now,' he says, and he starts opening all the cupboard doors. I sigh loudly and tell him that I just need a bath. He frowns and tells me to look again so we might unhitch ourselves from what it is that is weighing us down. I remind him that a lot of what I'm looking at is his, not mine.

'It's mostly your stuff,' I say, then add, because I'm feeling peevish, 'Your stolen stuff.'

He reminds me that *that stuff* is keeping us on the road.

'It's just driven us *off* the road,' I point out.

'And you are driving us apart!' he shouts.

I rub at my face hard. 'You've just asked me to tell you, so I told you,' I say. 'I know you don't like what you've heard, but you wanted to hear it and I can't tell it any other way. But what is really driving us apart is being attached to this fucking caravan and you not telling me where we're going with it.'

'And you didn't have to go downstairs and keep running,' he shouts. 'But you did.'

'I was sixteen! And I made it two miles down the road to Stoke station. Watched all these trains leave and never got on one of them.'

But I did go to the edge. Where the platform falls away. I was listening to the echoes of the train on the tracks. Have you ever really listened to the echoes on the train tracks? They can take you miles.

'And then I came back.'

'And never again acknowledged me, like you couldn't even see me, until one day you completely disappeared. Like you'd been rubbed out.'

'I'd started to show. I had to.'

It wasn't like Meg asked me to go. She never used the words, but closed doors on me instead. Something she'd never done. She was kind enough to loosen darts on dresses and let down hems on skirts, but I came to realise that she'd been in love too. Then, this one morning, I woke up and there she was standing at the end of my bed, and she told me she was going to go and think somewhere, and it would be no bad thing for me to do the same. 'Don't have my life,' she'd said. 'I brought you up better than that.'

She'd left me money on the kitchen table, in one of her brown envelopes, and I ran to the butcher's shop because, if nothing else, I didn't want her to leave me. I'd never once been on my own. And she'd done it alone. Why couldn't we? There was a sign gummed to the door. *Closed to take stock,* it said. And I just threw up. Couldn't help it. Couldn't stop it. Threw up so much I gave myself a nosebleed. It was all up the door – my sick and my blood, like my insides had just splattered out – and not a single person walked past to help me. I felt as if all that lace and cotton wool I'd been wrapped in for sixteen years had been unwrapped and there was absolutely nothing there, inside, and nobody around to wrap me back up again.

I went home. Took the money. Pulled out my suitcase from under the bed and did that same walk down to Stoke station. And I meant to get on a train. I watched the trains ticker past thinking there or there or even there? Out of the corner of my eye, the Bluebird had come to wave me off. *Good riddance to bad rubbish,* and steaming up like a pressure cooker. I realised then that she'd arrived for Meg, never me, because I was always going to leave her behind. Not the other way around.

Her name was Sylvia. She waited on Stoke station for girls like me.

At that, I realise I have not said her name in a very long time and struggle to remember her face. What I do remember is the phone we fed coins to in the hallway to call boyfriends and worried mothers and mothers like mine who wouldn't answer because there was never a phone to call. I used to pretend anyway. The dialling tone reminded me of those echoes in the train track. Then the door opened for another girl to leave for a wedding ring and closed as another one was brought in off the platform. A revolving door for the ashamed.

I don't know how, but Meg knew where I was. She left me packages on the doorstep full of the things I'd left behind. I put them all in a cardboard box and shut them away. She'd got someone else to write my name on the brown paper. She was a whizz with figures and knives, but could barely write a single word.

I took a secretarial course and a maths course at night. Shared a room with single beds and pink walls with a girl called Hayley with a cruel father and who was probably older than she said she was. No idea what happened to her. She used to iron her hair with egg whites and worked in the cloakrooms of the various nightclubs up Hanley, until her light fingers got the better of her. We planned on going to London. And then my waters broke. A month before I was due.

I pause to skip five decades.

'You know the rest, and here we are. An ordinary story at best. It happens to lots of us. And life trucks on.'

But he's not listening. He folds into himself and starts pulling out clothes of mine that he has hung on various wireframe coat hangers. I realise he has unpacked my suitcase.

'What's this coat?' he asks.

'It's a cape,' I correct. 'And you're angry with me, so please don't do this now.'

'Do you need it?' he asks, trying to make sense of it.

'I don't not need it,' I say, trying to remember the last time I wore it, because it's not my colour at all. Mustard really. A condiment I don't like, along with horseradish and mayonnaise, and this cape is a battle of those colours. Selwyn is looking at the label inside of it. He brings the washing instructions closer to his face.

'This is dry clean only,' he mutters. And he's disgusted by it. I can tell. He holds it out to me like it's a pair of wings I've been hiding from him.

I start to wonder where I would go if I really could wear those wings, and if they would be strong enough to get me to New Zealand. There are birds that fly that far. Migration. Hibernation. I realise I've been wearing wings for most of my life, and place my hands on the small of my back where they used to sprout. I was a moth, once, I think. I used to be able to see so clearly in the dark.

'Are we really heading for the other side of the world?' I ask.

Selwyn looks as if he's about to say something. I will him to say it. But he asks, 'Do you have an anorak? An anorak would be much more practical than this.' He throws the cape on the cushion aside of me and returns to the cupboard to rifle through my clothes again. 'And what about jumpers? Is that the only one you have?' He gestures to what I'm wearing. A grey cable-knit that grows with every wash. I reach over for the cape and put it on over my jumper. It's unflattering, because it widens me, drowns me, and I suddenly regret not giving it to Maisie. She'd been as cold as the dead.

'So many women whose clothes I would've liked to have snatched off their backs,' I say, smiling, but Selwyn still won't look at me in the cape, as if he knows something I don't.

Instead, he looks at my other clothes, sorting through them by clutching on to hems and sleeves, and feeling them for warts and blemishes, hard skin and infections. He seems to pick out a dress at random. It's navy blue with an A-line skirt, the faintest polka-dot, with the sort of pockets that resemble holsters.

'You're unpacking me,' I tell him. 'Don't make me feel like I shouldn't have told you. You wanted to know it all. Selwyn, please.' I try and grab his hand, but he pulls away. 'Am I to be thrown out too?'

'I told you that everything had to have a place,' he retorts. 'Nothing can be too heavy, too light. You've seen what happens when the balance is off.' He folds up the navy dress and puts it on the bar. 'Have you any other trousers other than those jeans?' He points at my legs, which makes me look down.

'I have a black pair,' I tell him.

He looks back into the cupboard, as if trying to locate the black pair of trousers.

'You know my clothes aren't the answers to the questions you want answers to,' I say calmly. 'But it's only fair that I get to sort through yours after you've sorted through mine.'

Selwyn sniffs loudly to this, and removes a floor-length floral chiffon dress, with an exuberant pussy-bow, from its hanger that I have never worn but keep in the suitcase because it's one that Meg gave me. She'd left it on the doorstep at Sylvia's, like she wanted me to remember that, even when a mother, I was still that little girl.

'This can never be yours,' he says aghast, holding it up to the light so I can see just how translucent the material is. Appearances are always deceptive, I think, but I still stop myself from making a quip about seeing right through me.

'She had me in dresses and gowns from the moment I was born,' I say. 'I don't know what else to wear.'

I think about the hair shirts I've dressed Selwyn in; how might he feel about sacrificing some of them to retain the balance? What about your wellies, your waders, all that heavy weatherproof gear? All those things that *you need*, and all those clothes you don't wear. We are blaming each other for so much. But, instead, I settle for reminding him that I am simply a woman with a past, as he is a man with a past; that our future might be as uneven as the road that has almost unhitched the caravan and forced us into this layby, but we have got this far. There's something to be said about that.

His reply is to hold up a ribbed burgundy polo neck two sizes too big that I am pretty sure is not mine. He remarks, 'Finally, something mindful of where we're headed,' and folds it neatly on the top shelf.

'Selwyn,' I say, 'it was fifty years ago. We can't let it weigh us down when we're already weighed down by all this bloody stolen pond equipment. All those fish.'

He looks at me, wears the sort of expression you have when you've found old Christmas cards from those no longer with us. He tells me that's why we're heading to Wrexham. 'I've told you before,' he says. 'Judd will tell me what to do.'

I'm not following him and tell him I'm not following him.

He says, 'Then nothing's changed.'

'Good,' I say quickly. 'Because things are just fine and dandy, aren't they?'

I watch him let an orange knitted scarf, that I swear I have never seen before, snake through his fingers and drift to the floor. He looks down on it, as if it's something he can't save when a salesman's job is to persist. 'Just remember that I have been the only one to never let you down,' he says coldly. 'And I'm still here, Ginny. I am still here.'

'I know,' I say quietly. 'And that's why I still want us to go to Wales.'

I move towards him and I take his hand. His skin is hard and his knuckles protrude like fungus growing on trees, and I wish he wouldn't bite his fingernails as much as he does, but they do wrap around mine, his fingers, and when I look down at our hands, our skin is soft, and we blend, like butter and sugar.

'From the moment I met you,' he murmurs.

'You were the boy next door,' I say quietly, honestly. 'I just wanted to know that there was more than the boy next door.'

He lets go of me, looks at me.

'But there wasn't, was there?'

'No.'

We lean into each other and touch foreheads, stay there for so long we have aged beyond who we are. We are a tangle of stories, Selwyn and I. Entangled and entwined and even in other stories that don't belong to us. But we play our part in them, all the same, and here we are.

'There's something I want to show you,' Selwyn says slowly. 'Something you need to see. But I need to see Judd first, sell the fish.'

I nod and let him lead me by the hand. We shut the caravan door behind us and get back in the car to carry on.

We almost miss the turn, for a sign I paid no attention to. I am supposed to be navigating.

'You make me feel like I'm driving in blinkers,' Selwyn chides. 'I used to know these roads like the back of my hand.'

He asks me, left or right? There's a roundabout coming up that wasn't there before, he mutters. I tell him right. It's just a hunch because I've lost my place on the map, which is one of those that takes a degree in origami to fold back up. He indicates. Takes a crumpled piece of paper out of his shirt pocket and tells me that we don't actually go into Wrexham itself because it's on the outskirts of the Erddig estate, but the lane is hard to spot. You'd quite mistake it for a dirt track. I remind him of what happened last time we went down a dirt track. He says, 'Surely there's nothing else to declare? What haven't you told me now?'

I hold my tongue. Selwyn will come back as a buzzard. He cannot leave a bone alone when he knows there's still meat on it. I look down at the paper he's given me. The writing isn't very clear – the pen seemed to be running out of ink – and I can't pronounce the words when written in a language I do not know. I wonder if he's made the words up to pretend like he's never been here before, when he has. I know he has. His driving has never been more assured.

Still, I wish I'd paid more attention in Geography. Seen where all the roads lead and which had the most diversions; understood how rocks can be split and life found inside. In History too. Not all battles are meant to be won. Losing is often no bad thing. Meg would say, *When we can't find the wood, we take a digger to the trees. The problem with you, is that you think you should know everything when there's nothing there for you to know.* And she'd be wringing her hands in her apron. *But it cannot be just us!* I'd wail. Because where were my uncles and aunts, my grandparents and their parents before them? She made me feel like our history began and ended with her. 'Aren't I enough?' she'd yell. Then, later, I'd say the same thing to Mia. 'Aren't *I* enough?'

I think of that photograph again, back in Loggerheads, those farmhands from up Mucklestone way, poor as crows with childhoods snatched by TB, and murmuring at me to find them, to not be kept closed away in a book. I think of that wake back in the pub and the distress we caused as Selwyn tried to give the widow his plate of tough meat; how I'd bumped into Teapot Marge from Joiners Square at the bus station with Mia. How Marge had looked down into the pushchair, then at me, and said, 'She's dead, you know? Pauper's grave because of you.'

'Ginny,' Selwyn snaps me from my thoughts. 'If you're needing to say it, then say it.'

'I'm sorry,' I say.

He says, 'Why are you sorry?'

And then he grimaces, like I've nicked him with a compass, swerves to dodge a pothole and comes to a sudden stop.

'We're here,' and he gets out of the car.

I'VE SEEN A LOT of new faces this past week, and here is another one greeting Selwyn like he's survived a kidnapping, or a bout of typhoid. As I get out of the car, having watched some terrific embrace between him and Walter Judd that I want to disapprove of, I tell myself that the best thing to do is to start hating him. Then I can let it all wash over me and it won't at all matter where we do end up. He said. She said. Neither here nor there. Whatever we try and be, we are not.

Walter Judd is a sunken waspish man. Even I look down on his bald head and protruding ears that must get sore as hell if sunburnt. He has a lot of faces – I've seen the smiling one, the cautious one, the still-not-sure one – and he takes my hand, shakes it as if he can't be bothered, and says he's pleased to meet me. No, I've heard lots about you, or it's good to put a face to the name, but like I'm a mystery to him. And unexpected. Everything he wears is brown – shirt, trousers, cardigan, boots – he's like an earthenware pot, and he looks as if life has been pretty peachy on the whole, he won't grumble, but still seems to be anticipating others to get out of the car. He then asks Selwyn for the road he used to get here, and did he mind for the state of the lane? They quibble a little about the A5, and Walter praises Shrewsbury's ring-road system, and Selwyn agrees: it has made a big difference because he zipped through. Which is a lie. Walter then rubs his two little fat hands together – no wedding ring, I might add – and asks to see the wares. He's been on tenterhooks all morning, he says.

'I feel like a kid at Christmas only expecting conkers.'

Selwyn looks at me and replies that he shouldn't be too disappointed. We all walk towards the caravan and I have butterflies, as if any disappointment will be blamed on me.

'So, you're the fish man?' I make conversation. However corny, I must fill this awkward silence. 'Do you have a pond too?' I sound like a child hoping to dip their toe in the water. He answers neither question, rather nudges Selwyn's arm. 'Selwyn tells me that you'll know what the fish have been fed?' I truck on.

'Feeding is a tricky business when there's carnivores,' he responds.

I try not to be repulsed and instead wonder what Walter really does to make ends meet, for this place is as dilapidated as the Corbet Hall. It reeks of missed mealtimes, unpaid debts, and damp washing. I pray that the Candy whatsitsface in the washbasin pedestal is what it's supposed to be; that Walter's got the cash and we can get on our way, for I hope to God that we don't have to go inside and spend the night.

Selwyn unlocks the caravan door and lowers the little steps for them to embark, because that's exactly how I see it from where I'm standing: we are embarking on the adventure of our lives if that ugly great candy fish proves its worth. This makes me so nervous I can't go inside with them. Instead, I choose to wait it out in the yard, counting pebbles underfoot like I'm trying to balance the books. Besides, Selwyn is the bargainer, the business smart, and if I'm inside with them I'll get the blame if it doesn't turn out to be what Selwyn thinks it is and I was right all along: a goldfish covered in purple felt tip.

A cat turns up. Tortoiseshell. Quite pretty, actually. Large amber eyes like burning cigarette tips. It mews and curls its tail about my legs before rolling on to its back. I can see it's both female and entirely placid, and, oh dear – that's an open wound. I bend down and start to stroke its belly while I look at the scabbed hole on its underside and ask for what happened. 'Has someone hurt you?' I ask, as if expecting an answer. 'Has someone had a go at you? Who came off worse, you or him?' I pause, lean back on my haunches. I have a lot in common with the cat, I think.

I look up as Selwyn and Walter disembark with grave faces. I don't need to ask. There are no more fish in the sea, it seems, and certainly not any swimming with pound signs. I stand up as Walter walks past me. I look over at Selwyn and hold out my hands. 'Is it not?' I ask.

'Whatever it is, it's not pregnant either,' Selwyn says solemnly. I ask where Walter's gone. 'To consult his books,' he replies.

'Has he offered us anything?'

Selwyn looks at me like I'm speaking another language. He comes towards me. I fear the worse.

'It's a sprat?'

'Ginny,' he says gravely, 'we can't find the plug for the tank.'

'The plug?'

'The way it's designed,' Selwyn says, 'the basin has been welded to the tank. There must've been a plug. A way to get at the fish. I don't know how it was installed.'

'If we can't get at the fish does that mean they've never been fed?' I ask.

'No, there's a way to feed them, and I have been feeding them,' Selwyn insists, twisting his mouth. 'Just not a way to release them. To get them out.'

'How many are still alive?' I ask.

'How many were put in and how were they put in?' he fires back.

I look disgruntled. 'Why are you asking me? I don't know.'

'Because the pedestal has been welded to the basin.' Selwyn is properly ticking me off. 'We need to get at them else they won't survive.'

I look around me. Walter doesn't seem to be coming back.

'He's not phoning the RSPCA, is he?' I say. 'Walter, I mean. He's not reporting us to the authorities?'

Selwyn looks blank. I look down at the cat and wonder how many lives it has left.

'What about the money?' I ask. 'Will Walter still want to buy them?'

Selwyn frowns. The fish are conkers.

'So that's it?' I ask. 'Journey over?'

Selwyn looks over me.

Walter is back. With a mallet.

Salesmen are strategic creatures. If there's a problem there has to be a solution, and to find that solution you have to work through the problem. The problem, however, is not the washbasin pedestal full of tropical rainbowfish and a doppelganger that isn't what we thought it was, but the fact that we cannot get at them to sell them. We cannot find a way to get them out. There's a small window to drop food through at the top, but this is no more than a fingerhole, and even Walter's fingers are too fat for it.

Another problem is that the basin has been welded to the tank. This is cruel. Walter has mentioned the word rehydration many times, that is, when did you last change the water? Selwyn has had to admit that the caravan was Louis's domain and he looks at me as he says it. This is animal cruelty. The problem with animal cruelty is that you can be put in prison for it. The fish, if we are not careful, will begin to eat each other. We are also at each other's throats.

I make a suggestion: perhaps there is something outside of the caravan in the exterior panels? Or maybe something underneath?

Selwyn shines a torch underneath the caravan. The two men look and then both settle back on their haunches. There is something here, Walter concludes – not a plug, but most definitely a tap, and something else. They give the something and the tap some thought then look under the caravan again. Selwyn asks for a piece of paper and a pen, and, like the secretary I never became, I oblige him with a small jotter pad and a Biro from my handbag. He starts to draw and occasionally Walter shines the torch under the caravan again and informs Selwyn where his drawing is wrong. Selwyn tears off the piece of paper from the notepad and starts from scratch.

Time passes. It is dusk, and I am wearing my cape.

Walter is wondering about buckets. Selwyn says that buckets are too big and what's needed is a tank, of sorts – something that the fish can drop into in a gush. Walter disappears into one of his many ramshackle outhouses. I think about the farmhands who once lived in them. I think about calling an ambulance. I don't know why.

Without Walter, Selwyn and I don't speak. It occurs to me that Selwyn and I work better when we don't say anything. I can hear his heartbeat then, and he can hear mine.

Walter is back with three washing up bowls and a roll of bin bags. He tries the washing up bowls for size and they fit. The two men pat each other on the back as if this is the solution.

'Good thinking,' Selwyn says.

They spend some time opening the bin bags and putting the washing up bowls inside of them and then they slot them underneath the caravan. Selwyn checks his drawing again.

He says, 'I guess we turn the tap then.'

He looks up at me and tells me to go back inside the caravan and run the tap in the washbasin. They need a flow of water to maintain the air.

I say, 'Just out of interest, where does the water go when we run the tap? Does it go into the tank, or somewhere else?'

Selwyn clicks his fingers and gets up. He opens a panel on the outside of the caravan and gets Walter to shine his torch inside. There are pipes, like intestines, and when I look I see that the water goes down the pipe and must end up on the ground.

'So, the basin and the tank aren't connected then?' I say. 'Else we could get the fish to swim down the pipe.'

Selwyn shines the torch in my face and tells me that the washbasin has still been welded on to the tank, which means the tank has a lid, which means smashing the washbasin off will fracture the tank and, if the tank fractures, it's likely to burst. He tells me to run the tap. I go inside the caravan and do exactly what I'm told.

The water is nail-bitingly cold and makes me shiver. I do not know what is happening outside when I am inside the small bathroom with the door closed. It occurs to me that I should open the door in case there's a rush of water upwards and I get soaked. I open the bathroom door and hear Walter use the word irresponsible. Selwyn keeps repeating, 'I should've checked. I should've checked. Why didn't I think to check?' I try not to look at my face in the bathroom mirror, in case it reminds me that my future is very small.

I hear a crack and shout out. No one answers me. I bend down and run my hand along the pedestal for hairline cracks and fractures. I can see nothing and feel even less. The water is cloudy and the fish inside of it dull, as if they've been switched off at the socket. As my eyes drift to the bottom of the pedestal to its seabed, I imagine uneaten bodies and mountains of tiny bones. We have committed a terrible crime.

'Look at yourself. Just look at yourself,' I say aloud. 'Look at what you've done.'

I force myself to look in the mirror. I tell myself this is not a punishable offence and I will not go to jail. Walter would not be going to all this trouble if he didn't think there was something to be made from the fish. Still, I hear nothing from outside. Just the water running in front of me into the basin and down the plughole. Then the plughole gulps. An air bubble. A spurt of water. They have clearly turned the tap and it must be happening.

I bend down to see if the water level is going down. I can see a rim, this time, like in a dirty bath, and I scratch my fingernail at it. I think how far we have come, and how far we haven't, in the scheme of things, as Selwyn says, and, as the crow flies, we aren't even fifty miles from home, and yet we are further away from ourselves than we have ever been.

The water level is dropping. Slowly, slowly, but dropping all the same. The fish go with it, as if they know that they're going to survive. I bite my lip and draw blood. I make scratch marks on my cheeks as I watch the water level drop. The water running from the tap is barely a trickle. I wonder how much time we have left to save them all.

'Selwyn,' I shout, 'is it working?'

I don't hear anything, so decide to go outside. The two men are lying on their bellies with their heads and shoulders under the caravan. The torch has been propped up on a box and I start to wonder of this secret life of Selwyn's that I'm starting to see in torchlight, the little flashes of his life on the road and the questions I have never asked of it.

I see that both men have removed their belts, the buckles, perhaps, digging in as they work on their stomachs, and they're grunting under the caravan, using the word 'there' a lot, and 'here'. Here and there is where we go, I think, when there is where we think we should be when here bores us silly. I start to feel sick and enjoy the taste of my blood from my bitten lip so much that I bite myself again. What if this isn't working, I think? What if we have committed murder on this grand and awful scale? What will Mia say when she is my one call from the cells and has to fly home? *Is this how low you will stoop to, Mother, just to get me home?*

All of a sudden, I am frightened of Walter Judd. He knows too much and has seen it all, too, and for one mad moment, I stare at the mallet that is lying aside of him. What if? I think. It would just be a quick blow and we could go, and he would get up in the morning for sure because I'm not that strong. It would barely cause a bruise. Mild concussion is nothing. Selwyn can give him a couple of his aspirin. My feet are walking towards the mallet and my eyes will not stop looking at it. I start to bend down. They've both forgotten I am there.

'What are you doing, Ginny?' Selwyn says, shining the torch in my face.

I stand up quickly. 'Helping,' I say. 'There's hardly any water running out from the tap and the level is dropping in the tank. Are they still alive?'

Selwyn tells me to go back inside. Is the water still running? How much water is left in the tank?

'Do you want me to come back out and tell you, or stay inside and just watch?' I ask. I feel like I'm repeating myself. Like I haven't been told properly what to do. He shines the torch in my face again and tells me to take the mallet with me. They're going to have to smash the washbasin off. This is not working as it should.

'But we need to save the fish!' I shout. 'Isn't that the point?'

And that's when it happens. Selwyn twists the tap. It comes off in his hands and we all start to scream.

I have never swept up dead fish before. I do it with a scarf over my mouth – the smell is like rotting bodies. Then Walter makes a bonfire out of them. Not many were saved. But after the tap had released a sort of raging water backdraft, the pipe running from the washbasin down the side of the caravan burst and the fish shot out of that. I have red blotches where they hit me in the face. Selwyn has a black eye. I couldn't catch them, no matter how hard I tried – even dead, they were slippery. I used my cape as a shield.

Only one washing up bowl has enough survivors for it to have been worth it, but Selwyn won't take Walter's money. He is too ashamed. Besides, we find there *is* a plug – it's like a little trapdoor in the bathroom floor at the back of the pedestal. Selwyn bad mouths Louis in a way I never thought I would hear, and Walter agrees. He is a charlatan. Selwyn says this isn't the work of a charlatan but of a parasite who feeds on small fish.

'I have been so, so stupid,' he says. 'Who did I think I was?'

Walter says, 'What do you want me to do?'

Selwyn bites his lip and gives it a little thought. 'You can't drown what's already sunk,' he finally says.

Walter makes us up a bed in what he keeps referring to as the 'other room' when the only other room I have seen is the small square we entered when we came in by the front door – a door to the left of us, a door to the right, both shut – and we all headed straight up the stairs in front of us like worn out children from a day at the beach. Nothing hangs on the walls to give him away, and it's a great deal cleaner than I expected, with its white plastered walls and beige carpet underfoot.

There's a brass bedstead, two pillows, and an old-fashioned eiderdown covered in periwinkles on the bed. The rest of the room is stark, but for a single table with nothing on it but a lamp. I am surprised for how much I like it. Besides, the caravan stinks, barely habitable really, and Selwyn has declared fresh eyes in the morning will be for the best.

Walter shows us the bathroom that we are free to use within the hour once the immersion has warmed up. He digs about in a woven basket and hands me a little bar of mauve soap, taps his bald head, and says, 'Sorry. No shampoo.' He points to where we can find extra blankets. He apologises for the curtains being thin. He gets down on his hands and knees and checks for spiders under the bed. He puts a bigger bulb in the bedside lamp and offers me a couple of Mills & Boon books from a shelf. I realise that we've been on the road so much we've forgotten about the niceties of a friend's hospitality. The little touches. The things that make your toes curl in appreciation. And that it really doesn't take much at all.

He offers us drinks. 'Hot milk, or something stronger?' And then to me, 'I have a hot water bottle, if you'd like? For your feet.'

I tell him thank you, something stronger, and I'm very hot blooded. He tells Selwyn he will be downstairs in the kitchen. Selwyn tells Walter he'll be down in a minute, then turns to me and says, 'You look bushed. You should try and get some sleep.'

I immediately take umbrage. 'I am never invited, am I?'

He says, 'It's been a traumatic experience for us all, Ginny.'

'And Walter offered me a drink too.'

The bruise about his left eye is yellowing. He'd also been hit under the chin and just aside of his right ear. He turns his back and punches out two aspirin from a packet and swallows them down without water. He looks like he's been brawling, and not come out of it well. And tired. Really very tired.

'It wasn't my intention for us to be staying here,' he says, with a small cough, like the pills are stuck in his throat. 'But here we are and I've not seen Walter in a very long time. It'll be boring for you anyway. What to do next and all that.'

The unfairness of this makes me cough too. 'What about what *we* will do next?' I snap. 'I thought we agreed no more boxes. We can't keep letting things hang in mid-air.'

Our eyes meet, and there's that thing he does where he pinches his nostrils together and sniffs. He still can't forgive me.

'Don't you see me?' Selwyn says. 'Can't you see what happened to me?'

He is struggling to remain calm. His eyes are so wide open I fear for what they saw. I tell him not to blame himself. Times were tough. Recessions are crippling. Small businesses, they don't stand a chance.

'It's a niche market, like you said.' And then I add, 'But they're just fish. We're still okay.'

Selwyn slams the bedroom door with such force, I fear Walter will kick us out and make us bed down among the bones and brine. He marches towards me so quickly, I back away.

'You have no idea, do you?' his voice rising. 'I *was* that business, Ginny. And I was that man you ran away from.'

'And I see that!' I shout back. 'You kept that business afloat, and he did you over, so of course you're pissed off. I'm glad you're pissed off. It's about time you were pissed off. I'm just sorry that it's taken a tank full of dead fish for you to see it. And yes, I ran away. But I came back, Selwyn. I found you. What does that tell you?'

'That your daughter had left you.'

'What?' I cover my eyes with my hands. 'What the hell does that mean?'

'You said it yourself. You hate being on your own. You devoted your whole life to Mia and then she leaves you and goes to him. Doesn't come back. I think you knew where I was, Ginny. I think you always knew where I was.' He stands to hold on to the bed to keep his temper steady.

'Oh, my God. Do you have any idea what you're saying to me?'

But then I realise that I want him to be angry. I want him to cry. For the fish. For the years. For the money. For the lies. For me. I want him to cry so loud it wakes the dead.

'I knew what Louis was doing. But you?' he shakes his head back and forth.

I am moving towards him and I am moving my lips but there are no more words to be said and he is trying to forgive me, I tell myself. He's trying to forgive himself too. I cannot ask for any more than that when catapulting fish have smacked us both in the face.

So, I kiss him. And I do so like a teenager, groping about. He kisses me back. I claw at his neck. I feel it. It could happen, the next bit. There is a bed. There is us. His hands beneath my jumper and around the small of my back pulling me in, closer, to feel him. Then he pulls away. Him, not me. Not here. Not now. This is not for now.

I let him go.

He will drink cider with Walter. The cider they drink will be both medicinal and too strong. Come morning they will stink of booze, not feel their legs, and will have slept in their shirts. They will have picked and plucked at Louis like vultures and Selwyn will have asked Walter why he doesn't see things happening under his nose. Is he too trusting? Too naïve? Why does he let so many people swim in his water? Walter will have asked Selwyn what he's going to do next. Their voices will rumble like trains underneath me, like traffic on the flyover, as I lower myself into such a scalding hot bath that my skin glistens with scales. Our bodies might not have come together but our minds have known no one else and let no one else come near. I have been fighting it. I have loved him all along.

I sleep so soundly that I thoroughly believe in my dream where we make it to New Zealand on the backs of tropical rainbowfish and I don't even have to wear goggles the water is so clear.

The Tenth Day

'Water beetles can fly, and they readily leave the pond, usually at night, to indulge in long flights in search of possibility. During the course, they occasionally mistake the wet road for a stretch of water and come to grief.'

~ *The Great Necessity of Ponds*
by Selwyn Robby

SELWYN REACHES OVER ME to look for painkillers in the glove box. He's sure he had some stashed in there. Because I'm sulking, and my face is awful sore, I don't help and tell him I have no sympathy when he's nursing yet another hangover, from his boozing with Walter last night. I am no doctor, but the succession of painkillers he seems to be taking is doing nothing for his stomach lining, or his liver.

'I have never seen you drink so much,' I chide.

He tells me to wind my neck in and be fair – this has not been the trip he'd planned. I roll my eyes and wave to Walter who is now in possession of twenty-two Parkinsons and an unidentifiable Basslet that will, if properly revived, make him a grand, and we can't even say, 'all in a day's work', either.

We're now heading for a campsite on the other side of Wrexham that Walter has directed us to where we can air the caravan for twenty-four hours then properly calculate the extent of the damage. I won't say that it stinks of fish because that is not the smell. Rather, it's castor oil, salt and vinegar, like something you might drizzle on a salad. Or pickle. It's both disgusting and so enveloping that it leaves you with something gelatinous on the back of your tongue, which has already made me gag and regurgitate my cornflakes. Ever the resourceful salesman, Selwyn found two face masks, which he and Walter wore to disinfect the van again while I sat on a rock and petted the cat. To my right idled what was left of the washbasin that Selwyn, channelling decades of pent-up frustration, ripped out from the caravan wall with Walter's rubber mallet and some sort of massive chisel. There is no pipework under the caravan any more either, so both toilet and bar sink are defunct. The mock Chesterfields are so mottled and stained you'd think we'd used them as human shields. Even the mattresses were not saved by their plastic body bags, just as some of our clothes and shoes on bottom shelves are riddled with watermarks and reek of gutted fish. Only the mermaids on the curtains, marginally higher that the Chesterfield beds, have escaped complete disaster. The rest of the caravan is intact, but soiled, a little like me. Its depreciation is such that not even the metal will provide enough kindling to light the light at the end of our tunnel. We are both broken and broke.

As we drive away, I start to unravel the map on my lap and try to locate where we are right now. Selwyn says, 'No need. I know where I'm headed,' and there it is again: his pronoun, not ours. And then he smacks the dashboard with the palm of his hand and calls himself stupid, a sucker. He should've known that he was pulling a pup. Why else would Louis have been so quick to let him tow it off as he did? It was supposed to carry our burden, not be the burden. I feel my face twist as I dare to ask about the pond equipment.

'Has any of that survived?'

The pieces of his face slot together enough to form a small smile. 'The beauty of pond equipment is that it's waterproof,' he says, a bit too sarcastically, then asks me to look in my handbag in case there are some paracetamol to be found. His head is thumping. I reach down for my bag and begin to root half-heartedly.

'Good that we still have the pond equipment,' I try and encourage. His smile remains awkward. 'Isn't Wales full of stately homes with ponds? All is not completely lost, surely?'

He stops at a red light. A hole in the lane and three workmen in hi-vis jackets and hard hats are looking into it.

'Did you find any tablets?' Selwyn asks.

'Why don't you want to talk about it?' I persist. 'What are you so afraid of?'

He covers his face with his hands and rubs his thumbs against his temples.

'Must we do this now?' he says.

The light turns green, we are good to go, but Selwyn does not move, like I'm asking him to go down a road he's never been down and needs to consider his options. *There are always options to selling,* Selwyn will say. *You never go in with one deal to make.*

'You must think there's something to salvage from the caravan,' I start up again. 'Else why would we be going to some campsite to air it out? It's not like you've decided to drive it back to the yard.'

He angles his head to look at me. 'What do you want me to say, Ginny? I failed. *It* failed. Is that what you want to hear? That I tried and couldn't do it?' And then, because he's feeling spiteful, 'Is that why you ran away? Because you thought I couldn't be a good enough father either?'

I blow out my cheeks and look out of the window. 'That is not nice,' I eventually say.

He apologises. Then apologises again. 'We're in hell enough,' he says.

'You know what your problem is?' I begin. 'You dug your own pond. One hundred per cent watertight, even in swell. No unknown species. No predators. No spawn. You cultivated it to never fail you. A ponder's pond. Except it's been there all the time, hasn't it? Lurking underneath, all secretive and sly. Something has been there that you've let grow and take over.'

He turns away. I've hit a nerve. If not all of them. The traffic lights have yet again gone back to red and there's a car behind us frustrated and flashing its headlights, clearly in a rush to be somewhere when we are not. I watch him wave his apologies at the driver behind in the convex wing mirror. Then he looks at me.

'There is something you need to see,' he says. 'Something I haven't told you.'

'Okay.'

'Now have you got any paracetamol, or what?'

I put my bag down. 'No.'

He sighs. The lights turn green. We get on our way.

And yet we drive all but a mile before Selwyn branches off to the left and then stops at the gate of a church. This troubles me. A country church built for church mice. Blocks of grey stone and a little pebbledash; a slate roof and just three windows. A short steeple with a weather cock that is slightly bent and heading south. It's an ancient graveyard too, mossed and entangled in blackberry vines, and all approached through a little wooden gate that hangs off its hinges. It makes me want to both burst into tears and shout up at the sky, *I've been a good person!*

Selwyn takes the keys out of the ignition and looks down on them in his lap, as if he's about to throw them away. He tells me to get out of the car.

I let him walk ahead of me, though he walks so slow and thoughtfully that an immense feeling of dread overcomes me. We walk silently through gravestones, partly sunk and toppled, so mossed they're barely readable, and drowning in dead leaves. The inscriptions have long been erased by the seasons and nobody, sadly, leaves flowers any more. It's how the past should be, I think, clipping at Selwyn's heels. Not nurtured, not revisited, but left to return to earth. Let the harsh north winds do the rest. Then Selwyn suddenly stops and kicks at the grass beneath him. There is a small stone, weathered and mottled too, but here the engraving is very clear:

Sioned Robby
Born 14.04.1946 Died 24.12.1963

I look at Selwyn.

He says, 'This is why we left the Corbet Hall.'

HUGH STRINGER – THE ELDEST son of Hugh Stringer Senior – and Selwyn's father had met at a livestock market and traded pigs. So grew a friendship that eventually led to Selwyn's father – John was his name – uprooting the family from Wrexham to live at the Corbet Hall just outside of Wroxeter. John, Sarah, Selwyn and Sioned.

Selwyn describes her as if she is me. She was almost too quick for the eye, he says. Yet she filled up spaces he didn't even know were there. She was someone who was everything and didn't know she was. Someone who could've been, but never found the way.

His sense of loss is so easily recalled and I can see it now, it practically bounces off his skull. This is what this has all been about.

For a long time, his mother thought me her ghost, we were so alike.

'She couldn't bear to look at you,' Selwyn tells me. 'She thought you were there to punish her. "Of all the houses they could've found us," she'd say. You had exactly the same hair.'

I try to say that faces change and do so much – they are never trapped in time, and that is a woman's downfall. That grief, as Meg always said, could become such a darkness that nothing is ever seen in light again. 'I wasn't the only long-haired dolly in Joiners Square,' I add.

Selwyn says not true. Even our bodies moved the same way, the angle of our hips, the turn of our feet. Sideways on, I was Sioned's silhouette.

'It was a relief when you left, truth be told,' Selwyn says. 'And you're right. The darkness then lifted.'

It occurs to me that all that black Meg wore was to mourn an old life too.

He sits down to tell me the rest of it and rolls cigarettes. As he talks, I concentrate on how he makes them and watch the way his smoke twists and curls into the air. He rubs his earlobes a lot. He shivers at certain words. The story is short, but feels long, and then it comes to an end. His sister drowned in the pond.

He blames the pondweed. There was so much of it down there, like an iceberg; it was always going to cause tragedy, eventually.

'It starts to stick like adhesive,' Selwyn tells me. 'It's a myth that it's just congealed algae on bladderwort. It has spines. They seek to attach themselves, to propagate. And the pond was saltwater, the remnant of an estuary. Those things were not planted. They'd evolved.'

It took hold and kept her there. No one knew what she was doing out there, if she'd fallen, waded in, or if she were pushed. By the time they'd pulled her out, one of the children thought she'd been killed by an octopus. You could barely see her face.

Selwyn stands up and rubs out his cigarette, tells me he should have brought flowers.

'You must understand,' he says, 'I had to go back, to the Corbet Hall. I just wanted one last look at the pond. There was something about that pondweed that was different,' he is looking up at the steeple as he says it. 'I'd never seen anything like it. Especially in saltwater. It made no sense. I studied it for years.'

I remember all the buckets in the backyard and imagine Selwyn poring over nature books in libraries in his shirtsleeves, rubbing his hand through his hair in frustration when the pages will not tell him what he needs to know. I try and tell him that sometimes death is not always scientific and it's probable that she wanted to die. I knew shame in abandonment. I can't say it didn't cross my mind when the start of a new life feels like the end. Especially when you're responsible for it. Selwyn glares at me, as if I was the one who'd given his sister the rocks to put in her pockets. It's the same look his mother would give me. Like I was to blame.

'Why are you looking at me like that?' I ask. 'When there's death without explanation, you seek explanation all the same. I get it. I do.'

'But you think I should go back there, don't you? Bring it back to life.'

'Not at all,' I say, feeling confused. 'To be honest, I can see why you don't want it. The place is pitiful. It'd take millions to rebuild.' I start to laugh. 'You do have a habit of inheriting what no one wants.'

'Then what's to become of it if I don't look after it?' He kicks up a tuft of grass as he says it.

I go for his hand. 'It's a house, Selwyn. It's not her.'

But he turns away. I tell him to look at me. 'Look at me,' I insist. 'You need to look at me because this is what is here, now. I am not inherited. I am here.'

And he looks at me, with tears, and says, 'Remind me when this became about you again?' and heads back to the car.

This is why Selwyn wants me, I think, as I watch him walk away from me. This is why we have arguments about the dishes, the bladderwort in the drain, about the burnt bits at the bottom of the oven that congeal and weld to the sides. I find a chip in a mug. A hairline crack in a plate. I put them both in the bin and Selwyn fishes them back out. Washes them. Uses them. *Look,* he says. *Good as new.* I use his toothbrush to scrub the bathroom sink out of petulance. Wonder why he doesn't store memories like he clings on to paperclips and screws. I think we were neighbours for less than a year, we've been reunited for less than a year, and there are fifty years between those years, which is more than some get to spend on this earth, which makes those fifty years a lifetime. And that's what we've both had. Two lifetimes. In different directions. We are each other's loving memories, that is all. It was never going to work.

'When you lose something,' Meg said, 'the first thing you do is think about how to replace it.'

'Then what am I?' asked the Bluebird.

'The other me,' was Meg's reply.

And that's what this is too. Selwyn wanted his sister replaced, so he replaced her with me and bodged it.

We get back into the car.

'Look,' I begin.

But he interrupts me. 'She *was* pulled under, Ginny,' he says coldly. He's looking right through me as he says it. 'She was asphyxiated. Eel larvae can do that. Swarms of it. It would've buried her alive.'

'Okay,' I say.

'And I had to go there. You do understand that. I had to go. One last time. But I couldn't go in. Not inside. I couldn't see her in there.'

I put my hand on his leg and hold it there for as long as he'll let me.

'It's okay,' I say.

'There was so much I wanted you to see there.'

'I didn't need to see any of it.'

'It'll be a graveyard,' he says solemnly. 'No one will ever know about it.'

'But we will.' My hand is stroking his thigh. 'You have to let the past be past.'

He holds on to my hand. 'Isn't that what we are?'

I smile. He's a tough old nut to crack. 'Not any more.'

And this time, when we kiss, it's the most natural thing in the world, and we let it happen, right there, in the car, by a graveyard, in the middle of Wales, and afterwards we start laughing, because what in God's name took us so long?

THE CAMPSITE IS CALLED the Good Meadow and boasts four gold stars on a tin sign, which I instantly assume is for its behaviour.

I have never been to a campsite before so do not at all know what to expect or what is expected of me, least of all what to do with myself while Selwyn hooks up a humidifier to a long thick blue cable. He then reels off chores I can do while he sets about raising the awning. This is not a word I know and I'm curious what the awning is. I have never seen one before and want to know what it does. He tells me it's the overhang, like Meg had over the butchers to stop the meat from sweating in the sun.

'We can sit underneath it and watch the stars,' he says.

I look disappointed and ask if there's something more interesting that I can do than fetch water from a well, or see what's in the site shop that we could have for tea. Both tasks make me feel like we are scavenging.

I watch him unleash the awning and wonder why he can do this so ably when he weeps like a baby should the central heating be on the blink. I watch him align the left and right poles of the awning as if negotiating between where we are now and where he wants to be. There was also an equally worrying familiarity between Selwyn and the site owner, Gavan, especially in their handshake. I told myself that the best salesmen never don't have customers.

As Selwyn works on the awning, I ask him about Gavan and the pond.

'Ginny,' he says soberly. 'You have got to stop being so suspicious.' And then, perhaps owing to the look on my face, he adds, 'I've had plenty to be suspicious about over the past ten months, but have you ever seen me looking suspicious?'

He's finished doing what he's been doing with the awning then starts doing something else with a line of rope.

'What can I do?' I ask. 'Surely, I can do something?'

He says, 'I've told you. Go to the shop.' He lights a roll-up with such a wild flaming match he singes his nostril hair. Then he takes out his wallet and gives me a twenty-pound note.

I leave him to it.

The site shop is not a shop but a large shed that reeks of creosote and wood shavings. Inside are two trestle tables with stuff for sale, and there's a lot of sawdust on the floor. I see they have sliced bread, eggs, butter, cheese, one pint of milk and some tins of chopped tomatoes and baked beans. It reminds me of the tombola at Hodnet and I wonder if I need to buy a book of raffle tickets and take pot luck. There is a fridge, in the corner, with a lead so long I can't even see where it's plugged in, and this fridge is empty, all but for two bottles of white wine. Which I decide to buy. Along with the bread and cheese. I'm not sure where you pay, there is no till and no one monitoring the tables, but as I start to walk out, Gavan calls me back with a whistle. I do not like to be whistled.

'Just the wine, is it? That'll be twelve pounds.'

Up close, Gavan is rugged and rustling, grey and nasally. There is something stuck to his bottom lip, a cold sore? Food? And he wears a single silver stud in his left ear. The rest of him is as you would expect for a man permanently outdoors. The trousers are brown, patched and worn, the jumper has seen better years, and the shirt is a jagged criss-cross of buttons hanging on and falling off. I notice he has three Bic Biros poking out of his trouser pocket alongside a screwdriver. There cannot be a wife. Gavan looks unapologetically alone.

I ask him if he might set us up with a tab.

He says, no. 'It's all upfront, I'm afraid. Cash only.'

'Has Selwyn already settled with you for the night then?' I ask.

He says, 'He's doing me a big favour measuring the carp.'

I blink too many times for my eyes to cope with. 'The carp?'

'Big carp,' he nods, as if announcing his American Indian name. He leans in. His breath smells of coffee. 'And too big for the pond.'

'I'm sorry,' I'm shaking my head and pursing my lips, 'Selwyn is here to measure carp?'

'Those that've outgrown the pond,' he says. 'Then he'll consult. Mediate. The guy who wants them plays hardball. I don't play hardball. I'm in watercress.'

I'm tempted to open the wine and down it.

'I'm sorry,' trying my best to not look like my retinas have detached, 'but are you telling me that Selwyn knew he was coming here?'

'I should hope so,' he laughs. 'I've been waiting on him getting here for over a month.'

This is like squeezing a stubborn core out of a blackhead – the root of this story is playing hardball too. I think of what's just happened between us in the car, then of all the fish that have slapped me in the face. I close my eyes and let out a deep sigh. Gavan tells me he still needs twelve pounds for the wine and another three for the bread and cheese.

If Selwyn were here, he would negotiate. He is the salesman. He is always the salesman and never really stops being a salesman because salesmen cannot be anything other than salesmen. Even when they're not selling, they're selling, and even when they are telling you a story of their drowned sister, they are only selling a version of it that you choose to buy. And boy, have I just bought it! This is where I've been going wrong, I think. I haven't been negotiating. I've been thinking that Selwyn is only selling his pond supplies to keep us on the road, when what he's really selling off are his lives. One after the other. He's been positively selling them left, right and centre, and I've been trying to insert myself in every single one of them.

And then there are the ponds. There are ponds everywhere and as far as the eye can see. Loggerheads had a pond. Trentham Gardens had a big pond. Hodnet had many ponds and the Corbet Hall had a death pond. Now there is another pond full of carp. Which Selwyn is here to measure, and which Selwyn *knew* he was here to measure, and I slap down the twenty-pound note on the trestle table and tell Gavan to keep the change.

I storm back to the caravan where I find Selwyn under the awning watching a pot of coffee brewing on a camping stove that he's parked up on an upturned cardboard box. He's sitting on a deckchair and I see there is one for me too. I have not seen these deckchairs before. His is red-and-white striped. Mine is green-and-white striped. Like toothpaste.

'You're measuring the carp then?' I sneer. 'When were you going to tell me that you are here to measure carp?'

Selwyn's response is to ask me if I found anything interesting in the shop.

I show him the wine.

He says, 'And what about to eat?'

'Bread and cheese,' I say. 'Gavan said you'd organised this a month ago.'

Selwyn leans down towards the coffee pot and lifts the lid. 'I'd forgotten I'd packed this,' he says, sniffing the fumes, not listening to a word I've just said. 'I can't remember when I last used it.' He leans back in his deckchair and puts his arms behind his head. 'This is the life,' he says, sprawling out his legs. 'The open air. Pot of coffee. We should've done this years ago.' He squints up at me as if I'm about to puncture his second wind. 'What?'

'Why didn't you tell me that you were here to measure the carp?'

'In case he didn't want me to,' he replies. 'I thought he'd looked up someone else to do it.'

'He says you're playing hardball,' I say. 'Negotiating on his behalf.'

'It's my job.'

'You sold pond supplies.'

'I still sell pond supplies.'

'And suddenly measure carp. Play hardball. Why have you never told me that you know how to measure carp?'

'I didn't want to jinx it,' he says. 'This could be a windfall. I'll get twenty-five per cent. The size of his carp. They're worth thousands.'

'You made out to Walter that you'd never heard of this place.' I remind him of their parting conversation this morning. 'He drew you a map. Now you're measuring carp.'

He looks at me wearily. Says no, he has never been here before, but yes, Gavan did call him up a few weeks back to enquire of his availability. 'Seriously, Ginny. It's been no more than that.'

'I thought we were on a clear road,' I persist. 'That's what we said. A clear road from now on.'

He sighs. This one could quite draw blood. 'Ginny,' he begins, 'why don't you just take a shower?'

'Why didn't you measure the caravan fish?'

'I couldn't get at them to measure them. Besides, they're aquarium bred. Carp are freshwater. Clever buggers. They grow only to the size of the pond. That's why you need to move them, to somewhere bigger, let them really grow.'

'Is that fair?'

'It's nature.'

'But you're asking them to keep growing. It's fish obesity. And cruel.'

Selwyn snorts with laughter. 'What is cruel is the way that tank was installed in the caravan.'

'And you are in no place to laugh at me, Selwyn Robby, when we are in this bloody field because you lied again.'

He holds up his hands. 'I didn't lie, Ginny,' he says. 'I didn't know if he needed me or not. Like I said, I was late.'

'Are you late for anywhere else?'

He gestures to the field in front of us. 'Gavan says there's still wild boar in that field. Hares. It's that time of year.' He pauses, screws up his eyes.

'For what?'

'Mating,' he has a very serious look on his face as he says it. I slump down into the deckchair and look across at the field. I can see neither boar nor hares, just a lot of long grass and a wood. Very small. And that's as far as my eyes will see. It is also dropping cold.

'We're here, aren't we?' I say in an ugly mood. 'This is Wales, isn't it? This is it.'

Selwyn reaches for my hand and squeezes it so hard that the rush of blood to my fingertips makes me faint.

Second chances. Sometimes you just don't want them.

To pass the time, I watch a woman haul herself from out of a tent over there and hear the words 'hairdryer'. I then turn my deckchair to face another way and see there are tents dotted everywhere. Some look like fallen pods from satellites, others are the size of retirement bungalows. I become preoccupied with an arriving family and watch their procedure from start to finish in a state of shock. There is so much negotiation to be had over tent poles and tent pegs, which go where and why, then out come the mallets, the curses, the bruised thumbs. Selwyn leans over to tell me that good tent erection is all in the strategy, but I'm exhausted just watching. Because once the tent is up, there's all this adjustment going on. Tightening up this. Slackening off that. Then the car boot is opened and out drops the rest of the stuff: blow-up mattresses, sleeping bags, duvets, pillows, cookers with gas bottles, kitchen shelves, pans, then a box of food. A folding table. Four matching chairs. The mother spends much of her time hitching up Christmas tree lights and flags, then here come the candles and tealights, the burgers and umbrellas. Wine is opened. Windbreakers go up. The kids have swingball, shuttlecock, boules and scooters, but all lie abandoned in the drizzle while they shelter in the car fixed on screens. An argument breaks out. Someone has forgotten to pack the tin opener, the tomato sauce. I overhear an argument in another tent so vicious I can't repeat it. Camping, I declare to Selwyn, is a test of human endurance, survival of the fittest. We watch the arguing family pose for photographs that they take themselves with outstretched arms. Everyone smiles for the camera. Then all those smiles fade and one child kicks the other in the shin.

I smell sausages sizzling in a pan and wonder how awful they'll taste. Meg used to sing hymns when making sausages. She'd do them with belly pork and stomach lining, a grind of salt and pepper. Then she would massage them. Cook them in hot oil up to their hips.

'I thought you were going to take a shower?' Selwyn says. He's pouring coffee into an enamel mug. I see that he only has one mug aside of him. It is a one-person coffee pot. Like sausage making was a one-woman job. Like mothering. Like measuring a child's feet. I look about me.

'Where do you go and do that?' I ask.

Selwyn points to what looks like a tin barn.

My heart sinks.

'I'll get my towel,' I say.

Outside the showers, at a pair of stainless-steel kitchen sinks, I find that the woman from the arguing family is stood aside of me. She smiles at me in the mirror, apologises for her screeching swarm, and asks me if we've just arrived. I tell her yes, and that I'm a little out of my depth.

'Three nights and counting,' she tells me, squeezing toothpaste on her brush. She has a very big mouth for the size of her face. 'It's our eldest's birthday, this is what he wanted to do and, God, it's a travesty. We should be on a plane.' Still, the boys are having a ball and she supposes that's what it's all about and that's why she must suck it up. She cleans her teeth, as if she's angry with them too, and I think of how Mia would ask about holidays and I'd tell her, next year, for definite. *You said that last year,* she'd reply. It had never occurred to me to buy a tent.

I dry my hair on my sodden towel and ask if there's a hairdryer.

She says, 'Not in this field,' and gives me a soapy smile. She looks as if she's waiting for something incredible to happen, a small jot of thanks, perhaps, would do, and I don't know what to tell her that she doesn't already know. She asks me if we've come far. I realise that my answer to that question is, 'Yes. So far that I can't remember where we even started. I couldn't even tell you how long we've been away.'

She smiles again and asks me if we're retired. 'You're in that caravan, aren't you?' she says. 'It looks quite the novelty.'

'Yes, but it's airing and useless. We had a small accident last night.' I cover my fish-slapped cheeks with my hands in case they give me away.

'You've got a roof over your head and it's going to thunder down later,' she says, wiping her mouth on her sleeve, and her smile is both loose and forced. 'Appreciate the trees, isn't that what they say?' She looks as if she's said something aloud for the first time. I watch her move her tongue around her mouth, as if she's something stuck in her teeth. 'Just wait until the owls start,' she warns. 'And then the foxes. It's brutal. And they call this a quiet campsite.'

'I live under a flyover,' I say. 'Quiet is not something I know.'

She half-smiles, half-frowns. 'Well, sleep well,' she instructs, as if she's older than me.

'Is it night time, already?' I'm confused. I wonder if I'm feverish. I place my hand on my forehead and can't decide if I'm hot or cold.

'You have been away a long time,' she says tying her hair into a low ponytail. 'What a lovely state to be in. That gives me hope.'

I go to tell her that it is not lovely, not lovely at all, because at this age you just want to keep the blood pumping and your bowels moving rather than driving about Wales looking for the roots of whatever made you and trading past regrets. But she's walking away from me like what I have to say doesn't matter.

I suddenly feel something twist around my legs, call it swimmer's itch, like something is dragging me towards the edge of a cliff, because that woman was snubbing me. Just like that young girl in Loggerheads with her troubled baby. And that woman in that quirky café back in Shrewsbury, who'd conned me into buying her lunch. Giving me *Coddiwomple* and all that. 'Hang on,' I find myself shouting. 'Just you hang on a minute.' She turns to look at me as if I've attached *kick me* to her back.

And perhaps I have, because that's what I want to do. I want to kick *something*, the thing that's been in my way. That teenage girl dressed in lace and wellington boots flushing the blood down the drain while her mother trimmed a pork shin and made eyes at a man that she wanted too. My mother was always in my way blocking my daylight. But then so is that teenage girl. She won't ever go away either. And I want to kick her and beat her and hold her by the throat, because I've called her the names, sat her down, made her recite all the bad things that happened – number one, number two, number three, four, five. But she doesn't listen, doesn't want to admit to it, wears polo-necks, long sleeves, jackets that button up to the neck, and trousers, these days, always trousers, *manly,* and morphing into her mother. But when this woman asks me, 'I'm sorry. Have I said something wrong?' I bottle it and tell her that I like her boots.

'They look very sturdy, even from behind,' I say, appreciating the thick soles and heels that look as if they can stick to the slickest granite. She says they don't quite fit and make her ankles sweat. I say, 'I could do with a pair like that.'

'What size are you?' she asks.

I tell her a seven. And a half.

She bends down and starts to unlace the boots. Then she walks back over to me with the sort of smile my daughter would give her mother-in-law's roast chicken.

'They're yours,' she tells me, as I look down at her sodden socked feet on the bare concrete floor. 'Then I've no reason to ever come out here again.'

After she's gone, I pluck up the courage to look at myself in the mirror in front of me. When you've stopped looking at yourself, you don't really think about yourself as something to look at, and that's what I was afraid of. But when I do look, and it's barely for a second, I don't see her, the one that's been mattering, only *me*. And I will go on mattering no matter what.

By the time I get back to the caravan, Selwyn has got a fire going. A few sticks, a log, in a pit. Another thing I didn't know we had. He has got us blankets and he goes to wrap one around me, like I'm an old woman, but I tell him I need to change my clothes. I'd not taken a fresh set with me to the showers. He is still smoking, which makes that one roll-up number fourteen, if I'm not mistaken, which means he has smoked four more than yesterday and is therefore getting into the swing of it. I go into the caravan holding my nose. I realise that we have unhitched ourselves from the caravan and for a second or two, I feel weightless. Then I see that Selwyn has laid out clothes for me on the back of the cupboard door. A pair of khaki trousers, fresh underwear, a black fleece and socks. A good salesman will sell you not what you think you need but what you actually want. I open the cupboard doors to look for something *I want* to wear, and try and put the caravan's smell from my mind. I see that another shelf is empty. I can't remember what was on the shelf and so poke my head out of the door and ask Selwyn, 'Have you sold something else while I was in the shower?'

'Gavan needed a pond hydrator,' Selwyn says. 'The algae's been suffocating some of the smaller carp.'

I start to wonder if he is speaking in code, that all his sales have been code for something else, something he cannot talk about – it's not the first time it's crossed my mind that Selwyn is ill, but I've talked myself out of that notion before and talk myself out of it again. They're only paracetamol. Just indigestion tablets. Aspirin.

I drip-dry my hair by the fire, wearing my new walking boots, and snip at the split ends with nail scissors in the faint hope of appearing tidy. I am also watching my clothes burn. The jumper I'd been wearing since Thursday. The trousers that'd felt varnished on to my legs. I throw in the bra for good measure, and find this apt. Selwyn told me not to burn my clothes and that we would find a laundrette when we got going again, but I felt like I'd been wearing that jumper and those trousers for so long that burning them was the best I could do for them. I wonder what else I should burn – it's very addictive – and think of everything I could've burnt, if I'd just had time to pack it; if I'd had my time over and been prepared. I might even have burnt my box and got rid of that too. I see Selwyn looking down at my boots.

'Where are those from?' he asks. 'I thought you didn't buy any shoes?'

'They were a gift.' I point at the tent that's been zipped up. 'She gave them to me. They fit like a glove.'

He seems perturbed by this. 'Does she know you have them?'

'She gave them to me,' I tell him again. 'She didn't want them.'

His expression deepens and his chin locks on to his chest. 'Why on earth would you not want boots like that?' he asks.

I shrug. Tell him to never look a gift horse, and lean down to hack at the bread as if cutting it with a chainsaw.

As we eat cheese sandwiches and gnaw on stale crusts like goats, I ask Selwyn about his sister.

'Don't tell me about her death,' I say. 'Tell me about her life. Who she was.'

Perhaps the wine has loosened his tongue because, at first, he talks a lot and I don't interrupt. An older brother, a younger sister, one protects the other, as the other looks up to the other, and he never worried because she was never out of his sight. I notice that when he talks about her, he does so in context of himself, like he was never not there. He stretches out a memory of them both shelling peas at the kitchen table, and remembers the pattern on the tablecloth; how their mother would rag her hair until the ringlets were permanent. Like all mermaids, she'd been learning to play the harp. She'd been clever, and could've been cleverer, but books just weren't her thing. She didn't want to live through other people's words but find her own stories. Then he stops talking and there is a strange quiet between us, as if the story he told isn't quite finished and the end is yet to come. I wonder if he's stopped talking about her to talk about me.

He says, 'You're really not that interested, are you?' and gives me the look of a man who can't find his keys and doesn't know how to tell me. 'There's not a sympathetic bone in your body.'

This gets my hackles up. I tell him that sympathy goes both ways and comes around again when someone deserves it.

He says, 'Then what about that photograph back in Logger-heads and how you ran away from it? You tore open your leg doing so. Given half the chance, you would've ripped it to shreds and burnt it.'

'I didn't want it,' I try to explain. 'That Linda woman should never have had it. I don't know what she was doing with it. Meg would've been horrified to know it still existed.'

'It's only a picture, Ginny.'

'It's not only a picture, Selwyn.'

'She was your mother!'

'And she had the colour bleached out of her because she became my mother! Do you think I want a photograph that reminds me of that?'

He frowns. He is looking at me, looking for me, looking into me, trying to find me out, as if I'm lost in that tiny little wood over there and screaming to be saved from trolls. He does that thing he does with his nostrils and sniffs.

'I wish you'd stop doing that,' I snap. 'It's disgusting. You're going to burst a blood vessel.'

He says, 'The problem with you, Ginny, is that you're actually made of glass.'

'And glass shatters,' I say quickly. 'So don't throw stones.'

He says, 'We're all guilty of fabricating our lives when they don't seem exciting enough.'

'And what's that supposed to mean?' I shout. 'You think Meg would make it all up?'

'Who was the Bluebird, Ginny?'

'What?'

'Who was she, really?'

I bite my tongue and taste blood. 'Don't do this, Selwyn. It's not what you do.'

'But who was she?' he repeats.

I look over my shoulder to see if anyone can hear us.

'*Who was she*?'

I shake my head at him. Something is burning down my cheeks. 'You have no idea what loneliness can do to a woman,' I begin.

'But I know what the death of a child can do,' he says slowly. 'And then there's the birth of a child too.'

He reaches for me from his deckchair, like I'm a long way away and possibly in a hole, but I move further away so he can't touch me. He tells me we were neighbours, don't forget, and those hope-thin walls of Joiners Square were stuck together with Sellotape. 'I could count your hiccups,' he reminds me. 'I could hear every word said.' And he holds up two fingers. 'Two voices, Ginny,' he reminds me. 'Two voices, never three.'

I wipe my nose against my jumper sleeve and leave a line that glistens against the fire.

'I don't want to do this,' I mutter. 'I don't know it all and I don't want to anyway.'

He grabs my hand and his skin welds into mine. He tells me he is here. Right here and going nowhere.

'Do you hear me?' he says. 'I am not going anywhere.'

I pull away from his hand and stand up. I don't know why. I don't need to perform. I look down at my new walking boots. Some other woman's shoes, some other woman's life. Living in squares and going around in circles. I pace back and forth and wonder where to stop, to start. 'I played along,' I tell him in a stagnant voice. 'How could I not play along when I'd go on and on about family and where were they all and why didn't we have any? And one day she said to me, "There are birds in the trees and rabbits in the burrows but not only the foxes leave their dens at night. You are my family now."'

I pause. I don't know why.

'She was only manly because she'd had to be manly. I was womanly because she didn't want me to be manly. Then we both became women, and almost at the same time, and one of us grew up and the other invented an imaginary friend. What did it matter? It filled all the emptiness until I imagined it wearing clothes and telling me things too.' Again, I pause, as if I'm telling it all in chapters and I'm waiting for him to catch up. 'Look. Boys got paid to work the farm. Girls stayed at home until they were distractions to farmhands. Those were your laws of the countryside, and they needed the money. They were scratching in the soil. So, they cut her hair and dressed her otherwise. Desperate times. Isn't that what Linda said? She spent the rest of her life peeling away at that country skin. I spent the rest of my life hardening mine.' I pause again, drink more wine. 'You pretty much know the rest of it from there.'

I think of the three faces in the photograph, two uncles I never knew. I can hear an owl. Something scuttling. *Nature is always more scared of us,* Meg used to say. *And it should be, because we are vile creatures. We only know how to torment.* I look over at Selwyn who is looking at me without blinking.

'I know where Grogan took you that day back in Loggerheads. I know that Mucklestone pond. Meg used to talk about it. It's full of the unbaptised.'

He starts shaking his head at me. His face burns against the fire and he rubs his whiskered chin with the heel of his hand. 'Are you telling me what I think you're telling me?' he asks.

I look away and into the night which is closer than I have ever felt it.

'She never told me a thing about who he was,' I carry on. 'I suspect he was some farmhand or other making promises he couldn't keep. I learnt not to ask in the end. All she'd say was that I had his nose and that her mother gave her enough bus fare for her to leave and find a new life for her and me.'

'But *you* didn't have to run away,' he says. 'Times were different. And I didn't want you to run away.'

My face feels clotted in false smiles. 'I didn't run,' I say. 'And times were not that different. Meg could've brought me up in Loggerheads. I could've brought up Mia in Joiners Square, but both of us knew we had to find something that was just that bit better, you know? It would've broken Meg's heart to watch history repeating. And she left me money, don't forget. Just as her mother gave her money. Two options. Run or get rid. It was the shame I couldn't deal with, yet shame is in our blood.'

He is still shaking his head at me, but if ever there were a truth it is that. And if folk didn't think it a shame – *those poor young things that look born together, not seventeen years apart* – because to cart about that much shame is surely why she wore so much black – then it was a crying shame that no man ever found it in his heart to parcel us up for keeps.

'You keep her shoes, don't you?' Selwyn asks. 'Those black boots, at the bottom of the wardrobe that you don't even wear.'

'Unless you walk a mile in another woman's shoes, how are you ever supposed to know where she's been?' I stretch out my arms as if it's the first time I've been able to do so and feel my backbone rise like bread. 'I don't try and understand the past, and, to be perfectly honest, leave it be. It's of no use to me. But I opened the door one day and there they were. Just sat there on the doormat as if asking to be let in. Next thing I knew, Marge was telling me she'd died. There is no more mystery to them than that.'

We watch the fire.

'Do you miss her?' he asks.

'Yes, I do. But I mourned her many years ago. Now, I want to let her rest.'

'I used to hear her shouting,' he presses on. 'Really yelling at herself. Smashing things up.'

'The Bluebird could give as good as she got,' I smiled. 'She kept my mother sane.'

'And yet it didn't keep you,' he murmurs. 'That's the saddest part.'

'Well, I dragged the past back in, didn't I? Made the big mistake when she'd been clever enough to avoid the pond.'

'Did she tell you that?'

'She didn't have to.'

He pours me more wine and offers me a smoke. I take both and ask him again about the pond back at the Corbet Hall. What did he think he would find there?

'Answers,' he says quickly. 'I'm only ever looking for answers to why people suddenly give up.'

I cough a little on the cigarette. 'It's why I didn't want that photograph,' I start up again. 'Meg hated that part of her life. It was so primitive. You'd hardly believe it. She couldn't wait to get out. Blot it out. Forget it ever happened. Though, I do sometimes wonder if she forced me to happen, you know?'

'And did you blot me out?' he asks. 'Is that what you did with me while bringing up your daughter alone?'

I blow a little more smoke into the night air and then spend a long time rubbing at my face, wondering how he got me talking like this. Salesmen only ever hit targets when you're out of arrows and you need to buy some more, and my body has taken enough arrows over the years. The scars they leave behind just won't heal.

'Look, Selwyn,' I begin, 'I come from dirt-poor people who wanted that little bit more. That is all. Just as you and Louis thought you could have that little bit more.' I pause to collect my thoughts. 'Here's how I see it. Some people can't get enough of life. Some people live in the wrong life. Some don't make the most of it, and some get a second chance at it, and that's why this is about us, Selwyn, having a life now. Not the one we should've had, but the one we're having here, in the car, by the church, then in this field in Wales.' I pause again, bite my lip, keep on going because I have to say this. 'We can't just be together based on two versions of a past that don't fit. You saw things one way, I saw them as another, but neither of them exists any more. I don't need answers and photographs, or to be driven back into a past I don't belong in – history is not happening now – but I can't be what you've been imagining me to be. My version of love is different to that.'

The look he gives me now is as if he's found those keys, but he doesn't want to go inside in case he doesn't recognise it and someone else is sitting in his armchair. He looks over my shoulders, as if expecting something to take shape – the ghost of all our losses maybe, mating hares, perhaps his sister's smile; Meg.

He says, 'The problem with regrets, Ginny, is that they arrive in the future with you. It's why you don't have to forget the past in order to forgive it.'

'And Meg just had an imaginary friend,' I finish. 'Which is no different from what you've been doing when you lost a sister and tried to replace her with me. But you must let them both rest, Selwyn. Let them rest in the peace that they found.'

I throw my cigarette into the fire and watch the little spark of light it makes.

'You must do the same with the Corbet Hall,' I say. 'That place needs to rest. Now, where are we sleeping tonight if we're still airing the caravan?'

He tells me, in the car. I can have the back seat. There's plenty of blankets. I tell him that the woman I met in the showers said it was going to rain. 'Like thunder down with rain.'

He tells me to open that second bottle of wine. 'Conk us out,' he says. 'Not feel the cold.'

He hands me the bottle and, as I take it from him, I start to look at him, like really look at him, look so hard into him that I start to sway. My limbs hang heavy, lived-in and tired, they've been holding on to the wrong things, and the boots on my feet are like balloons of air. I am lifting, looking down on him, this man who claims to love me much better than I love him, and I've been sloppy, I think. Missing things, important things, driving by, letting him snoop. This is what drowning must feel like, I think, as my grip on the bottle tightens; this must be how the pondweed takes hold. We have said it all and there's still more to be said. You have things to say, old man, but I don't want to say any more. Because it's not the answers from his sister that he's been looking for. It's the answers from me. This journey – it's all been about me. And thirty thousand pounds worth of pennies drop from the sky.

The Eleventh Day

'Every organism, in time, dies.'

~ *The Great Necessity of Ponds*
by Selwyn Robby

MEASURING CARP TURNS OUT to be a long-winded affair that involves something called a spreader net to catch them and then a tub of silt water that mesmerises them still. Apparently, Gavan tells me, you don't need to do either of these things, but that's why he wanted Selwyn to measure his carp. 'He doesn't just do things right,' Gavan whispers in my ear, 'he does them right by the carp. See how compliant they are?'

I watch as Selwyn measures from snout to the fork in the tail, before rubbing the fish moist and throwing them back. He then shouts out numbers to Gavan, a little like a dentist names your teeth. At one point, Gavan punches the air, as if he's the champion, and I wonder if I should go over and renegotiate the terms, when a seventy-one-year-old man in body-length waders is doing all the hard work. Then I remember that Selwyn and I are not speaking and are unlikely to do so ever again.

I walk the edges of the pond wearing my new walking boots in. At one point, I am asked to make tea by Selwyn, who is still speaking to me, and which I grumble at silently, because making tea in the open air takes forever and I am making a point of watching all this when all too often my back has been turned and next thing Selwyn turns up grinning from a sale and we are heading somewhere else because of that sale. I grind my new walking boots into the earth beneath me and feel planted. I wonder what it's like to live here – right here, in the middle of nowhere, and scratching out a life from the soil – what goes around really does come around – but then Gavan looks up from his notepad and shouts up that there's weather coming in and we should hurry up because carp will sink to the bottom in hard rain, like trout. I look up at the sky. It's bleak.

Selwyn hangs back over the tub again. For a long time, nobody breathes a word. I list all the things I hate about him in my head and have the urge to print them all on a leaflet and hand them out to my fellow campers. Tea. He makes mugs of tea he never drinks and leaves them just where I'm likely to kick them over. Jam jars. They're everywhere. On the windowsills. On the radiators, *fermenting*. In the airing cupboard, drying out. In the oven, *sterilising*. He leaves toast crumbs on the butter. Dries his trousers by weighting them to the mantlepiece in front of the fire with two rocks. He sleeps with his eyes open. He does that thing where he pinches his nostrils together and sniffs. He fibs. Constantly. And then there's the illegal fish tanks and a drowned sister, a rundown stately home, suddenly speaking Welsh, and measuring bloody carp. And don't even get me started on what I think about the fucking great necessity of ponds.

And then children, out of nowhere, with those fishing nets you buy at seasides, in blue and red, and a sinking feeling because now we must mind our language and remember our manners, except the children are squabbling about who has blue and who has red.

'I chose red,' says the one boy to the other boy, his cheeks like lamb chops, and he tugs on it, wanting it back.

The other boy, slightly taller, far wirier, clings on to the red one and pushes him. 'You always have blue,' he insists. 'You chose blue.'

And though he's smaller by an inch, the younger boy stands his ground, and jostles him back. 'I changed my mind,' he shouts. 'I'm allowed to change my mind. And you said. *You said*!'

Though what's been said never gets said and all that is said is that he must stick with his choice.

'It's just a colour,' says the taller one, the bigger boy. 'And you're spoiling things again.'

I start to smile. I want to laugh. This tug-o-war of fishing nets between brothers – the sort of chums who might share kidneys – and yes, one's red and one's blue, but they're exactly the same. *Exactly the same*. And both, if they're lucky, will catch the same fish.

A little more pushing and shoving and soon the nets are thrown aside for body blows, but Selwyn is between them to stop it getting to bloodied noses – he'd like to take a good look at these fishing nets, he wants to see the difference, he's been fishing all his life – and the boys stop to look up at him as if he is someone who reigns in their kingdom. Selwyn takes the red net in his left hand and the blue in his right and, no, he says, no difference at all, but let me show you something you might like to see.

He takes them to the edge of the pond. He bends down and does what I have seen him do a thousand times – in puddles, in ponds, in coffee jars – and makes a whirlpool with his thumb. And then the boys gasp because there, see? Only a baby carp, but curious all the same, and see how the circles make bubbles which make oxygen? And there's another one. And another. And if you're lucky, perhaps a diving beetle. On his haunches now, showing them what his father showed him, and he tickles the top of the water with his fingertips until he finds a water spider clinging to his thumb. It glistens. It looks made of glass. Further up the bank and Gavan tots up carp worth on his clipboard and smirks.

Money isn't everything. Wanting to live and with someone you love is.

I go back to where the caravan is parked and start to pack.

They walk towards me side by side like father and son, thick as thieves. Gavan acknowledges me with a nod and a lazy smile. Selwyn uses the words 'Plan B', there is always a Plan B, as there's always fish in the pond, and I can see that the sprites in his eyes have reappeared.

He says, 'Pretty buoyant, by all accounts,' and looks at me for approval.

I look away. I don't really care.

He lights a roll-up and rolls down his waders. Gavan pulls cigarettes from his jacket pocket. He shares Selwyn's match. He says something about money by the end of the month. He doesn't say how much. Selwyn doesn't ask. I keep quiet and wear sunglasses.

They sit in the deckchairs and talk about the carp again. In measurements. In volume. In their transportation to Anglesey, and as if they are politicians. They use words like strident, liberal, stump and flip-flopper. Selwyn tells Gavan about the fish tank in the caravan. He must transport them kindly, he says. Their worth can decrease by the minute and to remember what he said about silt packing. Gavan says, 'Fucking gimmicks drive me mad,' and he'll get hold of an oxygenated tank for an overnight trip.

'Less caravans holding you up,' he says.

He gives our caravan a small kick and asks Selwyn if he wants Stuart Fury to price her up. Selwyn checks his watch and reminds Gavan he has a train to catch. He looks over at me. Tells me that Gavan is heading back into Shrewsbury if I want to go with him. He'll show me the bus station where I can take a bus back to Hanley. He fetches his wallet out of his back pocket and begins counting twenty-pound notes. As he does, he tells Gavan that he's never trusted Stuart Fury, in all the years, and he's not going to start trusting him now.

'Just the carp,' he instructs. 'You take no less, and don't be greedy.'

They shake hands then both look at me like I'm part of the economics. Selwyn even puts on his battered reading glasses as if he needs to get a closer look.

I stare down at the bag I have just packed in temper and left idling by the caravan step. I realise that Selwyn's not offering me any keys and that I don't have my house keys, because in the rush I didn't think about how to get back in the house. I point to the bag and say, 'There's nothing actually in there, do you know that? You've hocked it all.'

'Ginny,' he says, 'emptying boxes is what being a couple is all about.'

There's a long and awkward pause, dented only by Gavan pulling himself out of the deckchair and muttering something about it being nice to meet me. He does not mention the train back to Shrewsbury as he walks away. Something tells me he already knows that he'll be travelling alone. Though he's kind enough to bend down and fiddle with his bootlaces, just in case I change my mind.

Selwyn pulls the empty deckchair closer to him, and says, 'Come on, Ginny. Sit down.'

I look at the empty deckchair and think of Meg. *Can't you see someone is sitting there?* Not so much an imaginary friend as a second stab at life. I sit down anyway, and feel as if I'm bundled up on her knee. I can smell lamb fat. She's baking one of her plain cakes, rustled up with whatever she's found in the larder, and her arms are dusted with flour. The kitchen's a mess, but she needs a sit down and she starts to say things about her own mother – my grandmother – who made things and cooked things and cleaned things and worked hard at things and kept all that she'd made in one of her bed socks which she gave to me and you. It's where our height comes from, Imogen. Your two left feet. Our strength. We called her the lighthouse. She saw everything coming and stopped it. Meg's father was another story bare in plot. He came into the room and the children were made to leave. She knew him only through the door cracks and his footsteps as he limped from room to room, humming and hunched. When I look at her face, it is streaked. She's doing her best, she would tell me. But it's just not enough.

It's right when they say that you don't know your own mind. My mother had an imaginary friend. I have her ghost.

We pass some time watching a family dismantle their tent. A holiday over. The kids already waiting in the car wanting to go home. Pegs pulled out of the earth. The canvas goes limp and lies down on the grass. Everything back in boxes. A binbag of damp washing. Postcards not sent. Home is where the heart is, and the plasma-screen TV.

'Marry me,' Selwyn suddenly says.

I shake my head at him. 'It isn't the answer, Selwyn.' I haul myself out of the deckchair.

He says it again, 'Marry me.'

I start walking away from him. 'You got me in the car under false pretences then lied, lied, lied!'

This time he shouts it, 'Marry me!'

I quicken my step. He catches up with me. 'Marry me. Stop begrudging us a life together.'

I swing around to face him and he puts his hands on my shoulders as if I'm to carry his world with mine. 'Marry me,' he says again.

The boots on my feet are giving me blisters. I realise they won't take me as far as I want to go and that I don't want to go backwards any more. Selwyn has bandages in the caravan. A salt-bath. He'll think if I walk away from him it'll be just another stunt. But he loves me under false pretences, thinks me someone I am not. The bandages he has will not be big enough to patch us up. Not this time. And then I realise I am buried within his arms and I don't want him to let me go.

I SIT. TO MY left, a great blanket of dark sea, black and troubled, holding off an army of rainclouds. To my right, two old dears deliberately trying to get Selwyn's attention by talking about their dead husbands.

Selwyn sits in front of me, swapping his knife and fork around, looking as if he's dislocated something – he's wincing and rubbing at his left shoulder, blaming the unhinging of the caravan from the car on the only gradient in the car park, where he literally seemed to hold it from running away with his shoulder blades. Another F has also dropped off. *Or our pond lie and beyond*, it now says. It makes me think I had a choice all along.

Selwyn is yet to convince me that he doesn't know Audrey White who owns this B&B on Llandudno's seafront, when that's most definitely not a twitch in her eye but the suggestive wink of a woman who's not yet done. She's also one of those snippy sorts who thinks me looking at her shoes is me pointing out her skirting boards are laced with cat hairs and that there's hoofmarks on her rugs. But I won't complain when we seem to be finally getting somewhere, and we've been given a room with a sea view and a teapot, and one also big enough for us to spend the afternoon on opposite sides: Selwyn at the table by the window doing the sums, me sprawled on the bed with the map, tracing how we got from A to B and all the detours in between.

I say, 'As the crow flies, we have barely gone a handspan.'

He says, 'My grandfather would walk it. Every Sunday night. Wrexham to Etruria. For work. What we'll be doing at this rate.'

He doesn't look as if he's joking. But he is looking down at my walking boots all the same.

'This buyer then, on Anglesey,' I say, looking at my reflection upside-down in a spoon as we sit for dinner. 'You know it's famous for its puffins, mussels and stone circles?' I pass a leaflet across the table, showcasing a caravan site called Red Wharf Bay, that I've found in the B&B's reception. 'This has five gold stars,' I say. 'And a laundrette. Perhaps it's my turn to find some work. Launder it all back to normal.' I give a small laugh.

He tells me we'll be in and out. And perhaps not coming back out with the caravan. More circles and these ones are made of stone.

'We're really selling it then?'

He shrugs and grimaces with a pain in his right shoulder now. 'We need the money,' he says. 'And it stinks. We'll never get rid of the smell.'

I think of the man with savage eyebrows at the trade fair and how Selwyn had rebuffed his offer of thirty thousand pounds. The tree had been bearing fruit back then. And Selwyn had been greedy. *That little bit more*, I think. We all just want that little bit more.

'But you're selling carp,' I remind him. 'Playing hardball. Taking twenty-five per cent.'

'I can't rely on that,' he mutters at his cutlery. 'Look at what happened to the fish. They made us nothing and have made the caravan worth less. It's time to flog it. Get what we can. That was always the plan anyway.'

'I thought the plan was New Zealand?'

He shrinks from the question as if it's hurting him. 'I don't think that's going to happen now, do you?'

'It depends on whether you want to go or not,' I fire back, but he looks up at me as if he really can't be bothered any more; like he and I were never meant to know this much about each other when he'd thought himself made of the same stones he sets the past in.

We have no other company in the B&B's restaurant, apart from the two old dears clucking about the cheap margarine for their bread rolls, and it's barely six-foot across, if not the same long. The other three tables feel as if they've been sat empty since 1974.

It isn't a very interesting place. Pink walls. Pictures of flowers. Over-pressed tablecloths. It doesn't feel filled with stories of customers old and new, but instead makes me think about what I might look like as I get older, and how soon that will be.

Age, the one that thing that outwits us every time.

I sink back into my chair and look out to sea again. I thought I was going to rush at it, but I just felt disappointed. And that whatever lurked beneath its waves would eat me alive. There are people on the beach skimming stones, walking dogs. I wonder for when Selwyn's spreadsheets stopped working out; if that convex wing mirror really did give him a better view, or blinkered it. I tell him it's no good losing his nerve right when I've found mine and I'm not mustard keen on going back to the monotony of making those ends meet when they never do, but here's Audrey with our food. She places Selwyn's plate in front of him first. A lamb rack with mash and red cabbage, and then steak for me – a medium-rare sirloin, that looks from the hind of a Welsh bull – that fills the plate, with chips she's crinkled herself. And I have a sudden image of Selwyn being here before – the way Audrey looks at him, and the way he looks at her, even the way they curve their mouths is the same, and I find I'm scrutinising his collars and cuffs for lipstick marks, imagining his slippers on her hearth. He was very specific about us coming here, to Llandudno, though palmed it off as the good night's sleep we didn't have in the car last night. He'd also left the room to call Stuart Fury 'to make a meet' as he called it, when there is a phone in our room. And I have not said yes, but perhaps, possibly, let's just see.

But then Audrey settles it by putting the tray under her arm and asking us what sauces we might like. She has ketchup, French and English mustard, and horseradish, which she makes herself, and there was a guest last week who took his chips all fancy with garlic mayonnaise, or perhaps you'd like mint sauce to go with your lamb? And I realise that it's her job to pretend to know us – this hospitality, this desire to please – just as it was my job at the B&B to welcome everyone as if they'd just returned from war. But Selwyn has made me doubt and jump to conclusions, to fear the worst and feel weighted down with suspicion – Hugh and Maisie, Walter Judd, Rachael, Gavan, and Ilma Cheadle – so what leaves my mouth without thinking is – *Sioned*.

'Sorry,' Audrey says, looking disheartened. 'I don't think we have that one.'

Selwyn glares at me from across the table. He waits for Audrey to leave the room to find him mint sauce, before he asks, 'Was that necessary?'

'Very much so,' I reply, happy to see blood ooze out of my steak. 'We're knee-deep in Wales and I want to be one step ahead of you from now on.' The knife slices into my meat as if it were butter. This is certainly a woman who knows her meat. 'Shall we have wine?'

Selwyn shakes his head. 'We need to start being careful,' he says. 'I want a clear head to recalculate.'

Audrey returns with his mint sauce. I tell myself that the tables haven't turned and times aren't that different, after all. Yet he is sparing with the mint sauce. He usually dollops.

The Twelfth Day

'There is always a space between two parts, however shallow the water, for the reeds to bloom.'

~ *The Great Necessity of Ponds*
by Selwyn Robby

I CALL MY DAUGHTER after breakfast, try to picture her pretty tanned face strained with relief. 'Christ, Mother,' she says angrily. 'I've been calling and calling. Where the hell have you been? I've been worried sick!' And I tell her. How we got here from there and those places in between. But there is no reply – the phone rings and rings – and her face fades. The distance between us is growing. I can no longer picture where she is, and yet she is my world.

I try the number again. As I do, I scold myself for not sending her postcards, from every place and every stop with airmail stamps. *Where to next?* The last postcard would read. Or perhaps, *We are getting there, slowly, and almost on our way.* I wonder if she has emailed me, if she has been calling my mobile and leaving messages. We talk all the time, and yet don't talk at all, and perhaps our silence, these past few days, has done us both good, because now I really do have things I want to say.

Selwyn comes in the front door with oiled hands, black-rimmed fingernails and dark circles under his eyes. He's been reattaching the caravan to the car again and it's clearly getting harder every time. He tells me that he wants to go up Snowdon. 'We can head into Llanberis off the A55. It's on the way to Anglesey. Of a fashion,' he says. 'Can't come all this way and not go up Snowdon.' Besides, Stuart Fury's suggesting a six o'clock meet somewhere outside of Beaumaris. I say fine, and wonder if this is what being a wife is really like.

Here's another thing I did not know: I did not know there was a train going up Snowdon. Selwyn didn't know that either. The train goes up and the train comes back down. It has been doing this since 1896. There is a café up there, too, right on the summit. We both look up at the mountains in front of us – thrust into the air by volcanic action, so the information booklet says, this is *an experience above everything else* – and then at the Mountain Goat already whinnying steam. We both appear so shocked at this level of industrial revolution that the man inside the kiosk starts laughing.

'You really didn't know?' he chuckles. His cheeks are very round and sunburnt. 'Where on earth have you two been?'

We look at each other. Where on earth have we been?

What I have realised is that it is completely true that we do spend around fourteen days of our life lost. That when you add up all the times you take a wrong turn, or find yourself somewhere you don't want to be, it really does equate to a fortnight of essentially being missing. And then you see something familiar, something you recognise, something that gets you back on track.

We sit aside of one another in the train carriage on hard seats, our thighs touching, and Selwyn lets me sit by the open window so I don't miss anything.

'It's important for you to see everything,' he says, and I wonder what this salesman will sell me now, and realise how much I want it.

We start to move. There are people waving to us as if we're off on some big exploration with just our fingers crossed, and it's touch-and-go that we'll make it back in one piece. A little girl on the platform – it's always a little girl isn't it? The pigtails, the pout, the polka-dot dress, the pinching of her little brother's arm so she can sit further forward on the bench and see it all first – I ready myself for her smile, her poignant wave, or thumbs-up, how I will look at her and think of me, of Meg, of her Bluebird and how it's all caught up with me, but she sticks her tongue out and blows a raspberry.

Yes, I think. That's exactly what I would've done.

There's a man telling us things as we go up. His voice drifts in and out with a loose connection on the microphone, and I listen to his scree facts, agree with the subdued browns of the rock. I look for the rare Snowdon lily and its fossilised cousins as you do for a four-leaf clover, and raise my eyebrows when he says that this was Edmund Hillary's training ground for Everest, and that we'll be three and a half thousand feet above sea level when we summit – which is what he keeps saying, like the experience will heal us – *when we summit.* I look at Selwyn and realise that he's fulfilling a dream.

The man on the microphone now points out where King Arthur lies, under a cairn of stones, and here's where his knights in full armour lie beneath him.

I say, 'That man has more burial chambers than Tutankhamun.'

Selwyn mutters something about little pieces scattered everywhere, and I wonder if, when we do summit, he's going to tell me something else – that we're going to have *that* conversation about what we want when we really do finally depart. Or arrive.

'I don't have a bloody camera,' Selwyn says, and there is definitely something about this train, the way it chugs and steams, this old-fashioned carriage full of those too old, too weak, too idle to make it, this journey, up Snowdon that makes me wish I had taken that photograph from Linda in Loggerheads, when I have no photographs, not a one, and that everything I remember is fading. I look at Selwyn aside of me who is transfixed: his right eye and his left eye snapping every shot they can – photographs we should be pinning to the fridge.

The man on the microphone talks about the slate. There's a lot of it. It's been mined for every roof, but it should be treated like a precious stone, because we can't keep taking it.

'There's something I need to tell you,' I say to Selwyn. 'It's one last thing. When something happened.'

And we are so close right now, so very close to understanding why we came together and have come back together, that I cannot tell him. I should tell him. There cannot be any more boxes.

'Selwyn,' I begin. 'There was this time, a week ago, no, two weeks ago, when I went to see Louis.'

He shushes me. 'Don't talk,' he says. 'Just look.'

'But this thing happened that'd already happened.'

And he shushes me again. 'Then leave it on the mountain,' he says. 'Don't take it up with you and don't bring it back down with us.'

But I'm reliving it anyway and opening the cast-iron gate to the Toogood Aquatics yard, which is not padlocked, as it should be at this time of night, when I told Selwyn I was somewhere else – in my mackintosh and headscarf, because the rain had caught me out. The gate grinds against the concrete and leaves a perfect white arc and the light in the Portakabin is dazzling. I walk towards it – perhaps he is expecting me – and I'm planning everything I'm going to say – I have written it down so many times I know it off by heart.

And still this train goes up. And we are surrounded by another world, a watercolour world, a superior world, and it stretches further than my eyes can see. I strain to see it all, in case I miss something, because I have never, in the whole of my restless little life, felt this size, like I could be flicked away any minute. *In the scheme of things*. God, you have to wonder. Because none of this is to do with us.

It stunk of petrol inside the Toogood Aquatics Portakabin. It took my breath away and I coughed. I had to use my headscarf as a mask. I don't know how much Louis had been inhaling, how long he'd been filling the Portakabin with it until the fumes took him over, or if it was a passing thought he was now trying to sick up, but I could hear him retching even before I opened the door. He was conscious enough to seem surprised to see me. His eyes were the same blue as a second-class stamp, the touch of his skin like algae. He'd stopped wearing his wedding ring and had even taken down the photographs of his kids. I found three empty jerry cans and lined them up with the wine bottles, took the matches off him then called 999.

'Where did you even come from?' he'd said.

I'm not sure he'd wanted to be saved.

I have not dared to do anything much with my life. We imagine all these different lives we could have had, could be living, and none of them are real. Though even when a life is real, we can barely believe it. *No one is that poor,* I'd say to Meg. *You make it sound like you were living like pigs. You make things up to tease me.* And she'd look over at the

Bluebird and say, *We know it's true, don't we? And the pigs were treated like kings.*

For a long time, I had my own story. That I had left Joiners Square to give my mother the chance she deserved. Selwyn would've been good for her. All that steadiness might have straightened her out, and she would've married him like a shot. They might even have had another child. She would pink like pork when she saw him. Her ears, at the tips, would go blood red and she'd stiffen with terror that she might have to speak. When she wept, which she did a lot, it was because he looked straight through her. When he came into the butchers, she'd pack out his order with offcuts she said would only go to waste. I felt like I'd stolen her shadow.

I went in the ambulance with Louis to the City General, where they wheeled him off with an oxygen mask. He looked frightened to death. They checked me out and then I called his wife, Marion, to tell her what had happened. She'd said, 'Well, bugger me. I never thought it would be you,' and put the phone down. So, I called her back and said, 'Did you not hear me? Your husband tried to burn everything down. And probably himself with it!'

'Oh, yes,' she said, with a frostbitten voice. 'I heard.'

She didn't come to the hospital, though I waited for over an hour, so I couldn't explain that whatever she thought wasn't true, and that this was nothing to do with me. In the end, I went and sat by his bed for a bit. I didn't like the thought of him waking up with no one there, and he's not a bad sort – you should see the flowers he leaves on his mother's grave – he just thinks he deserves better.

When he did come to, all sallow-eyed, sorry and humiliated, he made me promise not to tell Selwyn any of it. 'Not about the money, or what I did, or you.' And I'd said, 'What do you mean, me? I was coming to talk to you about the money. I wanted you to give it him back, not do an insurance job, or whatever it was you were thinking.' And he'd said, 'Then why are you sat here?' 'Because I found you trying to burn it all down and I wanted to make sure you were alright.' And he'd said, 'That's all?' 'Yes,' I'd said, 'that's all. And make sure you tell your wife that too.' And I'd felt insulted – how could he be that bloody arrogant to think that I'd stopped him for me? And he started to cry. I couldn't do anything about that, so I left.

I walked back from the hospital. It's all main road down to where we lived under the flyover, and then I kept on walking until I found myself back in Joiners Square. It didn't even look like a square, all its edges had rubbed away, and I walked round and round in circles and could not for the life of me remember if that was our house or if that was our house or if it'd been demolished and that was a new house in its place: number twenty-three was not where it should be, and number twenty-four hadn't survived either. And when you do something like go back to the house you grew up in to find it's not there any more, it makes you question if you ever lived there at all. Though there was something about that gap in the land that felt apt. A gap that only a six-foot chump with size ten feet and a heart of twenty-four carat gold could fill. It was a time and a place and then, it wasn't.

I walked round the block to where Meg's butchers used to be. It'd been a mousehole really: three customers deep and the fourth would have to wait outside. She weighed every chop, steak and ham slice in her hands – *feels like six ounces, it's a good two pounds of brisket that* – and took only what folk could afford to pay. Never once did she ask for a bit more than what she had in her apron pocket. I felt like I was behind the scenes of a play that closed early because no one came to see it. I flagged down a taxi and went home.

That was Friday. And then it was Monday, and that's when I got into the car.

I reach for Selwyn's hand and look down. I have no idea for where we are on the mountain and there's a strong smell of wild garlic, of lavender, of diesel, but also of the rose petals he mulched in a jar, and when I look down, the wrinkles on our knuckles disappear. Our fingernails are pinker, sharper. Our skin is softer. Our fingers entwine until I can't hold them tight enough. He is looking at me and he wants me to let go. I'm hurting him, squeezing him, my nails are digging in like ten tiny fish teeth and almost drawing blood. But I can't let go because I'm his pondweed, up in this world, inside these clouds, in all this green, this echo chamber; as he is mine. Look up to the sky and there's the greatest pond you'll ever see.

'Don't let me go,' I whisper.

A feather lands on my lap. But it is not blue. Bluebirds don't really exist.

ON THE TOP, SELWYN says, 'This is it for me. This is the panoramic view.' He turns to look at me. His smile has the sort of girth people get stapled for. So irritatingly handsome, so steady, so *Selwyn*. He was born for heights, I think. He has pulled up all his roots, cut away those branches from around his heart, and he seems so weightless he could quite fly away. He breathes in the mist and breathes out the last of the fog. All that we have said, and now all things done, what does it really matter when you find yourselves on the top of the world and exactly where you belong?

'You really did show me the world, Selwyn Robby,' I say, still holding on to his hand.

'That's good,' he says. 'Because I have something for you.'

He let's go of my hand and pulls something out of his back pocket. It is not the box the size of a wedding proposal that I've been expecting, but an envelope.

'I thought about wrapping it,' he starts to tell me. 'But then it's not really a present,' and he hesitates, as if he doesn't want me to look inside, after all. I clutch his hand again and tell him it doesn't matter, whatever it is, I don't have to see, because I'm starting to wonder if what's inside of that envelope is news, and bad news, a diagnosis perhaps – all those pills, that cold shoulder – and I tell him to put it away.

'Throw it away,' I tell him. 'I don't want to know. Not when we've got here.'

He looks confused and tells me it's something he's been thinking about for ages and that he should've wrapped it, that's all, and he hands it to me, steps back from me, covers his mouth with the palm of his hand. I start to open it. The contents are made of paper. One is a passport application. The other is a plane ticket. Auckland. One way.

I look up at him and look down at what's in my hands.

'These are for me?' I ask. 'You've done this for me? Where are yours?'

He takes his hand away from his mouth and chews his top lip.

'You're not coming with me? You don't want to go?'

He drops his shoulders and looks up at the sky with a deep sigh.

'She's your daughter, Ginny,' he says. 'Let her remain as so.'

'But I want you to come with me,' I say, putting the passport form, the ticket back into the envelope and giving it him back. 'I don't want to go without you.'

'You're not,' he says. 'Because you'll come back.'

'But there's no return ticket,' and I'm shaking the form, the ticket on to the ground on the top of Snowdon – let the north wind do its thing, I wish. Blow them both away. 'It's one-way, Selwyn. It's like you're sending me away and I don't want you to send me away. I want to go *with you*.' I pause. My mouth has gone dry. 'I love you.'

'And you know what I'd really love right now?' he says, smiling. 'A cheese and pickle sandwich.'

He is bright with cold and it's making his eyes water and if he wants to jabber on about his pondweed and bladderwort as we eat our sandwiches, then let him jabber on and I will listen. Not half-listen but completely listen, until I'm entranced. If he still wants to work when we get back, he can, and I will wait and I will make him shepherd's pie, and we will sit in our armchairs and remind each other of when it hailed in Loggerheads, when he took a mallet to the fish, when we stood on the summit of Snowdon and entered space. There's no place for us in New Zealand, I think. Me and Selwyn Robby, we're doing just fine right here.

'Fine,' I say. 'I could do with the loo anyway. But I'm not going without you, Selwyn. I will only take these if you have one too.'

He nods and reaches into his shirt pocket, pulls out a twenty-pound note.

'I'm so glad we did this, Selwyn,' I tell him. 'And I don't care about the caravan, or the carp and what they're worth...'

But he tells me to shut up. We have all the time in the world.

I head off towards the café and will always regret that, because by the time I get back, with two packets of sandwiches and a bag of salt and vinegar crisps to share, nobody can tell me for sure whether he fell or if he jumped.

One Month Later

MY DAUGHTER IS ON the phone talking to someone about pork ribs. They have to be Orrison baby back, she is saying. Riblets will not do. She motions towards the teapot on the table and hands me a mug. She's wearing dungarees, a white T-shirt, and her skin, usually the colour of fudge, is almost as dark as her father's. Her hair is short now, it feathers into her neck, and she sweeps her fringe behind her left ear. She's had her ears pierced again. Is barefoot, despite me bringing all those shoes for her. A cat circles her ankles. She's not allergic to them, after all. As I've said, it was easier to say that than tell her that it was another mouth to feed. I sit down at the table and pour myself a cup of tea.

Anthony comes into the kitchen. He leans his stick against the table and removes his cap. The sun burns his head these days, and he rubs at his skin up there, scratches where it itches. He's just been stung by a bee, he says. He holds out his thumb to show me, but I can see no redness on his exotic black skin. I tell him there's tea in the pot and to stop being a baby. He sits across from me and smiles, as he tells me his cows smile, but I can never see it. Cows, to my mind, do little more than graze the earth. And then we eat them. I look away. I've not come to see him and, once my daughter's birthday is over, I'm going back. I have things to sort out. A caravan to flog. A life still to live.

Mia puts the phone down and looks at us both. For a minute, she is Meg. She has her way of looking at me from under her eyebrows, as if she cannot believe we share blood – and though Meg was frightened of colour – brown, red, anything but black – Mia might've been her bluebird, if I'd chosen a different way. Still, there's no mistaking whose daughter she is. Selwyn was a lot of things, but he wasn't daft. I think he knew it from the moment he'd heard her voice.

'Happy birthday,' I say.

She says thanks. I ask her again if she's really fifty, because time is a jet plane down here.

She tells me to stop being smug, 'Yes, Mother, you are not yet old,' and hopes I haven't got her a present.

'Actually, I have,' I say, and she frowns. She had specifically said no presents, no cards. 'But this is neither,' I tell her. 'I'm giving you something back.'

It's wrapped in brown paper and string. Just as it was when it was first given to her. I almost can't watch her open it. It falls into her hand.

'My bluebird!' she shouts. 'Look, Anthony. It's my bluebird! This is as old as me! Oh, my word. Look at it! It really is my bluebird!'

Mia had given it to me the night before she'd got married. No husband wanted to share his bed with a soft toy, she'd said. Until then, it had never left her side and, from then on, never left mine.

'I used to tell this bluebird everything,' she says.

'I know.'

She glares at me.

'Little birds can't keep secrets.'

We hold each other.

We hold each other like it was the last time, the first time.

Then...

I let her go.

To this day, I do not know where that bluebird came from – a small ball of kingfisher-blue fur that chirruped when you shook its beak – but it was there and given to her on the day she was born.

'I think this is for you,' said the midwife who'd delivered my baby girl. All she would say is that it was found, at the bottom of my bag, wrapped in brown paper and string. 'I was actually looking for clean underwear,' she'd said.

I do not know how long we all look at that old bird. But we do. And time stops.

Mia gathers herself and tells me that the butcher has let her down. She has almost fifty people coming and no meat. I don't know why I find this so funny, but I laugh until I cry, and eventually Mia comes to hold me again, entangling me within her arms. We stick to each other. Like glue.

She is not coming home with me as I'd hoped, but staying. She has come here to learn, she says. To learn how to farm. To love. To be. It's all been willed to her. And there's so much room, she keeps on saying. So much to do here, so much to see. We never wake up to the same sky.

'We'd better Skype Selwyn,' she says, looking down at her watch. 'It's already ten o'clock.'

'Oh, he'll still be up,' I tell her, giving her hand a last squeeze and wiping my face with a roll of tissue. 'Besides, he goes nowhere very fast on those crutches. It takes him over an hour to get up the stairs. It's like living in an old people's home. He rattles with prescription drugs and never stops complaining. I should've left him up on the mountain.'

She smiles goofily and says she'll fire up the computer. Anthony nods his head, as if he's just agreed to something he's not aware of.

'What was he doing?' he asks me for the umpteenth time.

I had not expected Anthony to be this old. He rattles too. Looks not dissimilar to a wise old eel and made up of the things that the tide leaves behind.

'Pondweed,' I say. 'He was looking at a plant that looked like pondweed. Swears it's the stuff in a pond that we know.' I stop. I am making it seem like the pond is a very good friend who's just discovered they've got gallstones.

'There's a pond,' I start again, 'where Selwyn's sister drowned, and it was full of a pondweed that she became entangled in. Selwyn has always said it was a different pondweed because the pond is saltwater, and he's spent the best part of fifty years looking for it, trying to work it out, where it came from.'

I stop again. Anthony looks grave. I realise he's not wearing his hearing aids. I wonder if he even remembers re-heeling my shoes, gifting me those his customers forgot. I carry on.

'Anyway, it was there, on the side of the mountain, and he went to get some of it. But he can't remember whether he tried to make the jump, or if he mistook the length of drop, but one shattered shinbone, a fractured ankle, couple of broken ribs later…'

'And was it what you were looking for?' Anthony interjects.

'He has it breeding in a bin in our backyard,' I tell him. 'It's like living with an alien species. He's got me buying salt like we're gritting the M6. I keep expecting it to grab me by the throat. It's ferocious. It grows like rhubarb.'

Mia comes back in the kitchen with her laptop and I hear Selwyn's voice. He sounds tired, drowsy with pills. Mia is showing him the bluebird. It chirrups. Still. I can't catch all of what he says, just that he says, 'It looks exactly the same as when she bought it.' She turns the screen to face me.

'Here's the old fishwife,' Mia slights, putting the screen down in front of me. 'Charming and impetuous, that's how Shakespeare wrote her, his perfect heroine created from a big mistake.' She smiles at the screen and nips at my elbow, and I see Selwyn is sitting in his blue leather armchair surrounded by the paraphernalia of an old man, in knee-to-toe plaster with a map on his lap. I can tell that Val has been round, clucking and fussing. There's a gravy-stained plate aside of him and the ashtray shows cigarettes shared.

Simpering old duffer. I love him to bits.

'You've got to be bloody kidding me,' I say, pointing at the screen. 'What are you doing with that map? I thought we were selling that heap of junk?' He puts up his hands and asks me to hear him out. 'No,' I say. 'That caravan is a deadweight. It has to go. What happened to your buyer?'

He tells me again that he has never trusted Stuart Fury in all the years and is not going to start trusting him now.

'But there's somewhere I do want to show you,' he says, and he breaks into what we now call the Snowdon smile. I realise that we've landed on our feet with the carp. 'But I promise you, Ginny,' he carries on, 'this time I have it all planned out.'

Acknowledgments

Ten years ago, Ginny & Selwyn came to life in a different novel that didn't work out but nagged away all the same. I must, therefore, wholeheartedly thank Professors Helen Wilcox and Ian Davidson for their continued re-reading and ongoing support, and with special thanks to Professor Steven Price and Dr Andy Webb who forgave me for not being where I should. This is why.

I'd be lost for far longer than fourteen days if it wasn't for Philippa Brewster who never fails to steer me in the right direction, and did so into the Myriad pond. So, to Candida Lacey, Corinne Pearlman, Lauren Burlinson, Emma Dowson, and Anna Burtt, thank you and with love. The water is, indeed, warm as toast. And to Vicki Heath Silk, a beady-eyed bluebird who feathered my words beautifully. Thank you, x.

To my lifebuoys -- Jonathan Davidson, Kit de Waal, Kerry Hudson and Chris Power: What smashers you are and I am so very grateful. And to Phil and Becky; Debs and Neil; Ami; Hallsy; Len and Jim; Maz; the family Fenwick; Lord and Lady Moncrieff; the Norths and the Roberts and the Walkers; to Jackus; Petra; Auntie Sheila and Jim; Sandra and John Lane; Rachy and Pat; Dr Catherine Burgass; Professor Deborah Wynne; Tania Harrison; Cathy Galvin; Meg Hawkins; Luke Wright; Carl and Sam – a massive Snowdon smile to you all because you keep me afloat, x.

As ever, I'd not be able to write a single word if it wasn't for my mum, dad and Sarah who never stop filling my car with petrol. And to Dave and Nell, my pond life and beyond.

More from this author

It's Gone Dark Over Bill's Mother's
by Lisa Blower

Winner of the Arnold Bennett Prize

With a sharp eye and tough warmth, Lisa Blower strikes a new chord in regional and working-class fiction. In this fabu-lous collection of her award-winning short stories she makes the bleak funny, and brings to life the silent histories and harsh realities of those living on the margins.

From the wise, witty and outspoken Nan of 'Broken Crockery', who has lived and worked in Stoke-on-Trent for all of her ninty-two years, to happy hooker Ruthie in 'The Land of Make Believe', to sleep-deprived Laura in 'The Trees in the Wood', to young mum Roxanne in 'The Cherry Tree', the working-class matriarch appears in many shapes and forms, and always with a stoicism that is hard to break down.

'Beautifully written from inside – real people, ordinary homes. Set pieces, hilarious and tragic – the caravan site, the spring cleaning, the drinking game. Each is crafted to perfection. These are short stories to die for.' – Kit de Waal

'Her stories are at times the laugh-out-loud funny of Alan Bennett and, at others, the achingly sad of the great David Constantine.' – Paul McVeigh

Sign up to our mailing list at
www.myriadeditions.com
Follow us on Facebook, Twitter and Instagram

About the author

LISA BLOWER is an award-winning short story writer and novelist. Her debut collection, *It's Gone Dark Over Bill's Mother's*, pays homage to her Potteries childhood and features 'Barmouth' (shortlisted for the BBC Short Story Award), 'Abdul' (longlisted for the *Sunday Times* Award), and 'Broken Crockery' (winner, *The Guardian* National Short Story Competition). Her novel *Sitting Ducks* was shortlisted for the Arnold Bennett Prize, the Rubery, and longlisted for *The Guardian's* Not the Booker and the People's Book Prize. She is a Senior Lecturer in Creative Writing at Wolverhampton University where she champions working-class fictions and regional voices. If she had a pound for every time she has travelled the *Pondweed* journey, she would be a millionaire. She lives in Shrewsbury.